THE MUSIC BOX MYSTERY

Also by Joanne Pence

Ancient Secrets Series
ANCIENT ECHOES - ANCIENT SHADOWS
ANCIENT ILLUSIONS - ANCIENT DECEPTIONS
ANCIENT PASSAGES

The Donnelly Cabin Inn
IF I LOVED YOU - THIS CAN'T BE LOVE
SENTIMENTAL JOURNEY - A CERTAIN SMILE
TIME AFTER TIME

The Rebecca Mayfield Mysteries
ONE O'CLOCK HUSTLE - TWO O'CLOCK HEIST
THREE O'CLOCK SÉANCE - FOUR O'CLOCK SIZZLE
FIVE O'CLOCK TWIST - SIX O'CLOCK SILENCE
SEVEN O'CLOCK TARGET - EIGHT O'CLOCK SPLIT
NINE O'CLOCK RETREAT - THE 13th SANTA (Novella)

The Cook and Inspector Mysteries
DEATH ON A SILVER PLATTER - A QUICHE BEFORE DYING -
THE MARINARA MURDERS -
CLOSE ENCOUNTERS OF THE DEADLY KIND
DEATH BY DEVIL'S FOOD - THE TAVERNA AFFAIR

Others

SEEMS LIKE OLD TIMES - DANGEROUS JOURNEY
DANCE WITH A GUNFIGHTER - THE DRAGON'S LADY
THE GHOST OF SQUIRE HOUSE

THE MUSIC BOX MYSTERY

THE COOK AND INSPECTOR MYSTERIES

JOANNE PENCE

QUAIL HILL PUBLISHING

Quail Hill Publishing

Eagle, ID 83616

Visit our website at www.quailhillpublishing.net

First Quail Hill Publishing E-book: April 2025

First Quail Hill Print Book: April 2025

THE MUSIC BOX MYSTERY

1

———————

Angie Amalfi dashed down Nob Hill to a small jewelry shop on California Street. Gold lettering over the shop proclaimed Rose Jewelry, Ltd. An open sign dangled on the front door.

Inside, recessed lights shone onto walnut-framed glass counters set in a U-shape along the back and side walls. Gold and platinum-set stones and diamonds were tastefully displayed on black velvet. Atop each long counter was a rectangular mirror on a lacquered stand, while more mirrors discreetly hung from the paneled walls.

A white-haired man sat at a wooden desk behind the farthest counter. "Thank God you're here," Angie cried, hurrying toward him on Giacomo Ferre stilettos that matched her Donna Karen jade green silk suit.

He raised his head. Slowly pushing himself to his feet, he unhooked the jeweler's magnifier from his eyeglasses and placed it on the table. He was quite old, his back curved so badly that even standing upright, he seemed to be searching for something at his feet. He peered at her through bushy gray eyebrows, frowned, and shuffled closer.

"I hope you can help me." Anxiety made her voice shrill as she placed a box roughly the size of a shoe box on the counter and lifted off the lid. "Mr. Warner at the Music Box Repair Company said this one was more intricate than he was comfortable handling. He said you were the only person he knew who might be able to repair it."

His eyebrows lifted with interest at the name. Ralph Warner was the senior jeweler at the prestigious store. Gnarled hands rested on the glass countertop. "What kind of work is it?" His voice was deep, and he spoke with an accent, mixing his "v's" and "w's."

"I'll show you." From the tissue-lined cardboard container, she lifted out an elegant porcelain music box. "My fiancé gave it to me for Christmas. It's old, but it worked fine. It plays Für Elise and the couple spins in dance. I wound it up and was listening to it, when suddenly the music stopped and the couple won't move. I was afraid to force it. I feared I might break a spring or something. I do hope you can fix it for me!"

His gaze was fixed on the music box as she spoke. "Oh, my," he murmured, then looked at her with surprise. "Your fiancé gave you this?"

"Yes." She guessed an old music box seemed like an odd gift, but even she had to admit she was difficult to buy gifts for since she tended to buy herself anything she wanted. She hurried to explain. "It was his mother's. She died years ago, so it has much sentimental value. For him to give it to me means a lot, and it really is quite beautiful."

He lifted and inspected the music box. "Yes, I would agree it is."

She tried to keep the dejection and panic from her voice. "He explained it's not worth much, but still, I can't tell him I broke it. This is so upsetting! I could just die!"

She waited for a word, a reaction, but he gave none. She

stopped talking and watched his fascination with the piece. It was beautifully ornate, the gold leaf shimmering in the light.

He stared at the music box for a long time, then, moving slowly, he carried it to his desk and carefully placed it on a square of black velvet. He reattached his magnifying glass and studied the porcelain figures and gold design under a strong lamp. "Oh, my," he repeated.

"What's wrong?" Angie was practically stretched out across the top of the counter trying to see what he was doing. He hadn't even opened it to look inside. "Do you think you can fix it?"

Her words seemed to jar him out of his reverie. "Do you know where your friend, or his mother, got this?"

She didn't like the tone of that question. "It was in his family for many years. That's all I know."

He sat and carefully removed the base of the music box, and then used an eyepiece to study the inner workings.

"I can see why your usual repair shop did not want to touch this music box. It is not mere decoration, but a work of art."

She was stunned. "It's just a music box. I didn't think they were all that valuable."

"The quality of the craftsmanship is remarkable, the movements are precision made—the cylinder, pins, comb. Oh, my! The artistry elevates this to something rare."

Angie knew beautiful things, and suspected the music box was more valuable than Paavo thought, but this revelation caught her off guard.

"Do not worry," the shop owner continued, studying her reaction. "I can fix it for you. I am one of the few people in the country who can do it. It won't be cheap, though. I'll need to be careful not to damage it more."

"That's fine." She found her voice. "You don't know what a relief that is to me."

"Tell me, would you consider selling this piece?" he asked. "It won't be worth much more than it will cost to repair it, but I know some collectors of Russian artifacts who may be interested in it."

"Russian? The piece is Russian?"

"Of course. The design is unmistakably Russian. It is...er...similar to items exhibited at the Hermitage in St. Petersburg."

"Really? It's museum quality?"

"No, no. I mean the style, not the piece itself."

"Of course," she murmured. Still, she was bewildered. How could Paavo's mother have come to own such a piece? Angie had always assumed his mother was American. Was she wrong? Had the woman been Russian? "Well, no matter. I'm sure my fiancé would never sell it."

"You might ask him. What is his family name, by the way?"

"Smith. Why?"

The jeweler looked surprised. "I thought he might be Russian... that he might even be someone I know, since, of course, I'm Russian."

Angie smiled. She'd guessed that from his accent. "No. If he's anything, he's probably Finnish."

He glanced at her quickly, then turned back to the music box. "Finnish... I see."

"Excuse me?" Angie asked, puzzled by his reaction.

"Be sure to ask him if he's interested in selling. And if not..." He shrugged. "I'll give you a receipt for the music box." He handed her a sales pad. "Please write down your name, address, and telephone number in case I need to reach you."

Angie jotted down the information.

He wrote "music box repair," signed with a scrawl, and gave her a copy. She looked at the identification printed at the top—Rose Watch Repair, Ltd., Gregor Rosinsky, Prop. "I'll call you in a week, maybe more," he said.

"A week?" How was she going to explain to Paavo why the

music box wasn't in its place of honor in her living room where it had sat over the past month since he'd given it to her? "Please call me if it's ready any sooner," she pleaded.

"Of course," he said. He turned his back on her as he again walked to his desk, then slowly, painfully, sat down. "Goodbye.

———

Gregor Rosinsky waited until the woman had gone. He read the name and address she had written, then picked up the telephone.

2

———————

The next afternoon, as Angie headed back to her apartment after having had lunch with her sister Frannie, and then getting her nails done, she pondered ways to keep Paavo out of her apartment until she got the music box back from Rosinsky. Last night, she'd shown up at his home with a platter of manicotti, but she couldn't cook for him every night, she didn't think. And when they went to a restaurant, they'd usually end up at her place.

With a sigh, she unlocked the door to her apartment, opened it, and then shrieked.

———————

The top of Russian Hill was the highest spot in the northern sector of San Francisco. From there, cable cars made a long descent to the Bay with a view of Alcatraz in the distance. Tourists massed and drove their cars down the "crookedest street in the world." And there, Angelina Amalfi lived in an elegant apartment on the top floor of a twelve-story building owned by her father.

Paavo had always thought of Angie's home as a quiet haven in a world of brutal madness. That was why he'd been so shaken by the call he'd received from her earlier that afternoon—two hours earlier, in fact. Two guilt-laden hours as he was stuck in a courtroom waiting to testify in one of his cases.

As soon as his testimony ended, he was out of the Hall of Justice and hurried to Angie's apartment.

Only two apartments were on each floor, one on each side of the hallway. Angie's door was wide open. Paavo entered to find crime scene investigators combing the area. Closet doors and drawers were open, their contents strewn on the floor.

"Hey, Paavo!" Ben Chan greeted him while he hovered over a dusting of fingerprint powder. "We're just getting started."

"Good. I appreciate you coming by," Paavo said as he scanned the area for Angie without success.

"Your girlfriend's right next door. She's fine."

"Thanks, Ben." Paavo crossed the hall and pounded on Stanfield Bonnette's door. Angie's neighbor was the last person he wanted to see just then. On the way to becoming a young bank executive solely through family influence, the guy was a choice piece of work. Paavo found him obnoxious and lazy. Angie seemed to like him.

Instead of Bonnette, Angie pulled open the door.

She was just a little woman, almost a foot shorter than his own six feet two inches. He often forgot how small she was since she loomed so large in his life. Her skin was creamy, with the slight olive cast of the Mediterranean. Her hair would have been chocolate brown, but she had added some red streaks to it —highlights, she called them. He liked her natural color better, but that was the sort of opinion he knew enough to keep to himself. Her eyes were big and brown, the skin beneath them and on her brow pinched and drawn with worry.

As she looked at him, her eyes calmed, and she smiled. "Thank God," she whispered.

Relief filled him, and he opened his arms to her. "I'm sorry it took me so long. Are you all right?"

She took the comfort he offered. "It was a shock, that's all."

Cupping the back of her head, he held her close. With all the grim experience of a homicide inspector, he knew what might have happened had she been home instead of out when the break-in occurred. The harsh world of the streets reminded him of how fragile she was, how easily and unexpectedly disaster could strike, and how tenuous happiness could be.

Whoever broke into the building had to know how to get past the doorman, or how to sneak in through the garage, one of the service entrances, or an emergency exit without setting off alarms. Finally, they had to get past Angie's dead bolt lock. Professional tools would be needed to enter, not kid's stuff, although, for a pro, the security measures represented more of a minor inconvenience than a major obstacle.

Angie took a deep breath, then stepped back. Holding Paavo's hand, she led him into Bonnette's apartment and shut the door. "What did they steal?" he asked.

"Nothing, as far as I could tell. Either something scared them, or they just didn't like my taste." She forced a smile, but her face was pale and her eyes appeared even larger than usual. "When I arrived home, I noticed the deadbolt wasn't on. I thought I might have forgotten to set it, but as soon as I saw the mess inside, I turned around and ran over here to Stan's."

Stan was lounging on a gray and blue plaid sofa, one arm dangling over the back. He wore a turquoise short-sleeved polo shirt, his light brown hair flopping casually onto his brow. "I was sick today," he said by way of explanation for not being at work. The thirty-plus-year-old had a problem with his job—he never went to it. "It was a lucky thing, too," he added, with a flick of his head that made his hair fly back off his face. "This way at least *someone* was with Angie in her hour of need."

Paavo frowned and slipped his arm around Angie's waist. As

much as he'd wanted to come to her as soon as he learned that her apartment had been burglarized, he couldn't walk out of the courtroom.

The best he could do had been to talk Ben Chan and the crime scene technicians into checking out Angie's apartment asap.

Now her neighbor was rubbing salt in the wound. He shouldn't let Stan get to him, but the guy always did.

"Angie, you know I got here as soon as I could," he said.

"It's okay." Her voice was soft and warm. "I understand."

"We were fine, Inspector," Stan added. "Just fine. When the cops arrived, I was right by Angie's side as she went through her apartment to see if anything was stolen. I made sure she was safe."

Paavo tried to ignore Bonnette's taunts. "Did you see anything odd or hear any noise from Angie's apartment while she was out?"

"No. As I said, I'd been sick. I was in bed with the TV on."

Paavo turned to Angie. "How long were you away?"

"Three or four hours. I went out to lunch with Frannie. I came up with an idea for a business and wanted to run it past her. Finding a great job or starting a new business is my number one New Year's resolution." Her eyes caught his, and a light blush touched her cheeks. "Well, number two, actually, but who's counting? Anyway, Frannie didn't think gourmet dog biscuits were a great concept. So I had a mani-pedi, came home, and found the break-in."

Paavo didn't comment on her business idea. He had to agree with Frannie, though—the market for gourmet dog biscuits seemed a bit narrow. "I'd better go talk to the crime scene techs," he said, hesitating to leave Angie so soon, particularly after Stan's jab. But she knew it had to be done and sent him on his way.

Now that he had seen for himself that she was safe, he was

able to return to her apartment and feel some satisfaction that the technicians were there looking for clues to the break-in. So many home burglaries took place in this city that they rarely got more than the time of day from the police, especially if nothing had been stolen. Still, the victim was Angie. He wanted to catch and jail the lowlife responsible. He should get some benefit from his years as a cop.

"Thanks for helping here, Ben," he said.

"No problem, Paavo. Angie's a good woman, and as close to family as you can get without being family." Ben paused, then continued with weighted deliberation. "Of course, you can change that... if you know what I mean."

Paavo shot him an icy glance. Another cop playing matchmaker. He wanted to shout that they were at least engaged, but knew that would only lead to more ribbing.

Ben chuckled. Everyone loved kidding Paavo about his nervousness at the thought of actually getting married. It was more than that, though. Much more; more than he wanted to explain.

When he turned, he saw Angie in the doorway, her arms folded and her eyes sad as she watched strangers going through her designer clothes and expensive knickknacks and antique furnishings. Standing there in cream-colored slacks and a pink silk blouse with cream piping, to his mind, she personified delicate and refined. The strangest thing about her was that for some reason she loved him. Who was it that said a woman was a contradiction wrapped in an enigma? That was Angie.

Then he noticed one thing missing, but it made no sense. He went over to her. "The music box is gone."

She gasped. "Oh... no, no, it's not. I took it with me to Stan's. It's safe."

His eyebrows lifted. "You did? Okay, good. That would have been a weird thing for them to take."

"Yes," she said with a nervous smile. "Very weird, indeed."

He tore his gaze from her and once more surveyed her apartment, room by room. A nervous prickle touched his spine. It didn't look like a burglary; it looked like a search.

He returned to the living room. Angie was no longer in the apartment. She must have gone back to Stan's.

"What do you think, Ben?" Paavo asked.

"I'd worry, Paavo." Ben Chan had spent years with the SFPD robbery detail. "Between stereo and video equipment, a desktop and a laptop, not to mention a Fort Knox worth of jewelry in her bedroom, something should have been taken. But it wasn't. It seems they were looking for something specific. All the disruption was done in drawers and cabinets, and places like the top of her closet where she had boxes of souvenirs and the like."

Paavo hadn't wanted to hear a confirmation of his suspicion, but Ben's words rang true. This break-in wasn't random; it was personal. If whoever was behind it hadn't found what he was looking for, he'd be back. What could Angie have that was worth so much trouble? "Any evidence?"

"Nothing jumps out. We'll keep looking."

"I owe you, Ben," Paavo said.

"No problem."

Following the procedure he'd use if this were a homicide, Paavo canvassed the building, talking to neighbors and the doorman. No one had seen any strangers lurking about or anything at all suspicious.

Finally, he returned to Stan's apartment. Angie blanched when she saw his expression, and she stood up. He must not have been as good at hiding his emotions around her as he liked to think. "Why don't you stay at my place for a few days?" He tried to sound casual. "Just until we're sure that whoever came here won't return."

What little color she had in her face disappeared completely. "You think they'll be back? But why? What can they possibly want?"

"Most likely they won't return, but I'll feel more comfortable if you aren't here alone in case they do."

She nodded and went to her place to pack. "One bag, Angie," Paavo called. "We can always come back for more later."

Stan folded his arms. "She can always stay with me, Inspector. At least I'd be around to take care of her when she needs me."

"Bonnette, go f...fly a kite."

It was nearly ten o'clock before Angie finished packing and picking up the mess in her apartment. Although she'd been shocked to arrive home and find it broken into, that was hardly rare in city life. Nothing was stolen; no one was hurt. Life went on. On the other hand, if Paavo wanted to make a big deal out of it and have her stay with him for a few days, she wasn't about to complain. Look for the silver lining, her mother always said. And moving in with Paavo for a while was pure gold.

Of course, they'd live together once they were married and figured out *where* to live. She couldn't fit her clothes, let alone her other belongings, in his bungalow, and he refused to live in her father's building. And also, whenever she tried to talk to him about a date for the wedding, he asked how her wedding plans were coming along. They were moving slowly, but that was because they needed to settle on a date. At that point, he would change the subject.

So, here they were.

Now, she packed enough to make this a nice, long visit.

Paavo drove an old Mustang. Her car was a white Lexus mid-sized SUV—what she thought of as a "family car." Using both, they could barely manage to fit all her luggage.

Her Lexus roared to a stop behind his convertible. He was standing on the sidewalk wrestling with a large Fendi suitcase, trying to pull it out of the back seat. She realized that he, too, needed to think about a new car. She once tried to give him a brand new Corvette—sure he'd adore it—but he wouldn't take it.

She stepped up behind him, holding her laptop, and admired the view as he bent deeply into his car. He was a handsome man —tall, broad-shouldered, with a slim but physically powerful build. His cheekbones were high and pronounced, his hair dark brown, and dark brows and eyelashes surrounded the lightest blue eyes she'd ever seen. Some people called them icy. To her, they were beautiful. But there was also a world-weariness lining the corners of his eyes and in the set of his mouth that reminded her he was a man who had seen more than his share of suffering and sorrow.

A hard tug sprung the suitcase free from the tight space in which it had been wedged. "You really didn't have to pack so much stuff," he grumbled. "We're only across town from your apartment."

"I'd hate to discover I'd left something important at home. Besides—" she batted her eyes innocently—"who knows how long I'll need to stay? Anyway, my suitcases all have wheels."

Her gaze swiveled, following his to the stairs that led up to his front door.

"Once I put things away, you'll hardly notice how much I've brought," she said.

"You'll have plenty of time tomorrow to figure out where to fit it all. I have to go in early. Yosh is on vacation and Rebecca Mayfield has been helping with some of his cases."

"Hmm, what a little helper bee." Angie knew all about Rebecca's crush on Paavo. She especially detested Rebecca's implication that only another cop could understand and be good for him—and that Rebecca was that cop.

He lugged the two big suitcases up the steps and set them on the stoop while fishing the house key from his pocket.

"Actually, I had assumed you wouldn't be home much," she said. This was a good time to show him just how understanding she could be about the demands of his job. "I know how hard you have to work, no matter what's happening in your personal life."

He glanced at her quizzically.

"One of those suitcases is filled with books for me to read while you're out," she said. "I wasn't sure which I'd be in the mood for, so I brought a bunch of them."

"Ah... that explains it." He pushed open the door and stepped aside to let her enter first. "I wondered why your clothes were so heavy."

Flicking on the lights, she stepped into the living room and abruptly halted. "Oh, my God." She back-pedaled right into him.

One glance at her face and he hurried past her. Hand on his gun, he stopped in the doorway, then drew his nine-millimeter automatic and moved inside.

Ignoring his whispered demand to remain by the door, Angie followed close as he crossed from room to room. In the living room, books had been strewn onto the floor, sofa and chair cushions ripped open, and desk drawers overturned.

The bedroom had also been torn apart and the mattress slashed. This was far, far more frightening than what had happened to her own apartment. There was anger here, perhaps hatred.

"What is going on?" she cried. "Why would anyone destroy your things?"

"It looks like a search, followed by frustration."

As she wandered through the little house, she realized he was right. It wasn't random destruction as she had first thought, but where the search to her apartment had appeared slow and meticulous, here it was hurried and frenzied.

"Hercules!" he called. "Herc? Come on boy, are you all right?"

Angie's breath caught. His cat... he loved that cat.

"Do you see him?" she asked, standing in the bedroom doorway.

"No. They better not have hurt my cat," he muttered, his jaw clenched. They looked under the bed, in the closets and throughout the backyard.

She was afraid—and for Hercules, more afraid that they'd find the cat than that they wouldn't. If he had run and was hiding, scared, he should return home eventually, but if he was nearby, and unable to come when called...

They couldn't find him.

Finally, back in the living room, Paavo bleakly took in the damage, the ugliness before him. "Who's doing this, Angie, and why?"

3

———————

The bellboy wheeled in a cart with Angie's luggage and turned on lamps. Paavo put down his duffel bag and inspected their room at the Huntington, an elegant hotel at the top of Nob Hill. The walls were papered powder blue, and the cream-colored gilded furniture was imitation Louis XIV. The view overlooked Huntington Park and the exclusive Pacific Union Club, from Grace Cathedral to the Fairmont Hotel.

"Didn't I tell you this would be much nicer than sleeping on the floor at your place?" Angie asked, clearly pleased with her choice.

"This is much nicer than my whole house," Paavo remarked as he tipped the porter and locked the door.

"Very funny."

Now, in the hotel room, she looked exhausted. No wonder. It was nearly four o'clock in the morning. They'd spent hours waiting for the police to arrive. During that time, he'd packed a few things and changed out of his suit to Levis, a maroon pullover, and a brown leather jacket.

"Tomorrow I'll contact my cousin Richie," she said, flopping into a chair. "He might have a house or apartment on the market we can use for a few weeks."

"Let's wait until we see what's going on." He unzipped his duffel bag. "Most people get new locks or a burglar alarm after a break-in, not a whole new place to live."

She watched him a moment, then walked to his side and touched his shoulder, stopping him as he unloaded underwear into a bureau drawer. He straightened, and she eased herself against his chest.

"I think it's wise to be prudent—just as you said when you suggested I stay with you for a while. Oh, maybe I didn't think it was necessary at first, but now I do. My house, then yours? It's bizarre."

Paavo's arms tightened protectively around her. "Tomorrow I'll talk to Ben Chan, get him to check out my place for finger-prints and signs of entry." *And I'll look for Hercules.*

She seemed to study him. "Once he knows it's safe, Hercules will come home," she said, making him wonder once again if she could read his mind or his expression. Most people called him stone-faced, but not Angie.

He brushed a lock of hair back from her forehead, and ran his thumb lightly along her cheek, taking in the dark shadows under her eyes. She was so beautiful, so soft... and this hotel room was theirs to share...

"You'll be fine here," he said, setting her from him. "I'm going to take a shower and go to work. It'll be morning soon and I'll feel worse if I try to sleep for just an hour. This way, you can get some sleep."

She firmed her jaw and nodded. "All right." Her voice was a little too husky. She opened a suitcase and pulled out a satin nightgown when suddenly she threw it back into the case. "Just a minute!" Hands on hips, she marched toward him. "On second thought, it's not all right at all. Not at all. Someone broke into both our homes, made your furniture look like it'd been ground up by a Cuisinart, and you're going to work? You've got better things to do, like getting some sleep so you'll have enough energy to find the crook who did it and pulverize him."

"Angie—"

"Even if you're not worried about this, I am. Especially for you! What happened to your home, your things... I can't get it out of my head. If anything happens to you—"

He gripped her shoulders. "Take it easy." Moving his hands to her back, he drew her closer. "Nothing's going to happen to me, or you. We'll catch whoever's behind it soon. Besides, I needed new furniture."

He kissed her once, twice, then more, wanting to kiss away her anxieties. He thought of how she'd gone to Stan when he wasn't able to be with her after the break-in. Was he really going to be such a jerk as to leave her alone again? "Maybe that stuff I was going to do at work can wait a few hours."

Her arms circled his neck, and she held him tight, kissing him back while a fearful shudder rippled through her.

He led her to the king-size bed and lay down beside her. There was no way he could leave her now. Instead, he held her, loving her as dawn lit the sky. She fell asleep before he did. As his own eyes shut, he gathered her close, and tried to keep the nightmares from them both.

Even after thirty years, the view from his office window caused Harold Partridge's narrow chest to swell with pride. The world's cleverest engineers, computer scientists and programmers strode briskly through the Silicon Valley complex, their minds ticking with the latest inventions and the next enhancements to the worldwide business that was Partridge Industries.

His private phone began to ring. *Finally!*

He held it to his ear. "Well?"

"Not yet."

"Not yet?" Skinny arms began to shake. "Impossible! You missed it! You cretins! Imbeciles!"

"We didn't--"

A pulsating pain crossed his brow. "Do you think I'm doing this just for fun? It's important, goddamn it!"

"We understand, Mr. Partridge."

The words, so cloyingly spoken from these sycophantic fools who couldn't follow simple instructions, made his overly acidic stomach curl. "Don't call me again until you are successful."

"That"—the caller coughed nervously—"that might require more than you said the first time."

"I don't care! Do whatever it takes!" He slammed down the phone but kept his gaze fixed on it as he nervously cracked his knuckles one by one. The time had come to do what he must, what he should have done immediately, much as he loathed the idea. Fighting the tremor in his body, he picked up the receiver again and began to dial.

4

———

"You're going to get us thrown out, Angie." Connie Rogers leaned across the table and spoke in a loud whisper. Angie's best friend was in her early thirties, blonde, divorced, the owner of a small gift shop, and a grudging accomplice in too many of Angie's screwball schemes. Like now.

The two of them sat in Pisces, an elegant restaurant high on Nob Hill, newly opened and filled with a young and hip clientele. Angie was using her phone to make a video of the restaurant, their table, the menu, and the wine list.

"If I walked in with a camera," Angie explained calmly, "no one would object. It's the same thing."

"People with cameras take pictures, not videos of the food, the tables and the help."

"Look, restaurant reviews have to be made incognito." Angie placed the phone on the table. "If the reviewer is known, it defeats the whole purpose. So, we're here pretending to be casual diners who happen to have a phone. Who doesn't, these days? This way, instead of me taking notes and verbally describing everything I eat, we're simply discussing the meal as we go along, and I'm recording it."

"And then showing it to thousands of viewers on YouTube!" Connie scrunched her lips to the side like some gangster as an unsuspecting waiter sailed by.

"Shush! Not so loud." Angie looked from one side to the other. "What's the big deal? Video restaurant reviews are a fabulous idea. They'll catch on in a big way—in other words, I'll make it big. The public will love them much more than bland old online articles."

"We could be sued!"

"Don't worry. As I said, restaurant reviews are always written in secret, and all I'm recording is our dining experience, which is my right. You can also look at this as investigative reporting—photos and film are often used. Besides, I plan to only go to good restaurants with good food, ones that should appreciate the publicity. And if I do find something wrong, to sue because of a bad review would give a restaurant even more negative press. That's the last thing they'd want."

Connies lips pursed. "Somehow, this seems wrong."

"It's fine. Quiet, now. Here comes our waiter." She picked up her phone and aimed it at him.

"What are you celebrating?" The waiter grimaced into the lens as he served a salad of arugula, shaved Parmesan and sliced artichoke with olive oil and lemon to Angie. Connie's salad consisted of radicchio, scallions and olives in a balsamic dressing.

"Nothing, I simply want to remember my experience here. It isn't easy to get reservations, you know," Angie said promptly. It wasn't a lie. She had been waiting a week to get in, and wasn't about to give up her reservation no matter how many apartment break-ins she had to deal with.

"Oh? I had no idea. So that's why you're making a video?"

She chose not to answer. "Haven't you seen it done before?"

He peered down his nose. "Only photos. I can take one of you two if you'd like."

"No, thanks." Angie centered the lens on him. "Tell me, do you enjoy working here?"

His eyes shifted left and right. "I'm sorry, but I'm afraid some of the other customers are bothered by your recording."

"They are?" Sure enough, everyone was staring at her.

"If you don't mind..." the waiter said.

With a weighty sigh, she closed the recorder and laid the phone beside her plate again. "Sorry," she mumbled.

The waiter sniffed and then marched away.

"See what I mean?" Connie whispered.

"It's none of their business! Next time, I'll be a little more subtle, that's all."

"Hah! You subtle? That's the day I'll become the next Mrs. Brad Pitt! Anyway, why should there be a next time?"

"Because YouTube potentially will pay a lot more than magazines."

Connie tasted her salad and decided to add a bit more salt. Quick as a flash, Angie recorded her salting the food. "Your point?" Connie asked. Now, she was grimacing at the phone as well.

"When I realized I was actually *glad* my apartment had been broken into so I had an excuse to move in with Paavo, I knew it was time to do something about our living situation." Angie took a bite of salad and chewed thoughtfully before continuing. "I want to be with him. Despite the break-ins, we had a great day yesterday—we saw his friends at the police department, contacted his insurance company, then shopped for a new bed for him. Of course, this morning when I woke up in a beautiful hotel room—romantic, room service, every convenience at the touch of a button—and I found a note beside me instead of a man, I gritted my teeth. I swear, he doesn't have a clue. Not a clue!"

"You don't sound very worried about those break-ins," Connie said as Angie made a video of her salad and softly spoke into it about crispness and a slightly tinny flavor.

"In the clear light of day, I decided they were nothing," Angie said, the recording momentarily over. "I'm sure whoever broke in was searching for money, and something scared them away before they realized I don't keep money at home, and before they took any of my valuables. I'll bet they saw Paavo's name and address among my things. Maybe they thought we were together and figured since they'd been scared off from my place, they'd hit his? Who knows?"

"You're making a lot of assumptions, girlfriend."

"I'm sure the break-ins are no more than that. But if Paavo wants to worry about me, who am I to argue?" She winked conspiratorially.

Connie smiled back. "I get it."

"And that's where my restaurant reviews come in."

"Now, I don't get it."

"It's simple. The two of us *need* a house. My clothes, and cookware, and antiques simply won't fit into his small place. And there's no way he'll live under my father's roof." She didn't have to tell Connie that Paavo and Salvatore Amalfi didn't exactly see eye to eye about Paavo's relationship with Angie. "Do you know how much houses cost in San Francisco these days? That's why I've got to make money on my own even if I have to hire a movie crew to film these restaurants!"

"All so you can buy a house?"

"Eventually."

Connie swallowed a big mouthful of radicchio. "Frankly, I really don't see how you can think about buying a house with a man when there's so much you don't know about him."

Angie stopped eating. "What do you mean?"

Connie shifted uncomfortably. "Well... you don't really know him."

"Don't *know* him? How can you say that after all Paavo and I have been through together?"

"That's what I mean. Things have happened to you both while you've been together, but how much of him do you know?"

"You sound like my father," Angie cried, waving her fork in exasperation.

"Think about it. He keeps so much hidden."

"Hidden? Nothing's hidden about Paavo!"

"How much has he told you about his past?"

"Connie, he had a hard life. I can understand why he doesn't want to talk about it."

"Are you sure?"

Angie couldn't believe her friend was talking this way. "I thought you liked Paavo."

"I do, but you can't build a life together with too many unknowns—with hidden pasts. I know what I'm talking about. It's what killed my marriage. Along with my ex being a slime. But if I had known more about him, I would have known he was a slime before I married him. You've got to learn all you can about Paavo."

"I know about him!"

"Angie, you don't even know the man's real name."

She glared hard at Connie. "What are you talking about?"

"You told me he said his Finnish stepfather gave him the name Paavo." Connie jabbed the table with her forefinger to make her point. "Well, he didn't live with Aulis until he was four years old. What was he called before that?"

"Aulis might have given him the name when he was first born," Angie answered vehemently. "I don't know *when* Aulis came up with Paavo, and I don't care. I like the name!"

"Why didn't Paavo's own mother and father name him? Why some neighbor? Unless—" Connie gasped.

Angie felt a chill go through her. "Unless what?"

"Unless Aulis is really his father! Wow!"

"Connie, really! Paavo told me Aulis is definitely not his father. Besides, the two don't look at all alike."

The waiter approached the table. Flustered, Angie hit the record button on her phone again, grateful for the interruption. She had no idea why Connie was talking to her this way. So what that she had wondered about some of it herself...

That was unfair. Whenever she asked, Paavo told her about his childhood. Maybe not all the particulars, but then, he didn't know much about them.

Still, Connie's questions bothered her.

The waiter smiled as he served Connie grilled Washington State salmon on spinach cream sauce, and scowled fiercely at Angie and her phone as he shoved a plate of steamed lobster medallions with saffron, tomatoes, basil and thyme broth in front of her. Angie smoldered. He was probably afraid her camera would pick up some dandruff on his shoulders.

As soon as he left, Connie leaned closer to Angie and in a hushed voice said, "I know you aren't going to like it, Angie, but frankly, I never did give much credence to that story that Aulis simply took in Paavo and his older sister when their mother abandoned them! I mean, being neighborly is one thing, but how many people raise their neighbor's kids? It just isn't done."

Connie's continuous harping grew beyond annoying. "Will you stop, already?" Angie demanded.

"You're my friend, my best friend, and I think it's time you learn exactly what's going on here," Connie insisted. "I mean, you're engaged to the man, but before you two tie the knot, you've got to get answers to a lot of questions. To stick your head in the sand about this is foolish, and you're not a foolish person."

"Right now, I'm ready to stick a fork in my ear!"

"Damn it, Angie. You are a certifiable whack job where Paavo Smith is concerned!" Connie cried.

Angie began to sputter, practically speechless for a moment. "Did you just call me a *whack* job?"

Connie put her palms on the table. "A short pier away from going over the edge!"

The two glared at each other.

Suddenly, Angie grinned. "About to fall into the drink, eh?"

Connie chuckled. "Deep-sea fishing time."

Angie laughed, then shook her head helplessly. "I wonder where I can find a diver's suit?"

To Angie's amazement, Paavo was there when she returned to the hotel room. The day's court session had been cancelled, the crime scene unit hadn't found time to go through the fingerprints they'd picked up at his or Angie's places, and no new murders happened. He left work early to be with her.

The other inspectors must have gawked at him as if he'd sprouted wings.

They ordered room service for dinner. Dessert was memorable... and it wasn't even on the menu.

5

Paavo strode briskly down Post Street, past porn shops and massage parlors, past doorways filled with wide-eyed Vietnamese children. In daylight, kids could be seen in the area, darting about, playing, or huddling in clusters and watching the goings-on. Once the sun went down, they disappeared, and San Francisco's version of the zombie class took over those streets—hookers, pimps, and addicts, plus a few lost tourists who didn't realize that close to the theater district lay this corner of despair.

Double-parked cop cars, their dome lights revolving signaled which building the body had been found in. As a homicide inspector, Paavo's job was to find out why people's lives were suddenly taken from them, even if that life had been lived in a hellhole like this.

A sheet from the *San Francisco Chronicle* blew toward him and stuck against his leg. He was careful to step over puddles of urine that stained the sidewalk next to buildings. A few years back, the city had spent big bucks putting in fancy port-a-potties on sidewalks in tourist parts of the city, most big enough for wheelchair access. Unfortunately, that meant they were big enough for other uses, too, like quick sex and drug deals. There were no port-a-potties in this part of town.

A rank smell pervaded the building's entrance. Pale green paint covered the walls, a color that must have been given away by the barrel to tenements and jails. Lurid graffiti was scrawled over the paint.

"Two floors up, Inspector," the uniform at the door told him. "Elevator's not working."

They never were in places like this, Paavo thought, which was probably for the best because few owners of such buildings would pay for their proper maintenance anyway. Riding one could cause more chills, thrills and spills than found at Disneyland.

At the top of the stairs more enlightening graffiti about the sexual habits of various residents filled a long, dark hallway. The debris and dirt on the floor crunched as he walked down the linoleum hall. With his partner on vacation this week, he wasn't supposed to be going to death scenes, but handling paper work, court dates and investigating cases he already had. This week's on-call team, Benson and Calderon, were mired down in a double homicide that involved a doctor and his wife who had been big-time contributors to the city's mayor. Rebecca Mayfield and her partner, Bill Never-Take-A-Chance Sutter were the backup team, but they had already gone out on a homicide investigation when this third call came in. Paavo should have looked to see if the moon was full last night. If so, it would have explained a lot.

A patrol officer guarded the crime scene. Paavo signed the logbook, ducked under the yellow police tape, and stepped inside.

Before him was a typical tenement apartment. The walls were a dingy yellow and the single window so filthy little sunlight came through. A torn shade covered the top-half. The main room held an old sofa, coffee table, chair and TV, and a kitchenette in one corner. Next to it was the bedroom, and beyond it, the bathroom. Drawers had been pulled from chests and upended.

He was growing sick of that sight.

Despite the drawers, he noticed that, unlike most of these tenement apartments, the floor and furniture weren't covered with empty food containers and other garbage.

A little girl sat on a tattered sofa. She had long brown hair pulled back in a ponytail. Her bangs were thick, and cut straight across, a millimeter above blue eyeglass frames. The frames were the defining features on her face, which was pale and plain. Her hands were folded on her lap, and brown eyes stared at him through the thick glasses.

"Hello," he said.

"Hello." Her voice was firm, and no tears showed on her face. With her was a patrol officer Paavo knew, Georgina McNally.

"This is Jane Platt, Inspector," McNally said. "She was the one who called nine-one-one when she found her grandfather." McNally pointed toward the open door. "Jacob Platt is in the bedroom."

Paavo was surprised at the news that the calm-looking little girl had found the body. He'd seen adults fall apart over such discoveries. He didn't remark on it, but gazed at her and nodded his approval. Her eyes held his a moment, then lowered.

After a quick perusal of the living room, he carefully entered the bedroom. "Did you or anyone else touch anything, McNally?" he asked.

"Didn't need to," McNally said.

McNally certainly had no need to question the fact of the man's death. The floor was covered with blood, and in the middle of it, Jacob Platt lay, shot point blank in the forehead. The entry hole was small, with powder burns surrounding it. The way Platt had fallen made it possible to see that the entire back of his skull had been blown off. Paavo couldn't help but think about the young girl finding this.

The bedroom held a twin bed, a small, rickety dresser, the contents of it spilled onto the floor, and two enormous tables, standing side by side. Two high-intensity lamps stood on one table, plus some strange equipment. He recognized the soldering iron, wire cutters, fine-nosed implements, Bunsen burner and microscope. The RS Mizar tester was a mystery, as was something called a Ceres Secure Moissanite Tester. Things started to make a little sense with the Raytech/Shaw faceter, the Diamond Jem cabbing machine, a centrifugal magnetic finisher, and finally, a magnetic polisher, all implements he'd come across involving jewelry making and repair.

No jewelry, metals or gems were found, and he wondered if Platt had been killed for them. Judging from the equipment, Platt's business must have been lucrative at one time. And judging from its location, it was probably illegal, or at best questionable.

Officer McNally stayed with the girl while Paavo continued to survey the scene. He had no sooner finished when the CSU arrived. He went over to the young girl and sat down beside her. She wore jeans and a gray zippered sweatshirt over a red tee shirt. "How are you doing, Jane?" he asked.

"I'm all right." Her voice was soft, and she looked more shy than tearful. Wide-eyed, she watched the crime scene investigators enter the apartment.

"How old are you?"

She lifted blue eyeglass-framed eyes to his. "Nine."

"Do you live here?"

"Yes."

"Just the two of you?"

She nodded.

"When you came home, was there anyone in the apartment besides your grandfather?" he asked.

She shook her head. "I called hello, and when he didn't answer I looked for him." She shuddered. "Then I phoned nine-one-one."

Jane's eyes grew even rounder when the medical examiner, Evelyn Ramirez, walked into the apartment carrying a medical bag. She waved at Paavo, but after one look at the young girl's face, instead of making her usual ghoulish comments she went straight into the bedroom. Two med technicians followed. Paavo noticed that the child's breathing had grown heavy. She was a good actress, but apparently not nearly as unmoved by her grisly find as she pretended to be.

He placed his hand on her narrow shoulder. "Where can we reach your mother or father?"

"They aren't here," she said.

They aren't here. A sudden flashback struck, shaking him. That was how his sister used to answer whenever kids at school or teachers or others would ask about their mother or father. Older, and tough, and protective of her little brother, Jessica would never say, "They've gone away," or "They abandoned us," or what he knew she really wanted to reply to the busy-bodies who questioned them, to shake her fist and cry out, "We don't know who the hell our fathers are, and we don't give a goddamn about our mother anymore. So what's it to you, asshole?" Instead, she'd politely reply, *"They aren't here."*

"Do you have any relatives or friends to stay with?"

"I have an aunt," she said in her matter-of-fact manner.

"I called her already, Inspector," McNally said softly. "She's on her way."

"Okay, good." Paavo's gaze swept over the apartment. There was a limit to how long a kid could sit in a room permeated with the smell of her grandfather's death, and this little girl had gone way past that point. "Want to go outside to wait for your aunt?"

"Yes." Her face filled with gratitude and she stood. On the

floor was her book bag. She picked it up and hitched it to her shoulders.

As they left the apartment, his gaze caught the equipment-laden table in the bedroom. "Do you know what your grandfather did in there?"

"He made jewelry." She reached under her collar and pulled out a pendant on a gold chain.

Paavo stared in disbelief. The necklace was beautiful. It looked like something Angie might have owned—a large ruby with a small diamond on each side.

"It's just a fake," the girl said. "It has a flaw in it. That's why grandpa gave it to me to play with. He lets me play with all the pretty fake things he has."

⁂

"I really don't think this is going to work, Angie," Connie whispered, crouching behind a row of industrial size garbage cans.

Angie, also stooping low, said, "Once, just once, I'd like to hear a bit of encouragement from you."

"Maybe I'd feel more encouraging if my knees weren't getting so stiff I'm afraid they might never straighten," Connie whined. "I don't relish spending my life waddling like Groucho Marx."

Earlier that evening, when Paavo called to say he'd be working late, the idea for the perfect addition to her video restaurant review popped into Angie's head. She decided to act.

Now, both dressed in black jeans, black turtleneck sweaters, and black boots, she and Connie huddled in the alley behind the Pisces restaurant where they'd eaten the day before.

Angie checked and doubled-checked the setting on her phone. Too many times she meant to take a photo and ended up with a video and vice versa. "Just relax," she said to her fidgeting friend. "I'm trying to figure this out. I think that window looks in on the kitchen, but it's too high off the ground for me to see into. I'm going to have to get up on something."

"Forget it. Let's go home."

Ignoring her suggestion, Angie tugged Connie along in a half-crouch, half-crawl. "We need to move one of these big garbage cans to a spot under the window."

They found a can that was fairly empty, although it still reeked. Each took a handle and carried it to the spot Angie had indicated.

"That can isn't very steady." Connie nudged it and watched it rock.

"You worry more than Little Red Riding Hood facing the wolf!" Angie tried to hoist herself up onto the flat, round lid, but couldn't do it. The top reached to her armpit. "I need a boost."

"This is dangerous, Angie," Connie grumbled, bending over and clasping her hands so Angie could use them as a step.

"It's fine."

Angie stepped as Connie held firm and lifted. With a wobbly clatter Angie was atop the garbage can on her knees and turned to look at Connie. "Connie?"

"Down here." She sat on the ground rubbing her hands.

"Are you okay?"

"Only if you call being used as a ladder and tumbling on your butt okay."

"You're okay." Angie stood up on the groaning lid to look in the restaurant's window.

"What do you see?" Connie asked, rising to her feet.

"This is so cool! I'm looking into the kitchen!" Her plan was working.

"Fantastic!"

"Unfortunately, there's a rack in front of this window. It's loaded with pans and blocks most of the view. I'm going to have to go to the next window to the left. That one should work better."

"Come down, then," Connie urged.

"Look, this can wasn't very heavy. Why don't you just drag another one over here? Then, I'll just step from this can to the next one."

"We're on a hill, Angie. The cans are too unsteady for that."

"They're huge and half-full of garbage. They aren't going anywhere."

"Since when have I become Connie-the-garbage-woman?"

There were times, Angie knew, when silence was golden.

Connie wrestled another can into place. Angie gingerly stepped onto it. "Much better." She raised her phone and looked through the lens. "Testing. One-two—oops!" She ducked down.

"What is it?" Instinctively, Connie ducked, too. Her fierce whisper floated up to Angie.

"Someone's coming. Shush!"

Angie slowly raised herself up to peer over the windowsill. The heavy-set chef she'd seen earlier stood with his back to the window, chopping chicken. She had to get this on video. She put the phone up to her face, hoping against hope it was on the right setting.

The man's backside filled the lens. It was not a pretty sight.

"What are you doing?" Connie tugged faintly at her ankle. "Come down before someone sees you!"

"Quiet," Angie whispered back. "I need another can over there." She pointed to her left.

"Angie, I don't think—"

"Hurry, Connie! This is a great shot!"

She waited until she heard Connie say, "Okay." Keeping her eye on the phone's camera, she lifted a foot through the air, then toed the garbage can that Connie had put into place.

"The can has a little problem..." Connie warned.

Angie squared her foot on the new can.

"... the lid doesn't fit very well."

As Angie shifted her weight, the garbage can cover gave way. The part she was standing on plunged downward, somehow making the lid soar upward and become airborne.

Angie dropped like a stone. Connie ducked as the lid whizzed by like a B-movie UFO to land with a ringing clatter on the street.

When Connie looked up again, Angie was gone. She clutched the lip of the garbage can and looked down at Angie sitting in the soupy muck. "Get out of there! Someone might have heard you screech as you dropped."

"This is so disgusting!" Angie stood. She wanted to wipe her hands, but she had nowhere to wipe them. Finally, she gave up, grabbed the lip of the can and tried to hoist herself up. The gunk she was standing in and the sides of the can were so greasy she felt like she was trying to climb straight up an oil slick. "I need some help."

"Ah, I know what to do." Connie circled the garbage can to the uphill side. "Lean against the downhill side of the can."

Angie grasped the lip opposite Connie. "Why?"

"When it hits the ground, crawl out!" Connie yelled, pushing with all her might. The can began to tip.

"Noooo!" Angie's world tilted. As the sidewalk rushed up at her, she bobbed down. Garbage sloshed over her like a great, smelly tidal wave.

On its side, free from the confines of the other cans, Angie's had room to roll. And it did.

A high, slightly gurgling wail filled the night air.

Connie watched in mute horror as the can bounced down the hill, accelerating with each roll like some great planet spinning madly on its axis. Scraps of garbage whirled out onto the pavement, leaving a slimy trail down the alley.

Connie ran down the hill after it, waving her arms. "Angie! Stop!"

The wail grew higher and louder.

Finally, the can smacked into a lamppost and with a small, dying teeter, came to rest.

Connie dropped to her knees beside it, afraid to look inside. "Angie?" she squeaked. She gave it a little tap. "Angie? Are you still alive? Can you talk to me?"

Slowly, painfully, Angie crawled onto the street, and then sat woefully on the sidewalk wiping from her face and hair coffee grounds, eggshells, all manner of once-green vegetables, and what looked like the inner parts of a crab.

"Is there anything I can do?" Connie blubbered, wringing her hands.

"One thing." Angie sat woefully on the sidewalk. "Next time I ask you to help me..."

"Yes?"

"Refuse."

6

The next morning, Paavo sat in Lieutenant Ralph Hollins's office on the fourth floor of the Hall of Justice. The room was miniscule, tucked in a corner of the fourth floor Homicide bureau, although the Hall itself was massive, ugly, and overlooked a freeway. It was not your high-class real estate.

Paavo told Hollins about the break-ins at his and Angie's homes. "I can't figure out what they want, what they were looking for, or why they tore up my place after giving Angie's the kid glove treatment. It was almost as if they were pissed off, or irritated that they couldn't find what they wanted. Whatever it was."

Ben Chan finally had found time to check the findings from Paavo's house, but so far had nothing to report. The only good news was that his cat had come home.

"It sounds weird," Hollins said. In his fifties, with gray hair and a protruding stomach, he was in charge of Homicide, which gave him a close acquaintance with Rolaids. "Take the time you need and keep me posted. I don't believe in coincidence either." An unlit cigar was held firmly between his lips. He couldn't light it—not with San Francisco's no-smoking policy—but he could pretend. "Any leads yet on yesterday's Tenderloin murder?"

"No leads, but I found something interesting," Paavo said. "The vic had a record. Served time for armed robbery, burglaries, was even accused of some killings, but they were never proven."

"Killings? Plural? You talking organized crime?"

"Not sure. He seems like a loner—a guy who, now and then, got in over his head. We were told his name was Jacob Platt, but it's really Platnikov. Jakob-with-a-'K' Platnikov. He was born in Russia, came over here in the eighties. He was young and might have been involved with a Russian mob."

Hollins quietly watched cars zip by on the freeway. "They were in the city back then. We called them the Russian *mafiya*, adding a 'y' to the Italian name. He could have been part of it. Hell, I've heard their black market worked better than the Communist party. That's why it survived when the party went to hell."

"We're trying to find out what Platnikov was involved in," Paavo continued. "Based on something his granddaughter said, he might have been making forgeries of good jewelry. Whoever killed him might have been looking for the good stuff. We found no jewelry, real or fake, in the apartment, so my guess is that they found what they were looking for."

Hollins took the cigar from his mouth. "Jewelry? Have you talked to Mayfield about her new case?"

Rebecca Mayfield... the homicide inspector Angie called the 'little helper bee.' "Not yet. Why?"

"She's got a dead jeweler on her hands. A well-known and respected jeweler. The jeweler's name was Gregor Rosinsky— another Russian."

As much as Angie welcomed living with Paavo for a few days, staying at a hotel was extravagant.

Especially when he walked out and left her alone each morning. There was duty, and then there was being enjoyment-challenged.

She was walking a little slowly this morning, the bumps and bruises she'd gotten rolling around in garbage had stiffened over night. She took a couple Advil, then made an appointment for a locksmith to meet her at her apartment. New, maximum security locks would make it safe for her and Paavo to simply stay at her place until his new bed was delivered. A couple of days under Sal Amalfi's roof shouldn't bother him too much.

As she approached her apartment building, her nerves jangled, and her mind replayed Paavo's reaction to the break-ins. He was usually pretty sanguine about things, but this robbery-attempt seemed to shake him up. That troubled her.

When she reached her block, she scrutinized the sidewalks, the doorways, the parked cars. Being this close to home, she'd expected her uneasiness to dissipate, but it didn't. Driving slowly, she continued past her building. Around the corner, situated with a view of the main entrance to the apartments and the garage, two men sat in a dark blue Mercury. One raised a newspaper higher as she drove by.

Was it to cover his face?

What kind of people sat in their cars to read newspapers in a residential neighborhood? She didn't think she wanted to know.

As she circled the block, she called Stan on her cell phone.

"Look out your window," she said when he answered. "Two men are sitting in a dark blue sedan at the corner. Do you see them? Do you know if they've been there long?"

"Gee, Angie, I don't make it a habit to sit at my window and ogle parked cars." She heard him moving about. "I see the car. So what? Where are you?"

"I'm a couple blocks away. I'm just being a little paranoid, okay? I want to be sure those guys aren't waiting for me."

"A *little* paranoid? You've hung out with that cop too long. This is not normal behavior. I know you had a break-in, but--"

"Humor me. I'm going to park and walk slowly toward the building. If you see those guys get out of the car, tell me, and I'll run back to my car and get away."

"That's ridiculous! Why don't you park in the building's garage like you always do? It's secure."

"Not secure enough. If anyone is after me, I'm not entering some dark, creepy garage. Now, will you just watch, please?"

"All right. I'm watching. If I were you, I'd just put more locks on my door."

The only open parking space was a half block from her apartment. She took it, and then held the car's key fob with its remote start capability in hand. She might have to make a fast get-away.

"You still there, Stan?" she asked as she neared the building.

"I'm here. I see you. I can't see the guys in the car, but I see the car."

She froze. *What do you mean, you can't see the guys in the car?*

"Not from this angle. But if they get out, I'll see the doors open."

"Oh. Okay." She slowly began walking again. "So far nothing?"

"Nothing."

She was just two doors from her building, with each step feeling more self-conscious and foolish for having asked Stan to help.

"Angie, *stop!*" Stan's voice was hushed, urgent.

Her feet felt glued to the pavement. "What?"

"I moved to the bedroom to look. The blue car is empty. Of course, it could mean nothing."

Or, it could mean... She bit her lip, clutching the phone. How paranoid was she? They could be anybody. Two men looking for an apartment to rent, checking the want-ads. Or...

Oh, hell! She could meet the locksmith another day when her nerves weren't as wound up as a Slinky toy.

She turned back toward her car.

"Angie, run!" Stan yelled.

Aches and bruises forgotten, she didn't even stop to look back, but hit the remote to start the engine, then hurled herself at her car, jumped inside and slammed down the door locks. All she could think of was to stomp on the gas.

Heart-pounding, she glanced in her rearview mirror, but saw only the backs of the men's heads. She guessed they were hurrying back to their car.

Her Lexus left them in her dust for the moment, but she wasn't sure how long it would be before they caught up with her.

"Hello? Hello?" Stan yelled.

Her hands were too tight on the wheel to press a button to connect her phone to the car's speaker. She careened wildly down Russian Hill, tearing across level intersections and then feeling the car became airborne as the pavement dropped steeply after each cross street. The jarring as the wheels bounded onto the roadway made her wince, both for her car's body and her own. She felt like a stunt-driver in a Hollywood action film.

"Angie? Angie? Where are you? Can you hear me?" Stan was sounding desperate.

She glanced again in the rearview mirror. No dark car followed. With shaking fingers, she connected her phone to the hands-free system. "I'm here." She was breathless. "Did you see them follow me?"

"No. They went back to their car, sat a while, and then drove off."

"Thank God!"

"I tell you, you made a faster getaway than Bonnie and Clyde."

Homicide Inspector Rebecca Mayfield walked into the homicide bureau and sat at her desk.

Hangdog eyes that always made Paavo slightly uncomfortable peered up at him as he approached her. If it hadn't been for Angie coming into his life, the two of them probably would have been a bureau item. She was the type of woman that had attracted him in the past, the type everyone who knew him believed was right for him. On some gut level, he knew Rebecca and the bureau matchmakers had a point.

Although he'd recently learned that on Christmas Eve, while Rebecca was working, she'd met Richie Amalfi, Angie's ne'er-do-well cousin. To his astonishment, Rebecca didn't seem to hate the guy, at least not completely. But apparently, despite their interesting day, Richie hadn't called her, so she said nothing more about him.

Now, Rebecca gave Paavo the files he had requested on Gregor Rosinsky, the jewelry and watch repairer whose murder she and Never-Take-A-Chance Sutter had been investigating.

Back at his desk, Paavo began to read.

Rosinsky was seventy-two when he was killed. He'd been in the US fifty years. He had left the USSR as a teenager by way of China, working his way to Japan and eventually ended up in California.

He seemed to spend his early years in the US walking a fine line between legality and crime. His rap sheet showed several arrests, but he had spent less than a week in jail, and that was at the county level for passing bad checks. He probably would have been given a suspended sentence for the crime, except that he'd been allowed so many chances in the past.

Then, his arrest record suddenly stopped. That meant he had gone straight or had found protection.

Rosinsky was married, with two sons and a daughter. His wife didn't work; all three children were married. The daughter had moved to Phoenix and was a realtor, one son went to Los Angeles where he worked at Warner Studios, and the other, the oldest, was still in San Francisco, now calling himself "Rosin." He was an attorney.

Twenty years ago, Rosinsky had opened Rose Jewelry, Ltd. Small and exclusive, it earned a reputation for quality jewelry and watch repair.

Nothing in the file indicated why Rosinsky ended up on the wrong end of a bullet.

His death occurred at approximately eight o'clock in the evening. The store was closed, and he apparently had stayed to do paper work. Rosinsky's wife, worried when she couldn't contact her husband, had called their son late that night. She'd been particularly anxious because three nights earlier, someone had broken into the store. They must have been scared off because nothing had been stolen.

This time, strangely, there were no signs of a break-in. Rosinsky's body had been found in back of the shop. Whoever killed him may have entered from the backdoor, but if so, Rosinsky must have opened it for him. Paavo couldn't see a jeweler opening any door after hours unless he knew and trusted the caller. Rosinsky had known his killer.

If whoever killed him had stolen some of the jewels, the crime would have made more sense. That, at least, would have been a red herring and thrown the police off on motive. Right now, it looked like an execution.

Paavo read through the crime lab reports. A lot of finger-prints had been lifted in the back area. He doubted anything conclusive would show up, though. Since it appeared Rosinsky wasn't killed as part of a conventional robbery, it couldn't be investigated as that kind of case.

Paavo's instincts told him that this had been a professional job. Someone had wanted the jeweler dead.

He read through Mayfield and Sutter's reports on talks with friends, neighbors and associates of the victim, but nothing there was helpful. Something niggled at him as he read, and he turned back to the beginning of Rebecca's write-up.

Then he saw it. Rosinsky's wife had said the store was broken into three nights before he was killed, the day before his and Angie's homes were burglarized. It was an interesting coincidence, but nothing more.

7

———————

While Angie directed, Paavo drove her Lexus nearly to the top of Telegraph Hill, and parked on Montgomery Street near Filbert. While most of the hill sloped gently down from Coit Tower to Fisherman's Wharf and North Beach, the east side dropped steeply to the Embarcadero. Streets were no more than footpaths and stairways, and ended abruptly at retaining walls, hillsides or parapets. Sections of unpaved landscaping and terraced, private gardens made the area green and lush.

Angie could have danced with excitement, but kept mum about where they were going or why. After telling Paavo about the two men watching her apartment building, she knew she wouldn't be returning there until this situation was settled. He seemed to assume she'd move in with her parents for a while. She had a better idea.

The block of Filbert they walked down had no paved roadway. Instead, wooden stairs and walkways zigzagged along the hillside, surrounded by trees, vines, ferns, and a lush central garden.

About a third of the way down, she opened a small wooden

gate and followed a stone walkway through a tiny fern garden to a white cottage. Paavo wore a bemused but curious expression. Many of the homes on this hill had been miners' shacks when first built, but had withstood the big earthquake and fire of 1906, and by way of age and location, were now worth nearly as much as one of the mines might have been.

As she pulled a key from her purse and dangled it in front of him, he murmured, "Home Sweet Home."

"You figured it out!" Wearing a big smile, she unlocked the door, and stepped inside.

"I don't believe this," he said.

In almost no time, she showed him the little foursquare house. The front door opened to a pleasant parlor, with casement windows overlooking the Filbert gardens, and a brick fireplace on the right-hand wall. Beyond the living room an archway led to a dining area with French doors that opened to a deck. The kitchen was to the left of the dining area. The sole bedroom was to the left of the front door. Like the living room, it also looked out onto the Filbert steps and central gardens. A bathroom had been built off the bedroom, probably as an after-thought many years ago.

Angie could have put two of these cottages into her apartment.

"My cousin Richie is in real estate and he owes my father a favor," she said. "When I told him what happened to me, he gave me the place for a month. Two, if we want it."

"This is the same cousin whose business dealings are a bit—"

"Sketchy?" she suggested. "Yeah, that's the one."

"The same one who recently spent Christmas Eve with Rebecca Mayfield," Paavo said.

"Don't remind me. I can't imagine! Just be thankful they didn't kill each other."

Paavo didn't pursue it. "So where is he going to live?"

"He doesn't live here. It's one of his rentals. It's vacant now, that's all." She couldn't explain why the place was nicely furnished and stocked with food. Some things about Cousin Richie's life were best not to question.

"I don't know about this," Paavo muttered. Despite his uncertainty, he seemed to find the little house appealing. It invited comfort and relaxation. As he peered out the window at the Filbert steps and the lush, green garden that gave it a secure, almost tropical feeling, she thought he was weakening. "This is nice, but it would make more sense for you to leave the city and stay at your parents' house."

Her gaze gripped his. "Is that really what you want?"

"No," he admitted.

She smiled with relief. "It's settled, then. We'll stay here together, safe and comfortable, while you find out what's going on." Taking his hand, she led him through the French doors to a postage-stamp size deck filled with containers of flowers. The hillside dropped away beneath it. "Look at how pretty the geraniums and impatiens are, even at this time of year. It's like a touch of springtime, right in the heart of the city. This place will be good for us."

"To find out how incompatible we really are?" he asked.

Her arm circled his waist. "We know that already."

She's right about that, Paavo thought. He draped an arm over her shoulders. "It sounds like you've made up your mind." He knew a steamroller when one hit him—even if only a hundred ten pounder. He had to admit the thought of living here with Angie on a trial basis appealed to him. He even had to admit that living with Angie on a permanent basis was something he dwelled on at length.

"We're here. Let's enjoy ourselves." She faced him, her back against the railing. "I stopped at the grocery. How do grilled T-bone steaks with olive and oregano relish, pine nut and basil rice, steamed zucchini, and a romaine salad with Parmesan dressing sound to you? I thought it would be nice to stay home for dinner."

Home... he liked the sound of that. He placed his hands on her small waist.

"And after dinner we can go to your place and pick up Hercules," she added.

"Can I trust you not to spoil that cat, Angie?"

"Nope." She grinned wickedly. "And I'll spoil his master, too, if given half a chance." He moved closer, very much liking the gleam in her eye, and quite ready to let himself be spoiled any way she wanted.

Her phone began to ring. Her voluminous tote was on the walnut table in the dining area and she dug through it to find the phone. After listening for a minute, her face paled, she murmured, "Okay," and handed the call to Paavo. "It's Yosh. I thought he was still on vacation? Your phone is switched off or the battery's dead. That's why he tried me. He says it's urgent."

Paavo took the phone, a thousand questions going through his head at the word his partner used. Urgent in police lingo meant very bad news.

"Yosh, what's up?" he asked.

"It seems there was a break-in," Yosh replied. "At your step-father's." A long moment went by before Yosh added, "He was shot."

8

———

Seventy miles south of Tucson, US Highway 19 crossed the Arizona border into Mexico at Nogales. Other Arizona crossings were smaller, like the mountain pass from Douglas to Agua Prieta about a hundred miles east, or the blistering, barren desert crossing at Sonoita, over a hundred miles to the west. Around Nogales, the land consisted of rough desert, parched ranch land, a few paved roads, and lots of footpaths for illegal crossings.

On an expanse of land on the Mexican side, thirty miles southeast of the border checkpoint, in an area so remote and desolate not even cartel members dotted the landscape by night, stood a two-room adobe. The house and garden were ringed by a six-foot adobe wall with a flat overhanging stone along the top, and a solid wooden gate. Such a wall helped keep down the number of snakes, scorpions and tarantulas... and larger creatures... that might attempt to enter the house.

A woman walked out of the gate and shut it firmly behind her. Her tooled leather boots crunched on the umber-colored rock and gritty sand as she continued along the well-worn path from the gate to the nearest saguaro. She was tall and angular, her muscles toned from a daily routine of weights and running. Her gray hair was clipped short. Her eyes were green—the color of the cholla and Mexican sage that dotted the Sonoran desert she had learned to call home.

She didn't know if she could ever learn to truly love the desert. She'd grown up along the eastern seaboard, Maryland as a child, then to Massachusetts while a teenager, until she moved south again. She missed the greenery of that area, the thick foliage of the trees and bushes in spring and summer, the bright colors of autumn, and the peacefulness after a fresh snow. But most of all, she missed the water. Beautiful, blue, cool water. She missed the streams and ponds, lakes and rivers, of her childhood.

She had learned to respect the desert in all its craggy intensity, it harshness, and its desolation. It constantly tested and had made her stronger. The desert, more than anything she had ever known, taught her to abide.

A square metallic target holder hung from an arm of the cactus. She attached a new paper target to it. Then, just for the hell of it, she reached into the yellow straw pouch she carried, and lined up five tin cans in a row on the ground beneath the target.

The day before, she'd made her weekly jaunt across the border to Tucson. There, she did her shopping, picked up her mail if any, saw people rather than simply the desert critters that lived near her home, and bought gas for her car and home generator. Most importantly, she would go to a cafe with internet service and catch up on the world.

She had no internet or even a telephone at home preferring to live completely "off the grid." Her main conveniences were a well and a generator. She didn't even use her real name. For the past thirty years, she'd called herself Jennifer McGraw.

As she sat in the cafe with a burrito and a beer, after looking at the major US national newspapers, she then turned, as always, to the *San Francisco Chronicle*. She rarely found anything of importance in the papers, and never expected yesterday to be any different. Force of habit, and a perverse interest in the city's crime scene, kept her at it. With some shock she noted the murder of a jeweler during a robbery. It bothered her, a lot, but then she told herself a jeweler's robbery wasn't an unexpected occurrence, even if the jeweler was Gregor Rosinsky.

Ironically, she'd almost overlooked a much smaller article tucked near the obituary page about the murder of another elderly man, Jacob Platt.

Only as she read about that second murder, did her heart begin to drum and her nerves turn raw and tight. She wondered if the authorities had found out yet that the victim's name was really Jakob Platnikov? And if they had, did they realize what it meant?

Rosinsky and Platnikov… the past came rushing back at her.

Now, back on her land, she paced off exactly twenty steps from the target. Keeping her back to it, she first put on the poly-carbonate wrap-around safety glasses, then fitted the shooting muffs over her ears, and slung her magazine pouch over her shoulder. Last, she removed the Glock 19 from her shoulder holster, dropped the half-used magazine, and slapped in a new ten-rounder. The 9mm compact was less than seven inches long and five in width. It fit easily into her handbag, and was comfortable in her hand. She knew it intimately, knew every nuance of its high-impact resistant polymer grasp. She'd used it to practice with on numerous occasions. Soon, she would use it for more than practice.

She breathed deeply, head bowed slightly, feet wide apart, clearing her mind of the distractions of the day. A blue-black buzzard circled overhead. Near a dry creek bed, two cottontails scampered. She saw none of it, saw only the real target, not her phony paper one.

In one fluid motion, she spun to face the target, formed the isosceles position and fired ten rounds. The completed magazine dropped out, and she slammed a new one into place, then began moving leftward. As she did, she fired another ten rounds, then ten more as she worked her way back to her starting place.

Twenty-five of the shots were bull's eyes, the other five missing by scarcely an inch.

Last of all, she straightened, one arm extended, eye on the sight. She shot the five cans, watching with satisfaction as they "pinged" and flew up into the air, dropping down to land on the ground like so many dead men.

Green eyes, cold and hard, swept the barren landscape. She shoved another magazine into the Glock. She knew what she must do.

Cops were easy to find.

So were dead men.

She had waited long enough. It was time to act.

9

———

Angie hurried alongside Paavo from the parking lot to San Francisco General Hospital, a massive complex of old brick and modern cement-gray buildings. Her chest ached with fear. Aulis was the only family Paavo had left.

Apparently, a neighbor had found his stepfather and called for an ambulance. The police were contacted, and the responding officer knew Paavo. When he couldn't reach him directly, he phoned Yosh. The blue brotherhood in action, she thought, not wanting Paavo to find out about Aulis from some stranger.

The hospital was chaotic. Most of the city's emergency and trauma cases arrived there, hundreds each day. To simply get the desk nurse to direct them to the proper waiting room presented a challenge.

Seated on an aluminum and blue plastic chair in the bright yellow room, Paavo leaned forward, elbows on thighs, hands folded, and stared silently at the gray linoleum floor.

"Aulis will be all right," Angie said gently. She sat beside him, her hand lightly rubbing circles on his back.

His complexion had a sallow cast to it, his eyes filled with sadness. "Not many eighty-year-olds can survive a gunshot wound."

She had no words to ease his pain and blinked back tears. "I'm so sorry, Paavo."

His hands clenched. "Damn it! I should have thought of Aulis when they hit your place, then mine!"

"Don't! You can't blame yourself for this. Any connection between you and me makes some sense. Or between you and Aulis. But you and me and Aulis? There isn't any. It's got to be chance coming up all wrong—one of those horrible, random things, so much a part of city life, that end up touching all of us."

"I've worried about him living alone at his age."

She rested her hand atop his. "He's surrounded by friends and long-time neighbors, as he's told you whenever you've brought the subject up. He's happy in his home. This isn't your fault!"

He pulled his hand away and clenched it. "I'll know if that's true, once I know what caused this to happen to him."

"He's going to be all right." She tried desperately to give her voice conviction, but she failed. Like Paavo, she knew Aulis's age was against him. A head wound… She shuddered.

Needing to do something more than sit helplessly and wait in the excruciating silence of the waiting room, she went in search of coffee. Near the waiting room, a canteen area held a coffee machine. On the first floor was a large, busy cafeteria. The coffee tasted weak and oily in both.

Paavo was talking on his phone when she returned. He soon hung up and eyed the Starbucks label on the paper cup she handed him. "I was wondering where you'd gone off to."

She offered some lemon tarts and almond croissants, but he shook his head.

"Has the doctor talked to you yet?" she asked, sitting in a plastic chair beside him.

"No one has," he said bitterly, "except to say the doctors are with him. I tracked down the patrolman who took the call to go to Aulis's place. He said the apartment had been pretty well trashed, and that Aulis had lost a lot of blood."

Angie's outrage nearly spilled over, but she forced it in check. Paavo had always been her Gibraltar. She was the one who got emotional, and he would rationally calm her down. Now, he was the one hurting, and she had to help him. She wasn't sure what to say or do, so she placed her arm across his broad back and silently held him.

After a while, a buxom, middle-aged nurse entered the waiting room and walked toward them. Paavo's face paled. He slowly stood.

"You're Mr. Kokkonen's son?"

"Yes."

"I understand no one has given you much information yet. I'm sorry."

He nodded quickly.

"Fortunately, the bullet did not enter Mr. Kokkonen's brain. But it did graze the skull and caused some bone damage and considerable swelling from the impact. We will have to see how much trauma the brain suffered. He's in a coma. With his age, and this type of wound, I'm afraid the situation is extremely critical. You need to prepare yourself for that."

He nodded again, not answering. Angie watched his hopes fall when the nurse said there was swelling.

"The doctor will probably be with him another hour or so. You might want to grab a bite to eat, then come back later when we'll be able to tell you something more substantial."

"I see," Paavo murmured.

"Also, we'll need Mr. Kokkonen's insurance papers. Medicare will cover some of the expenses, but you might want to know all that he's entitled to and what it will cost. I suggest you bring his policy into the hospital as soon as possible so that our billings staff can go over your options with you." She shoved a set of papers as thick as the city's phone book into his hands. He just stared at them as she walked away.

"Christ almighty!" Paavo collapsed into the chair again, then slapped the papers onto the empty seat beside him. "He might be dying and she wants me to worry about insurance forms."

"The world is going crazy." Angie reached over, grabbed the papers and stuffed them into her tote bag.

"You go and eat," Paavo said. "I'm not hungry."

She gazed at the doors the nurse went through. Aulis was back there, alone and hurt, fighting for his life, and Paavo here, his heart aching.

"We'll wait." She took his hand.

"You, then me, now Aulis," he whispered, his hand tightening painfully on hers. "Why, Angie? It doesn't make any sense. What could we have that would make anyone interested in us, and why in hell would anyone want to hurt a sweet old man like Aulis?"

There were no words she could say. They sat in silence, Paavo's hand in hers, and she hoped the connection brought some comfort beyond his dark, lonely thoughts.

"Rosinsky and Platnikov are dead!" Harold Partridge screamed into the phone, his voice growing shriller with each word. "Do you realize what this means? Do you?"

"We're sorry, sir."

"Sorry? That doesn't begin to say what you'll be!" He had a strangle hold on the phone and wished it was their necks. "I still don't have the music box. It's got to be with the woman."

"She seems to be hiding. She hasn't returned to her apartment."

"I'm surrounded by complete, utter morons! Do I have to do everything myself? Her boyfriend's a cop, goddamn it! A homicide cop. Find her through him!" Partridge's voice was raw from yelling. It was good his office was soundproof.

"I guess we can try to find him and put a tail on him."

"Hell, if you can't find him any other way, you can always *kill* someone then wait while he shows up to investigate!" He hung up, his heart beating so hard and fast he feared for his blood-pressure.

Rosinsky and Platnikov. He took off his glasses and shut his eyes, fear and dread drenching him with sweat.

He wasn't about to let it start again; he would stop it, one way or the other.

10

The next afternoon, Sunday, Paavo parked in the driveway of Aulis's apartment building. As he and Angie got out of the car, the area seemed eerily quiet. Usually, neighbors milled about on the street chatting with each other, children played, dogs barked, and low rider cars generated a pulsating *thump-tha-thump* from bass speakers as they cruised by.

They were about a block from Mission Dolores, built by Spanish padres with Ohlone Indian labor at the same time as the Revolutionary War was erupting on the other side of the continent. This area was a touch of Mexico in the heart of the city, filled with *los restaurantes y las abarroterías.*

Aulis's apartment was located on ground level of a three-story building, at the end of a long, flowerpot-lined path behind the garage. Paavo unlocked the front door and walked in, leaving the door wide for Angie to follow if she wished. He wouldn't blame her if she preferred to remain outside. Being here, knowing Aulis lay hospitalized and close to death, chilled him to the bone.

Three steps inside the door a dark pool of blood stained the beige carpet. His breath caught.

Yesterday, investigators had swept through the crime scene. He was glad he had asked the CSU to go over Angie's apartment after the break-in there, as well as the one in his own home. Now, the crime lab could look for similarities between the three. There had to be some.

Yesterday, too, he and Angie had spent the entire day and most of the night at the hospital. Aulis remained in a coma in intensive care, and was allowed no visitors. His condition had not changed that morning, although Paavo was allowed into the room to see him.

The only joy in the past twenty-four hours came from bringing Hercules back to the little cottage. He was so ecstatic to be with Paavo again that every time Paavo sat down, all eighteen pounds of cat bounded onto his lap. Angie immediately treated the big tabby to a plate of fresh salmon.

Now, Paavo forced his eyes from the carpet stain to the rest of the apartment. The destruction so much resembled what had been done to his own home, for a moment he was unable to move. Sofa and chair pillows were slashed, drawers pulled out, books and magazines opened and strewn all over. A throbbing in his temples beat in sync with the heavy beat of his heart.

A quick walkthrough left him ready to explode in rage and frustration. Nothing, it seemed, had been stolen. He would talk to Aulis's neighbors, find out what they saw and heard.

Once he found out who was behind this, there'd be no stopping him. The bastard would pay in blood.

When he returned to the living room, Angie moved toward him. "What would you like me to do?" she asked.

"Nothing! Don't touch a thing."

He was immediately ashamed of his tone with her, especially when she gazed at him with quiet understanding. "I'll look for his address book," she said. "You'll need to make some phone calls, Paavo, to let his close friends know what's happened."

He hadn't thought of that. He stood again unmoving as a moment of excruciating silence went by. God, how was he going to get through this? He turned toward the bedroom.

In the top drawer of the pine highboy Aulis kept important papers. Paavo and his sister had been taught to never go near that drawer if they valued their skins. Aulis had a "system" and if the system was in any way disrupted, it meant he might not pay bills on time, not be able to find important papers, and in general, the stability of the world order would fall into disarray.

It was heartrending to see that most crucial drawer on its side, the contents littering the floor. Grimly, he righted the drawer, knelt down, and began to stack the papers.

He didn't have to dig too deeply through old tax filings, social security notices, property tax billings and other such documents before coming across the medical policy. Along with Medicare, Aulis had good coverage and should be well taken care of.

As he gathered up the rest of the papers and envelopes to return to the drawer, an envelope from the Ford Motor Corporation caught his eye. He added it to the stack. It was odd, though. Aulis had never owned a car. Didn't even like cars, Paavo thought. Curious, Paavo pulled it out of the pile and opened it.

Inside was a photograph and another, smaller envelope. He pulled out the photo, and his blood ran cold.

Three people stared at the camera. One of them, looking very young and very innocent, was his mother.

He knew her immediately, even though he had seen only one other picture of her. That other picture, one of his most valued possessions, showed him standing on her lap, leaning across a table and staring intently at a birthday cake with two candles. His hair was blond and wispy—it hadn't turned dark brown until his teens—and he wore canary yellow short pants with matching suspenders over a white shirt. His cheeks were puffed out, and he seemed to be blowing hard. His mother was holding him at the waist and laughing.

She was a pretty woman, her face fine-boned, with white, almost translucent skin. He couldn't tell the color of her eyes, which were Kodak-flash red in the photo, but her hair was auburn, shoulder length, and parted on the side. Her head was cocked and her hair swung free and easy except for a strand of it tucked behind one ear.

His only vivid memories of his mother were seeing her laugh in that picture and hearing her cry as if her heart had broken.

In this newly found photo, she looked very serious. Her eyes squinted against the sun, causing her brow to furrow, and her lips were set firmly. Her hair was loose and wavy, and she wore a jacket with padded shoulders over a colorful blouse and jeans, all very 1980s to Paavo's eyes. She held a black-haired, dark-skinned baby in her arms in a way that showed off the baby's frilly matching pink dress and booties. The baby had to be Jessica. She had big, shiny brown eyes and a knockout smile even at that young age.

The woman in this picture didn't mesh at all with the image he had of his mother. She was taller than he'd imagined, and bore herself in a stiff, cautious manner. Clipped to the waistband of her dress was an identification badge of some kind.

Beside her stood a hard-featured older man. He wore a similar badge clipped to the lapel of his suit jacket. His face was heavily lined and many shades darker than the woman's. His eyes were thin slits from squinting, his mouth turned down at the edges, and his brows crossed. His hair was worn in a short Afro, Paavo saw, and was as black as Jessica's had been.

Jessie had never known who her father was. It was hard to imagine this dour looking man being him, but the resemblance showed in the dimpled chin and in the widow's peak. How odd that Aulis hadn't given her this picture. But then, Paavo didn't know his own father either—only that he wasn't the same as Jessica's.

He'd always assumed that meant his mother was "just that kind of gal." Love 'em and leave 'em Mary Smith. She walked out on men and on her own kids. She was a real winner. Good old mom.

Sitting cross-legged on the floor, he reached again for the Ford envelope and shook it, dropping out the smaller white one still inside. On its face, in a cursive, feminine hand, Aulis's name had been written.

Inside were two sheets of paper. The first was a simple statement.

I hereby grant Aulis Kokkonen full authority to care for my children, Jessica Ann and Paavo Smith, until my return. This includes the right to authorize any medical care necessary.

Mary Smith

He snorted, surprised his mother had bothered with such legal niceties. Maybe she'd run off and left her kids with Aulis more than once, and the last time hadn't returned.

He put the sheet aside. The one under it was a letter, written in the same hand as the statement had been. As he read, his throat began closing, tightening, until he could scarcely breathe.

Aulis,

I'm a dead woman. I've failed. Take care of my children, dear friend. Enclosed are the documents you will need. Tell them nothing about me—absolutely nothing. It's the only way they will be safe. Kiss Jessie and Paavo goodbye for me. Please destroy this letter.

Cecily

Cecily? He stared at the letter, unable to believe its contents. Reading it again, he was hurled back in time and place. The old pain, the loneliness, the question *why*—all those feelings he had sworn he would never again allow himself about his mother or his past—washed over him. He was back at the age when he told himself that strong boys don't cry, the age he had taught himself not to shed a tear, ever.

He dropped his head forward, his eyes squeezed tight. *Kiss Jessie and Paavo goodbye for me.*

It hurt his heart to see those words.

His gave returned to her signature. Why had his mother signed her name Cecily? Her name was Mary. Mary Smith... so common a name he'd almost, *almost* believed it was false. But then if someone were choosing a fake name, he'd convinced himself, they would certainly pick something less blatantly phony than Mary Smith.

Over the years he told himself he was being too suspicious thinking her name was false, being too much the cop. Now, he wondered if he'd been right. Strangely, the name Cecily resonated with him. He had no idea why, but seeing it written there, hearing it in his head, made the hair on the back of his neck stand on end.

His fingers smoothed the folds of the letter. It was undated. What did she mean about keeping her children safe? Aulis had never given any indication of them having been in danger, but that would explain why he had taken them to L.A. shortly after their mother had abandoned them... not that Paavo remembered being there. He was so young it didn't much register on him which city he was in, but Jessica had told him about it. All he did remember was that Aulis seemed to move around quite a bit, taking him and Jessie from city to city, one small apartment to another, until they all became a blur to him. Eventually, they returned to San Francisco.

He didn't understand what any of this meant, but he did know that Aulis had kept his part of the bargain. He had told Paavo nothing about his mother.

11

———

"I didn't know what to do or say, Bianca." Angie was fighting tears as she sat in her sister's kitchen. Since it was Monday, Paavo had returned to work.

Angie told Bianca about Paavo finding the strange letter from his mother. "First, the shock of Aulis's attack, and then that awful letter!"

"There's not much you could have said. You were there for him, that's what matters." Bianca was the oldest of her four sisters, the one she went to when she was troubled. She was little, like Angie, but outweighed her by about twenty pounds. Where Angie's hair was short and wavy with auburn highlights, Bianca's was straight, chin-length, and dark-brown.

"There for him? Hercules is *there* for him. The man is hurting and confused. I've seen Paavo upset about his cases and maybe once or twice even about me, but nothing like this. You know how quiet he gets when he's upset, well it was silent movie time at our place last night. I kept waiting for a piano player to show up."

Bianca had just taken a blueberry strudel from the oven, and cut a piece for Angie and one for herself. "When Aulis gets better, Paavo can ask him about his past."

"And if he doesn't get better?" The two sisters looked at each other sadly. "If Cecily's letter—if that's what her name really is—is to be believed, Paavo's whole life, his whole childhood, is based on a lie. It was such a strange, frightening letter. She gave Aulis her kids! I just don't get it. How can any mother do that?"

"It's hard to imagine that such a story could have been kept quiet all these years," Bianca said, pouring hot coffee and then sitting across from Angie. "People know about such things, and talk."

For the first time that morning, Angie smiled. "That's right, they do. They'll know. Neighbors will know. Anyone around at the time will know!"

"Slow down! This happened over thirty years ago."

"I'm not saying it'll be easy. But we aren't talking Harry Houdini here, either. She was just a woman with two kids, and no husband. Maybe she was heavily in debt, or... or owed money to some drug dealers. Who knows? That would be a reason to leave town!"

"Poor Paavo," Bianca murmured. "What a thing to discover."

"It's got to have been really horrible or she wouldn't have left her kids, I just know it." Angie sipped some coffee, lost in thought. "I wonder if Paavo should be the one to find out? It could be potentially devastating for him. Aulis kept the past hidden for a reason. At the same time, it's important. It's the... the prelude, so to speak... of the good man he's become. I'm afraid for him, Bianca. Maybe I should see what I can find out."

Bianca was lifting a piece of strudel to her mouth, but put it down at Angie's words. "Aren't you supposed to be hiding until the police catch whoever has been lurking around you, or your apartment, or whatever?"

Angie pushed her piece of strudel aside, her appetite gone. "Oh, the more I think about it, those two guys might have been salesmen, or Jehovah's Witnesses, or even Mormons. I might have made a mountain out of something completely innocent."

"And Aulis's shooting?" Bianca asked, with a worried frown.

"Well..." Angie didn't even try to answer. Instead of mountains and molehills, she was clutching at straws.

"Ah, here you are," Ray Faldo said as Paavo walked into the photo laboratory on the second floor of the Hall of Justice. "I'm just about ready to print. Give me a couple more minutes."

Faldo was the best lab man in the department. He could work wonders with the equipment they owned, making it perform almost as well as top of the line merchandise. That was why Paavo had gone to him for help. Faldo stared into the scope of a photo enlarger, and slowly adjusting dials. "I made a negative of the photo," he said, "and now I'm trying to see how large I can get it and keep it sharp. I figured you'd prefer a print instead of a computer printout."

Paavo sat on a stool at the end of the counter where Faldo worked.

"Who are these people, anyway?" Faldo turned the magnification knob.

"I found the photo at a crime scene," Paavo said. "It might be important."

Faldo made a few final adjustments to the focus. "The woman's quite a dish. A little flat-chested for my taste—"

"It's the badges I'm interested in," Paavo said, interrupting.

Faldo gave him an odd look, then he placed an 8x10 piece of low contrast resin-coated paper under the enlarger, set the timer, and flipped it on. "Badges? Oh, yeah. Those that she and the guy are wearing. Christ, is he her husband? Looks old enough to be her father. They made a cute kid, though." When the exposure was complete, he moved the paper into the developer tray, and after a short while turned it face up. The enlarged photo began to appear.

"How's your dad doing?" he asked as he used tongs to move the print into the stop bath.

Paavo shrugged, tamping down his impatience. "Same. Still in a coma."

"Well, he's hanging in there. Good for him. I've been working with Ben on the CSU materials from the break-ins. Nothing. I hate to say it, Paav, but the guys who did it were pros. Keep your girlfriend out of their way."

"She's found a place to stay until this is settled."

"Good." Faldo washed the print in plain water, squeegeed it, and hung it on an easel. "Here you go."

As Faldo turned on the fluorescent overhead lights, Paavo walked up to the photo. He could see some kind of symbols on the badges, but they were angled in a way that made them hard to read, and were still a little blurry. "Can anything be done with these to make them clearer? I'd like to know what they say."

"I doubt it, but I'll give it a try. If you're just curious about the badges, I can tell you about them. I used to wear one of those myself, years ago, before I decided I'd much rather live here in foggy and damp San Francisco than in hot and humid Washington."

Paavo eyed Faldo with surprise. "You know what these badges are?"

"Sure." Faldo grabbed a sponge and wiped up some spilled developer solution. "And if I didn't, the building would be a dead giveaway for old-timers like me. It's the Old Post Office Building in Washington D.C.--12th Street and Pennsylvania Avenue. Years back, when the post office moved out, other federal agencies moved in, including the FBI's metropolitan office. The blue background on the guy's badge meant he was a special agent, so he probably worked there before the J. Edgar Hoover Building opened up in the late '70s. The way they're dressed, her hair style, I'd say the photo is from the eighties or so. Maybe he wanted to show the building to his much younger wife. She isn't an agent, of course—almost no women were, back then. But it's pretty darn certain both of them worked for the FBI."

Angie unlocked the door to Aulis's apartment. As she entered, she shuddered, finding being here as eerie this time as the last. An unearthly chill hung in the air, along with a musty smell.

The investigators had finished their work, so the cleaning service she'd hired would be coming by in about an hour.

Today, when she first arrived in the neighborhood, she knocked on doors and asked people if they'd seen anything strange, particularly a dark blue Mercury which was the car outside her apartment, before or since Aulis's attack. As casually as she could slide it in, she also asked if they knew his old friend, Cecily. To her questions, everyone's answer was the same: "No."

Paavo told her that Aulis had lived in the small apartment for only the past fifteen years or so, but he had lived in the area for most of his life.

Her earlier phone calls to several of Aulis's old friends— Paavo left the address book at their house after making calls about Aulis being hospitalized—gave the same results. The people she spoke with were all quite elderly and sounded confused and anxious about her questions. She felt bad about upsetting them and stopped calling. For the moment, at least.

Now, walking around the ugly bloodstain inside the apartment, she rubbed the goose bumps on her arms. Something despicable was going on here. She wanted to scream, "Stop! Leave us alone!" and to explain that there was nothing that she or Paavo or Aulis owned that anyone might want. But what good would it do to shout at the walls?

She'd brought in the mail and flipped through the bills and advertisements before placing them on the coffee table with others accumulated since the attack. Paavo would need to take care of the bills. She should try to find any unpaid ones while they were on her mind.

Suddenly, outside Aulis's apartment, car wheels screeched, followed by a loud thud. She ran out to find a man lying on the street near her car. His head was bathed in blood.

Neighbors poured onto the street. "A black car hit him!" A little boy informed anyone who would listen. "I saw it!"

A man dropped on his knees to the hit-and-run victim. Angie understood when he used the word "<u>muerta.</u>" The man was dead.

12

Beginning in 1974, the FBI slowly moved into the new J. Edgar Hoover Building, a two-and-a-half million square foot monstrosity located on Pennsylvania Avenue between Ninth and Tenth streets in Washington D.C. It stands seven stories tall in the front, but the rear rises to eleven stories. Of the more than seven thousand employees in the building, less than a thousand are special agents. Most employees work on maintaining files, running the Uniform Crime Reporting Program, indexing and confirming fingerprints, and handling freedom of information requests.

Special Agent Nelson Bradley stood at the third-floor window by his cubicle and watched a turbaned Sikh and a woman in a bright-hued sari emerge from a cab. His thoughts weren't on the couple, who meant nothing to him, but on the message slip in his pudgy fingers. He didn't like the way his fingers had gotten fat, or the way the rest of him had as well, or the way his hair had thinned, and the years wore heavy on his face.

Simply reading Paavo Smith's name on the message slip had

made his hip begin to throb, adding to the generally aging and decrepit sentiment he had about himself. He hadn't heard from Smith in years, not since San Francisco happened. That was how he thought of it—*San Francisco happened.*

He went back into his cubicle. The blue burlap-covered partitions that divided the agents' desks made him feel like a rat in a maze. A Northern Telecom multi-buttoned telephone set, filled with features he didn't understand or care to use, waited silently for him. He hated his desk-bound job, but it was all he could do ever since going out to Frisco on a special assignment with a gang task force. Several Vietnamese families working in computer hardware manufacturing had been victims of home invasions. The FBI found an informant within the Vietnamese community and set up a sting operation. Bradley was a part of it, and when the sting went south, he was nearly killed. A couple of homicide cops, Smith and his partner, Kowalski, happened to be in the neighborhood investigating the latest home invasion murders when bullets started to fly. Kowalski had called for reinforcements as Smith went into the house with the agents to see if he could help. Smith found Bradley with his leg and hip torn up and bleeding badly. He pulled Bradley out of the back-door and toward an ambulance that answered Kowalski's call. Seconds after Bradley was clear of it, the house went up in a firebomb. The two other agents had been killed.

Bradley had heard that Kowalski, too, had been killed a while back. It was too bad. He'd been one of the good guys.

Bradley owed his life to Paavo Smith. He didn't like being in debt to anyone. He liked it even less than he liked being stuck here at a desk job in headquarters when he'd always been a field agent. No wonder he'd put on so many pounds. But at least they hadn't been able to retire him on disability like they had wanted to do. He had fought them. Leave it to the bureau to turn against you after you had given your all, he thought bitterly.

Always on his mind were the two guys who never had a chance for disability, Harris and Lane. They'd only been dead two weeks, he'd heard, when two new special agents were given their desks. Nobody cared, it seemed. Just him.

He returned Smith's call, and was given a strange request. Smith wanted to know if, some 35-40 years ago, anyone working for the FBI in Washington had been named "Cecily." That was it, just the one name.

He told Smith it would take a while. For him to act on such a request without higher up authorization was strictly illegal. He'd have to access employee records, which were protected from routine searches by anyone other than the personnel department.

He'd manage. Once he hacked into the database, he'd have plenty of time to manipulate it until he found what he needed. In fact, he had time for a lot of stuff these days. The work the Bureau gave him was garbage, something to keep him from twiddling his increasingly pudgy thumbs all day long. They wanted to insult him, to force him to ask for disability retirement, to somehow get rid of him.

No way. He'd stick around just to needle them. It was fun. It was payback.

"He's been moved out of intensive care," the nurse, a slim, blond woman in a crisp white uniform, said as she led Angie through a maze of corridors to Aulis's new private room.

"That's wonderful!" Angie cried. She felt as if her prayers had been answered. "He's awake, then?" she asked.

"Not yet. He's still in a coma," the nurse said. "But it's a light one. He can breathe on his own, his vital signs are strong, so he doesn't need the special equipment in intensive care. He's just not awake. We nurses call it a twilight sleep. The doctor will give you all the medical details, I'm sure."

"But overall, this means he's getting better?" Angie urged, trying hard to find some positive news.

"Let's just say, it's a good sign. Now, we have to wait and see how he is when he wakes up."

"You're saying he *will* wake up."

As if jarred by the question, the nurse stopped and glanced sympathetically at Angie. "At his age... the doctor will be able to tell you more."

Their gait was slower this time. "What has your experience been?" Angie asked.

"In my experience"—the nurse seemed hesitant—"in my experience, it's pneumonia, not the coma, that you have to be worried about. For older people, having to lie on their backs, being unable to move, fluid collects in their lungs, and sometimes, there isn't a thing we can do about it."

"I see." The graveness of it was all but overwhelming. The two continued on in silence.

In the hallway, two nuns stood talking. They both wore traditional, floor-length black habits with a white coif against their faces under a black veil.

"Here we are." The nurse turned into the private room right where the nuns were standing. Their proximity gave Angie a chill, as if Aulis might be closer to death than anyone had been led to believe.

The nurse bustled about the room, quickly checking Aulis and scanning his chart. "I'll leave Mr. Kokkonen in your hands," she said, then was gone in a flurry of white.

Angie went to Aulis's side and held his hand as she greeted him. She told him that she and Paavo were well, and looked forward to him getting better and going home. She said a few more words, then stepped back, saddened that she could see no change, no reaction at all in the old man. She covered her face in her hands.

"Are you all right, dear?"

Angie glanced up to see one of the nuns in the doorway. She was an older woman with an angular face and plain, rimless glasses. Her hands were folded, her expression curious but serene.

"Yes," Angie said. "It's just that I'm so worried."

The nun entered the room. "I'm Sister Ignatius. I visit our Catholic patients here, along with Sister Agnes. But I'm afraid I don't know this man."

Angie placed her hand on Aulis's. "His name is Aulis Kokkonen. He's Lutheran, but I'm sure he wouldn't mind your visits or your prayers."

The nun smiled. "Well, thank you. I'll be sure to stop by, then, on my rounds. Is he a relative?"

"No... not yet. I'm engaged to his... his son."

"Ah, I see," the nun said warmly. She studied the bandages on Aulis's head. "What happened to him?"

"He was shot."

"Oh, my!"

"It was a robbery, we think, at his apartment." As Angie began to explain what had happened, the thought that niggled at the back of her mind sprang forth and her eyes filled with tears. "First my apartment was burglarized, then Paavo's—that's my fiancé—and a few days later, Mr. Kokkonen's. I'm so scared that the three burglaries might be related. If so, it all started with me." She took a Kleenex from the bedside table and wiped away her tears.

"Why you?"

"I don't know! That's the problem. If it was me, why? I don't understand the connection between Paavo and Aulis and me with these robbers. Yet, they struck my apartment first."

The nun's warm expression was surprisingly calming. "It's

not your fault, dear. You can't know what would possess someone to go after another person."

"Thank you, Sister," Angie intoned, the nun's words making her feel a little better. She even felt a twinge of good old Catholic guilt over her initial reaction to the two nuns in the hall.

"It does sound as if you and your friend need to be careful, however," the nun cautioned.

"We're trying to be," Angie replied.

"Good. I'm glad." She glanced at the clock on the wall. "Oh, gracious! I must go, now. I'm sure Sister Agnes must be ready to leave without me. We can't be late for evening prayers."

"I'm glad to have met you, Sister," Angie said. "My name is Angelina Amalfi, by the way. People call me Angie."

"I'm sorry for your friend," the nun said, and then she was gone.

The room felt emptier and colder. As Angie watched over Aulis, she said a few prayers as well, for Aulis, for herself, and especially for Paavo.

Paavo glanced at the clock on the once white, now-in-need-of-paint wall in the Homicide bureau. Nine o'clock. At night.

The detail was empty, everyone gone but him. Mayfield and Sutter had been here until about ten minutes ago when a new case landed in their laps, a domestic dispute gone bad. Neighbors had called the cops, but by the time the uniforms got there, all was quiet. They found the wife dead in the kitchen, the husband missing.

FBI Agent Nelson Bradley had phoned earlier and told Paavo he'd best be able to access the personnel info when only the night shift people were around. They were the forgotten people. There weren't many of them, and no one bothered, at that time, to peer over anyone else's shoulders to check on the validity of their "need-to-know" the data they were accessing.

A friend in personnel had given Bradley the password and access codes to get into those files without raising red flags in the Integrity Branch. One disaffected employee helping another, Paavo thought. He guessed it was some sort of bureaucratic sense of justice.

Now, he awaited Bradley's call.

The evening quiet gave him a chance to make a few phone calls to speed up the identification of the hit-and-run victim outside Aulis's apartment when Angie happened to be there. Paavo didn't like the preliminary findings, that the victim—slim, late thirties, no distinguishing characteristics—had no identification on him, and no fingerprints on file. He was a John Doe, and unless something dramatic turned up, he'd continue to be one.

The only interesting information came from a med tech at the scene, who had noticed the victim's teeth. Several were missing and the ones still in his mouth were decayed. In Paavo's experience, most people with bad teeth ended up in a dentist's chair at some point. The only ones he'd seen who hadn't, were generally from poor, third-world countries.

Witnesses couldn't agree on whether or not John Doe was heading toward Angie's car or Aulis's apartment when struck by a black car with no license plates. Something in the features caused everyone to believe the driver was a woman with short hair. Just what it was about the features couldn't be agreed upon, and the consensus was that the car sped by too quickly for anyone to get a good enough look at the driver to attempt a composite drawing.

A few people also noticed another car, a black... or brown... or dark blue one, leave the scene immediately after the accident, going in the opposite direction from the hit-and-run driver. No details could be given about that driver, either.

The phone rang shrilly, and Paavo started. "Smith, Homicide."

"It's me."

Paavo recognized Bradley's voice. His spine stiffened. "Any luck?"

"I searched the personnel files going back from thirty to forty years ago searching for the name Cecily," Bradley said. "Thank God it isn't that common a name. Anyway, there were three. I think I've got a good idea which one you want."

"Tell me."

"Well, first, let me ask you about the one who worked the longest for the bureau. She was in her forties during that time— Cecily Drury. She was a typist for thirty years, and retired at age fifty-five."

"Not her."

"Then I've got a sixty-year-old librarian, Cecily Reiner, who spent a year reassigned from DOJ to put our library in order."

"No."

"This is it, then. Cecily Hampton Campbell, a young woman, only in her twenties, married to a special agent, Lawrence Campbell. She was hired to work in Ident—that was the old fingerprint identification section. It used to be a big paper operation with thousands of people, most of them women. It was like an assembly line. Anyway, she left Washington and was transferred to the San Francisco Field Office. Her record shows deceased. So does his. She died over thirty years ago."

Paavo's hand tightened on the receiver. That was her. The woman he'd spent a lifetime wondering about. To learn her name, hear of her marriage... her death... hit him a lot harder than he would have imagined. Cecily Hampton Campbell. "You were right. That's the one. Would you send me her file? His, too."

"I'll need another day or so," Bradley said. "Files this old are in storage. It could take a while to get them. Of course, you know I shouldn't send them. This is confidential information."

"I don't think so." Paavo's voice was harsh, jagged. "There's no privacy act for the dead."

As soon as he hung up the phone, he searched California and then national death records for Cecily Hampton Campbell.

No record existed.

13

———

Angie constantly monitored voice mail and text messages for one from the music box repairer. Well over a week had gone by and Mr. Rosinsky hadn't yet tried to contact her. She called him, but the phone simply rang and rang. She wanted her music box. Fortunately, after telling Paavo it was safe at Stan's house, he didn't ask again about it.

Since she was going out anyway to take some video shots of a new downtown restaurant with the unappetizing name of Les Chats—having nothing to do with chats, but was French for The Cats—she decided to swing by Rose Jewelry and find out what was going on.

As she drove slowly by the shop, searching for a parking space, she saw a CLOSED sign hanging on the front door. Taped below it was a note. She left her car double-parked and ran up to the note. It gave a telephone number in case of emergency. Back in her car, she punched in the number on her cell phone as she drove.

"Lyons, Bernstein and Rosin," the receptionist's voice said.

"Hello. My name is Angie Amalfi. I'm a customer of Rose Jewelry, Mr. Gregor Rosinsky's shop, and it's closed. A sign in the window says to call this number. Do you know what's going on?"

"I'm sorry to tell you, Mr. Rosinsky passed away," the nasally voice said. "His son, Martin Rosin, is handling business matters. Would you like to speak with him?"

"He died? How awful. Had he been sick?"

"Not at all. I'm sorry to say, he was the victim of a robbery and was killed."

"My God!" Angie was shocked. How hadn't she heard? But then, with so much going on she hadn't watched local news on TV or even read an online newspaper in days.

"It was a terrible tragedy." The woman spoke with all the emotion of announcing the weather. "I'll put Mr. Rosin on the line for you."

When Rosin answered, Angie offered her condolences before telling him about the music box she had left for repair.

The son had a list of all the jewelry and watches that were awaiting customer pickup, but after looking it over, didn't see her name or any reference to a music box.

A description of the music box was no help. Rosin hadn't seen anything like it in the shop.

"That's impossible!" Angie cried in a panic, trying to remember what she had done with Rosinsky's receipts. How was she going to tell Paavo she had lost his present on top of everything? "I was given a receipt."

"Would you read the number to me?" Rosin said. "I have all my father's business papers here. I've been getting calls for days from customers."

Her tote bag! "Just a second, I think it's right here." One-hand on the steering wheel, the phone crammed in the crook of her neck, she rummaged through the bottomless carryall, her car only occasionally crossing the double-yellow line as she pulled out grocery and things-to-do lists. A red light allowed her to search two-handed and find the receipt safely tucked in her wallet. "Got it!" she whooped, just a little while after the light turned green again. She read out the information as the driver behind her seemed to be having some kind of fit—his face looked contorted and his arms waved spastically. She zipped away from him quickly.

Rosin put her on hold to check for her receipt's numbers. After a long wait, he came back on. "The store's copy with that number is missing," he said with undisguised surprise. "I have the one before and the one after, but that page was removed from the sales book."

She was first stricken, then furious. Her car weaved from one lane to the other as she screamed into the phone. "Removed? What do you mean, *removed*? Where is my music box? It's important to me!"

"I'm sure it is—"

"It's a family heirloom!" She pounded the wheel instead of steering with it. "It was given to me by my—"

"Miss Amalfi, calm down! Give me your phone number," Rosin said soothingly. "I'm sure we'll find it. I'll contact you as soon as we do."

"I just don't understand how it can be missing," Angie protested, unsuccessfully trying to calm herself. "I heard your father was killed in a robbery. Could my music box have been among the things stolen? God, oh, God, how will I ever get it back?" She stamped her feet, and the Lexus lurched and jerked and nearly hit a startled pedestrian.

"Nothing was stolen, miss," he declared, his voice increasingly obstinate. "Perhaps my father took the box home to work on. I'll search. Now, you say you didn't pick it up, but might someone else have done it for you? After all, the store's work request is missing."

"Someone else? No! No one even knew it was broken"—then she remembered mentioning it to Connie—"except a girlfriend, and she wouldn't have gotten it."

"Did you check with her?"

Apoplexy threatened, and she nearly ran a red light. "Of course I didn't! The repair work wasn't even paid for. *No one picked up my music box!*"

"I'll call you. What's your number?" She'd barely gotten the last digit out of her mouth when he hung up.

She slammed her phone shut, dropped it in her tote, and looked up to find honking cars and cursing pedestrians all around her.

Just stepping inside the little house soothed Angie's overheated emotions. Not only had Rosin sounded like a pompous blowhard talking down to her, but at Les Chats, the food looked and tasted like something Roto-Rooter flushed out of a clogged drain.

Rosin would find her music box or discover what it was like to meet a master nagger. A crazed pit-bull was wishy-washy by comparison.

She made herself a cup of tea and brought it out onto the deck and sat. It was a perfect place to calm down. She loved living here—and knew she loved it because Paavo was with her. She realized, too, that she was merely playing house with him.

But playing it was better than not living with him at all, especially during this time when he was so upset about Aulis, and, much as he didn't want to admit it, his past. He tossed and turned each night, and at times seemed to dread going to sleep. She had never known him to be afraid of anything.

To her surprise, she, too, had fears about the outcome of his discoveries about his parents. Before he reached his journey's end, the path he was taking could lead to overwhelming or disturbing places, psychologically, if not physically. Somehow, she would help him through it.

As she sipped her tea, her mind turned to poor Gregor Rosinsky. She could scarcely believe he had been murdered. He had seemed like an interesting old man. Robberies were so common—too common—in this city. That was a reason she liked this little house. Since it was on a street too steep for cars, if anyone came here to rob, they'd have to lug the stolen goods up or down the stairs to a getaway car. Not very likely. But then, she always used to feel safe in her own twelfth-floor apartment, and look what happened. There, she'd been specifically targeted. She was sure of it. Just as Paavo had been, and Aulis.

And Rosinsky? Why was his copy of her receipt missing?

All of Paavo's warnings to her came back again. She nervously raced through the house checking the locks on doors and windows, and then double-checked the revolver Paavo had put in the nightstand for her if anyone tried to force his way in while she was home alone.

After locking the French doors to the deck, she lounged on the sofa, and tried to read the latest issue of *Vanity Fair*. The umpteenth article on Nicole Kidman and a fashion layout from Milan had all the staying power of cheap lipstick. Feeling cold and lonely, she snuggled into an afghan and waited.

When her tall detective walked in the house, his blue eyes found her and he smiled, and the world became right again. She ran to him with a hug and kiss. After Rosinsky, she didn't want to hear any more about death and sadness. At times, she wondered how he stayed sane in his job.

So she chattered brightly about books and movies and TV shows, phone conversations she'd had with her mother and her oldest sister, her visit to Les Chats, and her video restaurant reviews. The first one was finished. All she needed was to edit it and put it up on her YouTube channel. Or, better, to make a new YouTube channel. Or, maybe a local TV station would like to show her work? She should send out some queries.

Not until dinner was over and they were nestled side-by-side on the sofa did Angie bring up her troubling discoveries.

"I have a confession to make," she began, pulling nervously at a loose thread on a needlepoint pillow.

He looked startled. "A confession?"

"It has to do with my Christmas present."

"Do you want to retrieve it from Stan?" His voice was soft, his eyes resigned even though he didn't like having anything to do with her neighbor.

"No, that's not it." The thread was getting longer and longer.

"It was a silly present. I should have gotten you something new." He sounded embarrassed.

"Paavo—"

"Stupid of me. I'm never sentimental—"

She tossed the pillow aside and grabbed his shoulders. "Will you listen? I love the music box. The only reason I don't have it is because it stopped working. Maybe I wound it too much, I don't know, but the dancing couple stopped moving and the music stopped playing, so I brought it to a vintage music box expert to have it fixed."

"Okay," he nodded, waiting for what he sensed would be the other shoe dropping.

"When I went to get it back, I learned the shop owner had been murdered. His name was Gregor Rosinsky."

His eyes widened at that news. "Rebecca Mayfield is working on Rosinsky's case."

"I learned he was killed during a robbery, and my music box is now missing! Rosinsky told me it is actually a valuable piece."

"It's valuable?" Paavo looked incredulous. His brow furrowed. "Where did you get this information?"

"When Rosinsky checked it over, and said he could fix it, he said he was amazed at the quality of the workmanship. He said it could be in a museum, the Hermitage, in Russia—although he soon changed his tune and said it wasn't that expensive. In his next breathe, he asked if I'd like to sell it, so I suspect it's more valuable than he wanted to admit."

"That's hard to believe. Where would my mother have gotten such a thing?"

"Good question," Angie said.

Paavo stood and silently refilled their coffee cups, lost in thought. Only when he sat again did he speak. "Another man with a connection to fine jewelry was recently murdered. He, however, was on the other side of the line—he was a forger."

"A forger? I don't see the connection."

"He was also old, and of Russian descent."

"Old and Russian...it sounds like the music box," she murmured. "And Rosinsky."

Blue eyes met hers. "I know."

"You think there's a connection?"

"Gregor Rosinsky's shop was broken into the night before your place and mine were hit. He was killed three days later, as was the forger, Jakob Platnikov."

Angie took this all in. "Two Russians were killed—an antiques restorer and a forger, an antique Russian music box vanishes, then you, me and Aulis have our homes ransacked, looking for something," she said, and then all but whispered, "It's all connected, isn't it?"

When he made no reply, a chill went through her. Of the people she'd just mentioned, two were already dead, and the third might be dying.

14

———

When Nelson Bradley called Paavo at 7 a.m., and said he had the requested files, Paavo was in the house getting ready for work. Not that he had slept in. He had hardly slept at all, but kept reworking the strange information about his mother's music box.

He wanted to read the documents on something larger than his phone. Angie had, of course, set up a fancy all-in-one printer in their temporary living quarters, and it served as the answer to his prayers. He asked Bradley to send the documents to Angie's email.

As soon as the email with attachments arrived, he began to print out the documents.

Paavo picked up the first page and began to read. *It can't be,* kept running through his head. All these years he had carried an unflattering image of his mother. To find out that she had been a government bureaucrat, married to an FBI agent, just didn't fit it. Didn't fit it at all.

But then, Bradley's words that Cecily Campbell was dead didn't fit his image of her either.

It was peculiar, but even though she had walked out on him

and his sister, even though she had made it clear she didn't care about them, and didn't want them in her life, he always felt that someday, somehow, their paths would cross. And then he could ask her, *why?*

When Jessica died, he'd been positive their mother would show up for the funeral. He remembered standing beside Aulis, trying to keep his face stiff, not letting anybody see how hurt he was, or how angry. At the same time, he wanted to look around, to see if a strange woman was in attendance. He wondered if he'd recognize her, if she'd look like Jessica, although he couldn't imagine anyone else being so pretty.

Jessie had been beautiful and fun. She was one of the few people outside of Angie who could get him to make an out-and-out belly laugh. And make him angry. Yes, he was furious at her. Furious at the type of people she decided to hang out with, the type that caused her to overdose at age nineteen. Furious at her for dying.

He shut his eyes, trying to tamp down the emptiness from losing her that would never go away. His mother hadn't shown up that day. That was when he knew she was never coming back. He hadn't cried about her since he was a little boy, but alone in his room, on the night of Jessie's funeral, he had cried for the loss of them both. He was fourteen years old. After that, he toughened, and never shed a tear for either one again.

He took the documents from the printer, folded them in half, and walked out onto the deck to sit.

Angie, in a satin nightgown and pink robe, placed a hot mug of coffee beside him, her eyes heavy with concern, then she went into the house, leaving the French door partially open. She understood what was going on and understood this was a time to let him be alone with his emotions.

He took a sip of coffee and unfolded the papers.

Their words were too cold, too mechanical, to be about a

parent. They had a bureaucratic, impersonal ring—true government files, all dates and facts, about a stranger.

At age twenty-two, Cecily Jane Hampton, both parents deceased, took a job as a clerk-typist with the FBI. Six months later, she married Lawrence Campbell and a year after that, Jessica Ann was born.

He stopped there for a moment. Jessica Ann Campbell. How odd that he'd never known that. She never let on. She'd been nine years old when Cecily walked out. A nine-year-old understands a lot, and recognizes when it is necessary to hide, and to create a false identity. The realization of all that Jessie must have known and kept hidden from him was staggering.

He continued reading. When Cecily was 24, her marital status changed to widowed. Three years later, at 27, she transferred to the FBI's San Francisco Field Office. Nothing appeared in the file for six years until the annotation "deceased" was entered. That was it. No explanation, no embellishment.

No nothing.

He turned to Lawrence's file. Campbell had been an agent, twenty-three years older than Cecily. He saw Campbell's photo —a tall, distinguished-looking black man in a suit and tie, standing ramrod straight, as if he'd been in the military. The file showed his parents' names—Jessica's grandparents. Paavo wondered if they had still been alive when Jessica was a child, and if so, why they had never contacted their granddaughter, never sent her a Christmas present or birthday card. He could look up information about them; a lot of personal data was available to him in his position, but some things were better not knowing about. Some things could do nothing but open old wounds and cause more heartache.

Lawrence Campbell had died of a brain aneurysm at age forty-seven. Until the time of his death, he'd apparently been a healthy, active man. Survivor benefits had been paid to his daughter, Jessica, until she was age nine, when the folder was annotated "Suspend benefits until new address received. Checks returned. Unable to locate."

Paavo stared at that a moment.

Cecily had walked away from her children years ago, leaving that strange letter with Aulis, and changing her name to Mary Smith.

What had happened that made the FBI think she'd died, and was it true or not? Why was Jessica's name changed, and her whereabouts hidden, so she no longer even received survivor's benefits from her father's account?

Paavo searched for answers in Cecily Campbell's file. He worked his way through tedious reports on her progress as an employee, but found nothing of note. She was rated as competent and hard-working, a team player, not one to take risks, and followed protocol. Generally, the reviews were uninspired, unhelpful. Her supervisor in San Francisco was shown as Eldridge Sawyer, and his reports were second-signed by Tucker Bond.

Paavo went back inside. As he tapped into his cell phone's address book, he caught Angie's anxious expression from the living room and motioned her to join him.

"FBI," a woman's voice answered.

"I'm trying to reach an agent named Eldridge Sawyer," he said.

"Thank you." After a short wait the operator came back on the line. "I'm sorry. No one by that name is here."

"I see. What about Tucker Bond?"

Her response was immediate. "One moment, I'll connect you."

A second pleasant female voice came on the line. "Mr. Bond's office."

"This is Inspector Smith from the San Francisco Police Department. I'd like to meet with Mr. Bond as soon as possible."

"Can I tell him what this is concerning?"

"A former employee, Cecily Campbell."

"Let me check his calendar." She put him on hold. About two minutes went by before she came on the phone again. "He has a few minutes available today at twelve-thirty."

"That's fine. Can you tell me what Mr. Bond's exact title is?"

"Certainly. He's the Special Agent in Charge."

"Thank you." Paavo hung up the phone. The SAC was the head of the San Francisco office. So, Bond had moved up in the world over the past thirty years. He wondered what had become of Cecily's boss, Eldridge Sawyer.

Angie was bursting with questions by the time he hung up. "Did you find out anything?"

He handed her the FBI files. "There isn't a lot here."

She scanned them quickly. "I wonder where she lived? No address is shown."

"So I noticed. There are names, though. I'm starting with one of her bosses. I wonder how much he'll remember about her."

Angie's eyebrows rose. "Judging from the pictures I've seen of her, whether he admits it or not, he'll remember her."

<hr>

Although the FBI files didn't show Cecily's address, Angie had a good idea how to find out where the woman had lived, or darn close to it. Despite the many lies Paavo had been told about her, Angie was fairly confident that Cecily and Aulis had been neighbors. What else could a young widowed FBI employee and a middle-aged Finn have in common? Hmm, Angie decided not to pursue that, especially in view of Connie's brainstorm about the two of them.

The cleaning service had done a nice job on Aulis' apartment. Still, being here made Angie's hair stand on end big time. And the fact that the last time she was here, a man near her car and the apartment had ended up wearing a toe tag, only added to her nervousness.

She dashed into the bedroom and flipped through papers and old envelopes until her eye fell on one postmarked thirty-three years earlier from the Pacific Gas and Electric Company with stock certificates.

The address showed Liberty Street in the city. She had no idea where that was. Several more recent envelopes had different addresses, even some in Los Angeles and Bakersfield, but Liberty Street was in the correct timeframe.

Not until she was back in her car, doors locked, did she breathe again. Google Maps gave her the information she needed. Liberty Street wasn't far.

As she followed the strange GPS directions, she discovered why she couldn't get there by the most direct route, along Sanchez Street. An imposing cement wall, with stairways on both sides, blocked the way. She had to circle around, and approach from the opposite side.

The street was quiet and narrow, high on a steep hill, with a barrier at the far end to prevent cars from going any further. Most of the homes were elegant Victorians, some badly weathered, and others "gentrified." A couple of modern houses looked overbearing and sadly out of place. Near the end of the block, she found Aulis's old address in a two-story Victorian. A long staircase with an ornately carved wooden banister led up to a covered front porch with four doors. An overhang on the porch mirrored the ornate carvings of the banister. As with many older buildings in the city, the house most likely had once been an elegant single-family home that was divided into apartments. Such apartments used to be inexpensive places to live. No more, though.

Getting out of her car, she lifted her tote bag to the shoulder of her marigold-colored Ellen Tracy suit, and picked up her phone and purse. Nobody would slam the door on a stranger wearing a sophisticated Ellen Tracy.

She knocked on the door to Aulis's old apartment. A barefoot young woman in jeans and a tee shirt, a toddler on her hip, opened it.

"Hello, there!" Angie said brightly. "My name is Angie Amalfi." She thrust a business card into the woman's hand. One good thing about not having a set business, her cards were generic. "I'm working on a special feature for *San Francisco Magazine* on people who have lived in neighborhoods for many, many years. Like, say, thirty years."

"Oh?" The woman stuffed the card in her pocket and pushed a strand of brown hair back off her face. The butterfly clip high on the back of her head wasn't doing its job. "That's not me."

"We're giving away a year of the magazine to everyone who helps us put the article together. Do you happen to know any neighbors who have been here a long time?"

The woman looked blankly at her. "We just moved in last year." She put her little girl down inside the house and stood blocking the doorway so the child couldn't get out. "I've never heard of that magazine."

"You haven't? It's quite wonderful. Can you tell me about the other people in this building? Have they been here long?"

The woman rolled her eyes upward as if the answer might be printed on the underside of the porch roof. This was no candidate for Mensa. "Well, I live upstairs in back. The guy below has been here a few years, but he's only twenty-eight. A gay couple lives in front. They've been here five years at most. I guess the oldest is Terry, above them. Her and her old man bought the building ten years ago, or something like that."

"Have any of them ever mentioned some Finnish people living around here?"

"Finnish people? What do they look like?"

Angie was getting desperate. "What about neighbors? Can you at least tell me if any of them are old?"

"What are you, pimping for AARP or something?" the woman asked.

Angie tried hard to be nice. "I'm just trying to do my job. *San Francisco Magazine* wants that article."

"I don't know any old neighbors, and even if I did, I wouldn't tell you." She cast a sneering albeit envious glare from Angie's suit to chestnut-colored high-heeled Ferragamos. "I don't want your old magazine, anyway."

Angie stared at the door that had just slammed shut in her face. She could scarcely believe it.

Maybe she needed a better cover story? She drove around the neighborhood until she found a Valu-Mart.

Two hours later, she was heading for home with ten of the fifteen boxes of chocolate mint patties she had bought to intro-duce herself as a new neighbor just wanting to say hello. Most people weren't home, and of those who were—all young—few would take the candy or even listen to her spiel. You'd have thought they were afraid she wanted to poison them or something.

The public could be so rude!

Up ahead, a sign on a building caused her to slam on the brakes.

15

———————

Paavo entered the Federal building at 450 Golden Gate Avenue. It was a plain, boxy-shaped, beige, building, the width of the entire block, protected by a concrete barrier and cyclone fence that reached into the street so that no cars could park nearby. The FBI offices were on the thirteenth floor. Bond's secretary motioned him to sit in a well-appointed reception area.

Within three minutes, he was ushered into a corner office and introduced.

Tucker Bond had just taken the lid off a small cottage cheese container, and had two packets, each with two soda crackers, side-by-side on his desk. He put down the lid, fastidiously wiped his fingertips on a napkin, and stood with his hand outstretched.

Paavo's first impression of Bond was that the man didn't look at all like the FBI agents he usually dealt with. They tended to be broad-shouldered, and thick-chested, with close-cropped hair and wearing a black or dark gray suit.

Bond looked like a hawk, gaunt, with prominent cheekbones, a thin, beak-like nose, and wavy gray hair. His navy blue suit fit like an off-the-rack special offer. A white shirt and a light gray and navy striped tie completed the ensemble. Compared to him, Paavo felt almost fashionable in his gray Nordstrom's jacket and black slacks.

Bond's grip was strong, and as Paavo regarded the steel-like nature of his eyes, he realized the gauntness was the sort he'd often seen on long-distance runners, practitioners of exercise and dietary asceticism. He seemed to be all sinew and muscle, fastidious restraint and monk-like intensity. Just as Paavo studied Bond, the man scrutinized him in return.

"I took the liberty of finding out which department you worked in, Inspector Smith, after receiving your request to meet." Bond's voice was surprisingly mellow. "Homicide. I was quite intrigued."

"I'm here about an employee you had many years ago."

"Yes, Cecily Campbell." Bond picked up a white plastic spoon. "I hope you don't mind that I'm eating my lunch? This was the only time I had free today."

"Go right ahead."

"I remember Cecily." Bond stopped talking as he ate two heaping spoonfuls of cottage cheese, then grasped the red-cellophane tear strip on the crackers and opened a packet. "I haven't thought about her in... God, twenty-five years or so. What does she have to do with Homicide now?"

"Perhaps nothing, although there may be some connection between her and a case I'm working on."

Bond's mouth compressed. "Your superiors weren't aware of any such connection."

Paavo tensed at Bond showing his muscle with the higher ups so quickly. "My superiors don't work my cases. I do."

Bond gave a slight nod as if to grant him a *touché*. "So, Inspector, does this mysterious case of yours involve the Bureau?"

"No."

"Given that, I don't see how I can help you." He shoveled more cottage cheese into his mouth. At this rate, the container was almost empty.

"Tell me what you remember about Cecily Campbell."

"It's been a long time. One thing, however, I remember well. She died. It was tragic. Very tragic." Bond ate a cracker in two bites. Paavo's mouth was feeling dry just watching him.

"How did she die?"

Bond scrapped the last bites from his cottage cheese container, then tossed it into his wastebasket. "An auto accident."

"There's no death certificate on file."

"Impossible. It must be lost. Some bureaucratic screw-up, I guess. Her husband had been a special agent. When he died, she requested a transfer out here." He ate the second cracker and then threw away the cellophane wrapper. After dropping the unopened packet into a desk drawer, using his napkin, he meticulously brushed the cracker crumbs into his hand, being sure not one escaped his notice. He tossed both the crumbs and napkin into the wastebasket. Desktop tidy once again, he faced Paavo. "She worked as a research clerk. We have a lot of them."

"And so," Paavo said slowly, "she transferred here, worked for you, then died. That's all you remember?"

"She didn't work directly for me. Did you know that?"

"I understand her direct boss was Eldridge Sawyer," he said. "I'd like to speak with him as well."

"Mr. Sawyer is no longer with the Bureau." Bond's voice was clipped. Obviously, the SAC didn't like how much information Paavo had obtained.

"Do you know where I can find him?"

"As a matter of fact, I don't. Sawyer quit the Bureau a number of years ago. We lost track of him after that. If you find him, do let me know. I'd like to see him again."

"Why did he quit?"

"Nothing serious. There's a lot of stress in this job. It happens."

"What about the others?" Paavo asked. "Are there other people still working here who knew her?"

"A couple, perhaps, although by now most had the good sense to retire, I'm sure. I'll have the records reviewed, and if I find any employees who worked with her, I'll have my secretary contact you with their names."

"I'd appreciate it."

Bond stared off into space a moment then said, almost gratuitously. "She was an excellent employee."

The bland words, the blasé tone sliced into Paavo like a razor. Here, he finally met someone who knew and worked with his mother, and the guy acted as if she was nothing. Perhaps he had expected too much, hoped for too much. After all, it'd been so long and, as Bond said, the Bureau had dozens and dozens of clerks.

Against his better judgment, he asked, "Do you remember anything at all about Cecily Campbell? Her character? Her personality?"

Bond stared at him as if trying to decide how to respond. "She was young and impressionable." He paused a moment. "And a bit on the emotional side." He stood. "I'm sorry, but I have a meeting to attend now."

Paavo handed him his card. "Thank you for your time."

Back at his desk, Paavo emailed a list of clerks and supervisors named in Cecily's file to Nelson Bradley at FBIHQ. It would take Bradley little time to let him know if Tucker Bond was telling the truth about a few of them still working for the Bureau.

While waiting for Bradley's response, he searched for

addresses and phone numbers of any who had retired and still lived nearby.

Eustacia Florian, who had been Eldridge Sawyer's secretary, was listed on Noriega Street. A woman with a young-sounding voice answered his phone call. He introduced himself and asked to speak to Mrs. Florian.

"The police?" the woman sounded frightened. "What's wrong? I'm her daughter."

"Nothing's wrong," Paavo said. "I have some questions regarding a case I'm working on."

"My mother's involved in a case?" She sounded incredulous.

"It concerned her former employment. If you could tell me when I might reach her?"

"Now I understand. What a relief—for me, anyway. I'm sorry, but I doubt she'll be able to help you."

"Why's that?" he asked.

"My mother's in a nursing home. She has Alzheimer's."

16

Angie followed the matronly woman down the dark hallway to a sunny room at the back of the small house. A man sat by the window, eyes closed, a blue blanket over his shoulders and a green plaid covering his lap. His frame was slight and his hair billowed like tufts of white cotton.

"Henry!" Mrs. Eschenbach shouted. "Henry, are you awake?"

The old man's body jerked from the aural assault. "Huh?"

"The young woman who phoned is here to talk to you." The wife bellowed like a foghorn.

"Okay, okay." Sharp blue eyes turned toward Angie. "Come over here where I can see you."

Angie hurried across the room to a chair facing him. "Thank you so much for allowing me to come by, Pastor Eschenbach."

"It's no problem. My days aren't very busy anymore. I'm glad to hear Pastor Meier remembered me. It's been years since I was well enough to minister."

"He spoke wonderfully of you," Angie said. It was true, too. When she spotted a Lutheran Church not far from Liberty Street, she entered and spoke with the current pastor. He directed her to Pastor Eschenbach who led the congregation from the 1975 until 2005. "He thought you could tell me about a Finnish man who used to attend your church, Aulis Kokkonen." She waited a moment, and when she got no reaction, she added, "He used to live on Liberty—"

"I remember Aulis," Eschenbach said. "A nice fellow. I haven't seen him in many years. I'd complain that he stopped going to church, but then I did, too!" He leaned toward her and whispered. "The fire-breathing dragon who showed you here says I'm too old."

Angie thought it prudent not to comment. "Did you... did you know any of Aulis's friends?"

"Oh, yes. There were some other Finns, younger than Aulis I believe, but they were all good friends. Once in a while—not often, in the ways of young men—they would all show up for service. Aulis attended regularly, and he always brought his two children."

Angie's heart leaped. "You knew his children?"

"But of course! We—"

"Henry!" Mrs. Eschenbach's voice was stern. He glanced up at her. Angie hadn't noticed her hovering in the doorway.

"What is it?" Angie asked, looking from one to the other.

"Let me think," the old man said. "It seems they were his sister's children. Yes, that's right. She died, and he raised them. They were very well-mannered."

Well-mannered? There was a lot more than the kids' manners being remembered here. She was quite sure that wasn't what he nearly said before his wife interrupted. "So, you must have known Cecily?" she asked.

"Cecily?" He glanced at his wife.

"Mary, I mean," Angie said.

"We didn't know Mr. Kokkonen's sister, if that's what you're asking." Mrs. Eschenbach moved into the room. "Why are you asking these questions?"

More than ever the sense they were withholding something filled Angie. "I'm asking because Aulis is in the hospital. He's not doing well, and he seems to want to talk to some of his old friends. I don't know how to find them, so I'm trying this way."

"Why don't you look in his address book, or at old cards and letters?" Mrs. Eschenbach gazed at her disparagingly.

"He doesn't keep them," Angie replied sweetly.

"Neither do I," the pastor said. "My wife takes care of all that."

As the couple seemed to communicate wordlessly, Angie hoped they would open up to her.

"It's quite sad," the wife said, "but we don't have the information you seek."

"I will pray for my old friend." Pastor Eschenbach's gaze was warm.

Standing to leave, she took his hand. "Please, if you think of anything at all that might help, call and let me know. I would appreciate it so very much." She placed her card by his side.

Mrs. Eschenbach walked her through the house. "Miss Amalfi," she said, holding the door open for Angie to leave, "My husband is old and sick. You are not welcome here. I suggest you stop asking questions and stay away from us."

The good news was that Tucker Bond hadn't lied. The bad news was that, of the people named in Cecily's personnel folder, four were dead, two were clerks who merely processed paperwork, Eustacia Florian was in a nursing home, and he couldn't find Eldridge Sawyer in any directories, DMV files, or, for that matter, death records. Thinking back on Bond's strange request, he wondered if the FBI had also tried to find Sawyer and failed.

Paavo had hoped to use those people as leads to Cecily's peers, the ones who best knew her and could tell him what was going on in her life that made her run away and change identity. There were two possible scenarios. One, since there was no death record on her, despite how frightened and desperate her note to Aulis had sounded, she had survived the ordeal and chose not to contact her children. Ever. Or, if Bond was right, she was dead. Either way, end of story.

There was no logical reason for him to pursue this one step further.

On his desk was a ballistics report on the bullet that killed Jacob Platt. He focused his attention on it, and then compared it to the one removed from Gregor Rosinsky. Both were 9 mm. 147 grain hollow points, but not fired from the same gun.

He left the Homicide for some street work on Platt's investigation and ended up within a few blocks of Eustacia Florian's nursing home. Her daughter indicated she still had a few lucid moments now and then. If he caught her at such a time...

Even as he explained to the home's supervisor who he was and why he wanted to speak with Mrs. Florian, he cautioned himself against getting his hopes up. Not even his caveat prepared him for how bad it would be.

Eustacia Florian, a Filipina, had a face crisscrossed with wrinkles and hair cut so short her scalp showed in patches. She sat atop the bed, fully dressed in black slacks and a yellow top, wearing green slippers instead of shoes. As he entered the room, black eyes bored into him.

"Mrs. Florian." He approached her slowly and showed his badge. "I'm Inspector Smith. Nothing is wrong. I'd just like to talk with you a few minutes if I may?"

A thin hand reached out and snatched the badge from him, turning it upside down and over before giving it back. "Do I know you?"

"No, we've never met. I spoke with one of your old bosses, Tucker Bond."

"Mr. Bond? Do you know Mr. Bond? He's very smart. Very

smart." Her eyes sparkled. "He's a little sweet on me, you know. He always gives me the biggest bouquet of flowers on Secretary's Day."

"That's very nice," Paavo said, sitting on a chair near the foot of the bed. "I'd like to talk to you about someone who worked for your boss, Eldridge Sawyer, years ago. Her name was Cecily Campbell."

When she didn't respond, he wondered if he should continue. "Do you remember Eldridge Sawyer? Or Cecily Campbell?"

She gazed at him. "Do I know you? I met the FBI Director once, you know." She sat up tall. "He came to San Francisco. We had to scrub the office until it shined. He came right up to me and said, 'Hello, Eustacia. Good job. We'll make you a special agent soon.'" She beamed. "Do you know the FBI Director, too?"

Paavo stood. This was a good idea, but wasn't working. "Goodbye, Mrs. Florian."

"Cecily was just a clerk, you know," Eustacia said, clasping her hands. "She wasn't an agent. Mr. Bond liked to give her special jobs."

He sat down again. "Do you remember Cecily?"

"I complained to Mr. Sawyer, but he told me to keep my mouth shut! I hate him!"

Paavo couldn't quite follow her rambling. "Tell me about Mr. Sawyer."

"Mr. Sawyer left. He ran away." She put her finger to her mouth. "Shush!"

Sawyer seemed to be his best bet to learn about Cecily. Paavo leaned toward her, keeping his voice low and modulated. "Where did Mr. Sawyer run to, Mrs. Florian? Do you know where he is?"

"He's with... he's with..." Her eyes darted down, then to the side, then up, and around again.

He leaned forward. "With who?"

"I need my planner. Where's my planner?" She jumped off the bed, opened a drawer and began to toss her underwear, piece by piece, onto the floor. *"Where's my planner? WHERE'S MY PLANNER!!!"*

Paavo backed out of the room. "Nurse!"

Angie met Paavo at San Francisco General. He'd managed to talk the SFPD into posting a guard outside Aulis's door for a few days, at least. After sitting with Aulis and meeting with his doctor, they returned to the little cottage making a slight detour through Chinatown for some food-to-go. There was no news yet on the break-ins—no identifiable fingerprints, no witnesses. So far, the only hard evidence was the slug that grazed Aulis was a 9 mm., the same as the slugs found in the two Russians, although the markings showed different guns were used.

Paavo was putting out plates for their dinner when Angie handed him a glass of Chablis. "First, let's take a minute to relax, and for you to tell me what you learned from the FBI today."

Standing in the kitchen, sipping the wine, he gave her a brief recap of his visits with Bond and Mrs. Florian. "Cecily Campbell was a clerk," he concluded. "It's a dead end, not worth pursuing. What happened thirty years ago doesn't mean anything now, anyway."

Despite his words, his disappointment was obvious. "You don't know that yet." She tried to be encouraging. "Her old boss might remember. Did you try to find him?"

"I did, with no success. Bond said the guy's 'troubled.' He could be anywhere, new name, and everything."

"Hmm, he sounds like Cecily," Angie observed. "What if she ran off with him?"

"I would imagine Bond would remember a scandal like that. He's convinced Cecily's dead. He's probably right."

"It sounds like Mrs. Florian thinks Sawyer's whereabouts are shown in her planner. You should find him."

"It doesn't matter. Cecily left, why should I care what the reason was?" Paavo's voice turned hushed. "I never should have started this wild goose chase."

Angie turned her back on him as she put on water for tea. His conflict between wanting to know his past and dreading it was clear. "I also did a little... checking... myself." She glanced back at him. Sure enough, a dour expression had formed on his face.

"You did what?"

"I went to the apartment Aulis lived in when Cecily was a neighbor. Unfortunately, no one there remembered him, let alone her."

"You saw the old house?"

"It was pretty, an area with lots of steps instead of sidewalks." Their eyes met. Could that have anything to do with the quick, obvious appeal this neighborhood had for Paavo? Some harkening back to his childhood?

The tea was soon ready. Over mu-shu pork, bok choy with beef, chicken chow mein and Hunan style prawns, Angie told about her visit with the Eschenbachs, and the wife's strange warning. "He said Aulis had several young Finnish friends. Do you know about them?"

"The only Finnish friend I know is Joonas Mäki, but he lives a few hours away, up the coast in Gualala."

"Well, there were more."

Together, they cleared off the table. Then, as Paavo put on after-dinner coffee, Angie cast her phone to the forty-inch TV to watch her restaurant videos.

"Maybe I should try to track down Sawyer," he said, joining her in the living room. The coffee maker hissed and gurgled as it brewed. She simply loved how domestic Paavo was becoming.

"It couldn't hurt," she said.

"What's that?" He stood behind her, watching the TV.

"I wanted a behind-the-scene shot of a restaurant's kitchen. That's the chef's butt--"

"Gross."

"Like bread dough that rose too far. This part is a little shaky because I was moving to another can to see better."

"Another can?"

"Don't ask. This is—hey, wait!" She hit rewind.

He moved closer. "Did I see what I thought?"

Her heart was pounding. "I think so." She played the tape again, then hit pause at the key frame.

As she had struggled to keep her balance and still take a video of the kitchen, the phone swung wildly in her hands, capturing the surrounding alleyway. A man stood in a doorway watching her.

He was also the man who had been killed outside Aulis's apartment, right next to her Lexus.

With horror, she now had proof of being watched and followed. And she had no idea why.

17

———

"Here it is, Inspector." Mrs. Florian's daughter handed Paavo her mother's planner. He sat in the living room of the modest home.

"It's more than a calendar," Jill Florian said. She was attractive, with a small, upturned nose, pouty mouth, and large brown eyes. Her long, black hair hung free and reached nearly to her waist. "My mother used to carry it back and forth to work every day. She would write notes and reminders, and often said if she ever lost it, she may as well shoot herself." The daughter's eyes filled with tears. "No wonder she was so agitated when she couldn't find it."

"I'm sorry," he said.

"It wasn't your fault."

The planner was one of those 5x8 multi-ringed binder types with lots of tabs that sort your life into a variety of categories—appointments, priorities, projects, finances, and one for addresses and phone numbers. He turned to the calendar section. It was dated 2014. "Is this when she retired?"

"No. She retired in 2004. She bought replacements for ten years, but as you can see, there wasn't much to fill them with."

He flipped to the address portion. The pages were yellowed with age, and the ink for the top entries on each page had faded into browns and purples, while those near the bottom were darker. The planner looked like it might have been used for a good portion of Mrs. Florian's career.

The address book's "S" section was several pages long, with cross-outs and additions, asterisks and arrows from names to addresses and annotations. A short way down the first page the name "Sawyer, Eldridge" was shown, with a South San Francisco address and phone number. He copied down the information, then hunted for a more recent entry for the man. There was none.

He thumbed through the pages to the "C" section. Near the top of the page was Cecily Campbell. The whole entry had a diagonal line over it. His heart skipped a beat seeing that—the reality of his mother's life. He wondered if Mrs. Florian did that after Cecily died.

Cecily's first address shown was on Ocean Avenue. It had been X'd out and an address on Liberty Street added below it. That must have been where Angie went. He wrote it down.

Cecily's name had an asterisk beside it. At the bottom of the page was the referral: "*C's friend, Finland expert—Prof. Susan White," and a San Francisco phone number. He copied them down as well. *C's friend...*

He wondered why Mrs. Florian would annotate Cecily's friend, or that she was a Finland expert? All that must have had some importance to Sawyer or Bond.

He looked through other addresses, finding lots of names and companies and experts and cryptic notes. An entire career's worth of contacts existed here, carefully noted by a secretary with dreams of becoming one of the FBI's special agents.

Paavo took a long detour back to Homicide, all the way to South San Francisco and Eldridge Sawyer's house.

Except for color, the small, plain house perfectly matched every third one on the block. The elderly owners had bought it from Sawyer nearly thirty years earlier. It hadn't been an easy purchase, they told him. Sawyer demanded he be paid in cash, and he had refused to allow his Social Security number or driver's license number to be added to any of the documents. "The guy was unhinged," the homeowner stated bluntly.

Back in Homicide, he ran more checks on Sawyer, but still came up blank.

Then he did the same with Professor Susan White.

To his surprise, she had a rap sheet. There was nothing recent, but years earlier she had managed to get herself arrested on twice in Bosnian and Serbian War protests.

Nothing was making sense to him.

Paavo's shoes echoed in the empty hallway as he searched for room 308C, the office of Professor Susan White. It had been surprisingly easy to find her. When her old phone number didn't work, he called San Francisco State, the University of San Francisco, and finally U.C. Berkeley, where she was listed as a tenured professor in the History Department. Her specialty was twentieth century Russian and Eastern European history.

She agreed to meet him after her last class ended. The heavy Bay Bridge traffic made him late. He knocked on the frosted glass door.

"Come in."

A woman in her sixties sat at a large desk, a computer behind her. She wore light make-up and her blonde hair pulled up in a loose knot. She had the well-toned look of a woman who pays close attention to her body and her diet.

"Inspector Smith, SFPD." He held out his hand to her. "Thank you for waiting."

She removed her reading glasses, and studied him with such absorption, it took a moment before she noticed his hand. "Inspector, you weren't one of my students, were you? You look familiar."

"I'm afraid not." He explained that he was trying to find out about someone she may have known long ago, Cecily Campbell.

"Cecily?" Her hazel eyes caught his. "I remember her well. We used to meet all the time at the library at SF State."

"At the library?"

"Yes. She was a law clerk, and I was a new professor at my first job."

He was confused. "A law clerk? I thought she worked for the FBI?"

White's eyebrows rose. "Good God, I don't think so. She was as opposed to government policies as the rest of us back then. She didn't work for them."

"I must be wrong. What can you tell me about her?"

The professor's intelligent gaze assessed him a moment before she responded. "She was about my age. That's what started us talking. Most of the professors were 'old, white guys,' and the students much younger. I learned she was widowed with a young daughter, new to the area, and I was divorced. She was fascinated by politics and the effect of Soviet policies on Eastern and Baltic European history, my specialties."

"Plus Finland, right?"

She cocked her head, but then her eyes narrowed. "Yes. Why do you ask?"

"What else can you tell me about her?"

"Probably not much. She was bright and witty. Over time, after I took the job here in Berkeley, I lost contact with her. I heard she died a few years later."

"Do you know how she died?" he asked.

"An accident. An auto accident, I believe."

"In the Bay Area?"

Large, questioning eyes captured his. "I don't really know."

It was a long shot, but he had to ask. "Did you know Aulis Kokkonen?"

She pursed her lips. "The name sounds familiar. I'll ask again—why?"

"Just trying to tie up some loose ends."

She leaned back in the chair. "It was a long time ago. I'm sorry, but I don't think I can remember anything more."

"It's important, if you can help—"

"I'm sorry."

He stood, not even sure why he had come here. What had he expected to learn? He handed her his card. "If you remember anything, call me."

She read it. "Paavo?" Her head jerked up. The tone of her voice stopped him at the door. An eternity passed as the two regarded each other and slowly the furrows on her brow smoothed. She tapped the card against the desktop a moment, as if unsure how to begin. "You came all the way to Berkeley for a reason. Now, why don't you sit back down, please, and tell me what this is *really* all about?"

The tautness of her posture, the intensity of her gaze, made him decide to tell her the truth. He sat and faced her squarely. "I've recently learned that Cecily... Cecily was my mother. I'm curious about her. I heard you were her friend."

"Oh, my," she whispered. "You don't know anything about her?"

He shook his head. "What I thought I knew seems to be a far cry from the truth."

"Yours is possibly the strangest request of my career." She pressed her fingers to her cheek a moment. "I don't know how much I can help you, but let me start at the beginning."

He sat stiffly, scarcely breathing.

"As I mentioned, Cecily shared my interest in the Soviet Union," Professor White began. "A number of us on campus sympathized with the dissidents there and in the eastern European satellite nations who wanted to be free. Cecily joined us. She particularly talked about Finland and its sub rosa dissident movement. I knew some Finnish students, well, former students by the time she met them. It turned out there was a vacancy in the building where two of them lived, and she needed a bigger place, so I brought her along to see the apartment, and meet them. She fell in love with both."

Her expression silently questioned if this was the kind of information he sought. He nodded.

"Where was the building?" he asked.

"In a nice area up near the top of Sanchez. A small street."

"Liberty?"

"Yes! That's it. This all took place so long ago…"

"Please continue."

Her hands folded atop the desk. They were strong, capable hands, without rings. "Aulis Kokkonen—since you mentioned his name and Cecily's, you've brought back memories. I do remember he lived in one of the apartments, but he was older, not caught up in helping the dissidents. The *samizdat* movement was going on at that time. Do you know what that was?"

He shook his head.

"I'm a professor, so now here comes a lecture, but I'll be quick." She smiled. "It simply means 'self-published.' Essays and newspapers against the government were being illegally copied in Russia so the dissident movement there could grow. To get equipment to make the copies—keep in mind, Inspector, that typewriters, let alone mimeograph machines and small printing presses, were nearly impossible for common people to own in that country—the dissidents looked to sympathizers in the West for help."

"And the Finns were such sympathizers?" Paavo asked.

"Correct. They believed that only by undermining the Soviet government itself, would Finland, which was under the thumb of the USSR, become free. As history proved, they were right."

Paavo nodded, absorbing the information. "Who were the Finns?"

"I'm trying to remember their names. There were four of them, thick as thieves. Let's see. Of the four, one Americanized his name—Sam? Yes, I'm sure that was it. He was quite the live wire. One was quiet, a little guy. One was tall and thin and had thick eyebrows that went straight across his face. He was a little older than my former students—although not as old as Aulis."

"Joonas Mäki?" Paavo asked, his voice hushed.

"Joonas. Yes, that sounds right. Then, there was the fourth man." She gazed at Paavo with a strange smile. "My God, when he and Cecily met—I remember that evening—I think it was love at first sight. The two had eyes only for each other. Me and Sam and the little guy kept jabbing each other in the ribs, watching the two of them stare at one another, yet scarcely saying a word." She chuckled. "They never even noticed us."

"What was this fourth man's name?"

She pressed her fingers to her brow, her eyes shut, trying to dredge it up. After a while, she dropped her hands in exasperation. "It'll come to me in time. I know it will."

"Can you describe him, or tell me what he looked like?"

A touch of sympathy, then resignation, came into her eyes, and she reached for her purse. After rummaging around inside it, she took out a small mirror and handed it to him. "Look." Her voice was gentle. "Now I know why you're so familiar to me."

18

"**I** remembered!" The woman's excited voice all but sang over the phone early the next morning. "This is Professor White."

Sitting at his desk in Homicide, Paavo's heart began to pound, and his hand tightened on the receiver. "Yes?"

"I was watching Leno on TV last night and a commercial came on for Formula One racing. One of the drivers is Mika Häkkinen. That jarred my memory."

She pronounced the name MEE-kah HAH-ki-nen.

He waited, holding his breath.

"His name was also Mika. Mika Turunen." Then she said words that Paavo never imagined he would hear. "I remembered something else. I'm almost certain I was told that Cecily married him."

"I can't tell you how much I appreciate your seeing me," Angie said as she walked into the elegant Pacific Heights home of retired De Young Museum curator, Donald Porter. Her jeweler at Tiffany's, the man who suggested she bring her music box to Gregor Rosinsky, had contacted Porter on her behalf after she told him the box was now missing. Porter had a particular interest in Russian artwork.

He led her into a living room crammed with antique furniture and nineteenth-century paintings. She paused in the doorway to catch her breath at the opulence before her.

"May I offer you some sherry?" he asked, crossing the Sarouk carpet to an ornate mahogany liquor cabinet.

"No, thank you." She sat on a Chippendale arm chair and handed him a photo of her music box. She'd taken pictures on Christmas Day of her decorations and the music box was already on a shelf. She had enlarged it, then made a print. "Here's the photo I told you about," she said. "Gregor Rosinsky was quite surprised to see it and gave me the feeling it's very valuable."

"I knew Gregor well," Porter remarked, studying the photo. He stood tall, with a thick head of pure white hair. "It was a great tragedy that he was killed. He did fine work. You said he had this music box, and it's now gone?"

"I believe it was the only thing taken in the robbery," she said.

He, too, sat. "Well, if this is authentic, the thieves made off with something that could easily be valued at upwards of a half-million dollars."

"You're kidding me!" she cried.

"I never joke about art."

"How could something so valuable end up in"—how should she put this?—"private hands? I mean, it was a gift to me from someone who had no idea of its value."

"I must confess, you have me intrigued, as well, about the music box's history. I'll go to my sources to see what I can find out. I will say, if it was in a Russian museum, many were looted under the Bolsheviks, as were many churches and private estates. Smuggling was a huge business in the former USSR."

"I've heard a little about some *samizdat* movement," she added tentatively, recalling Paavo's words to her about his visit to a UC Berkeley professor.

"Oh yes, but that was long ago, back in the 1960s and '70s it flourished, although remnants of it continued through at least the '90s, I believe. I'd call it a Soviet civil rights movement. Since censorship was heavy in the USSR, the anti-Soviet dissidents published their own magazines, books, and flyers promoting freedom. Of course, that was a dangerous position to take. It is known that many of the dissidents had to steal artwork and smuggle it out of the country to the West to get money for their activities. That was quite common."

Angie was a bit stunned to hear all this. "Do you think my music box might have been smuggled out in that way?"

He gave her a toothy smile. "That's as good an explanation as any."

19

─────────

At San Francisco's Hall of Records, Paavo resolutely filled out a form to request a search for a marriage certificate. He would see if there was any actual proof to the professor's story. Cecily's FBI files made no mention of any marriage. It might have been another of his mother's stories —like being a law clerk—one that she told people to look good.

A bored clerk gestured him to the seats in the hallway with an even more bored assurance that he'd be called. While waiting for the marriage records, he decided to fill out another form. Why not be even more of a fool?

After turning in the second request, he sat back down on the wooden chair to wait.

A Mexican woman with three children stood at the table filling out papers while her children tugged at her arm, pulled the hem of her dress, dangled from the table, and ran along the polished tile hallway then dropped to their butts to see how far they could slide. An old man stood at another table, his hands shaking as he slowly, carefully checked his application.

Three other people sat nearby, expressions of varying tedium on their faces. All three glanced at the tall, stern looking detective, then quickly lowered their eyes. Did he look so much the cop, he wondered.

The clerk called one person, after a while another, and then the third. Paavo's assumptions that they were pretty much on a roll proved wrong when he had a long wait before finally hearing his name.

Prepared to be told simply that no record existed, he was momentarily at a loss when the clerk thrust a sheet with an embossed seal into his hand.

He walked back to his chair before looking at it.

It was a marriage certificate between Cecily Hampton Campbell and Mika Turunen. Much to his surprise, he found himself doing a quick mental calculation between his birth date and the date of the marriage. Eleven months. His breathing grew shallow and fast.

As if from far off, he heard his name being called again. He looked up. The clerk was glaring at him as if he'd been saying his name for some time.

In his hand, he waved another piece of paper.

Mechanically, Paavo retrieved the result of his second request. His ears were ringing, his temples pounding, as he headed straight out of the building and over to the Civic Center plaza in front of City Hall, scarcely looking at anything around him.

He sat on the bench and stared a moment at the pigeons. Earlier, someone must have scattered breadcrumbs, because the birds were still bustling and bobbing to find a few morsels here and there. He didn't think anyone had time for things like feeding birds anymore. When he was a boy, sometimes he'd go to the park with Aulis and toss them tiny bits of dried bread. Other times, Aulis would bring him to the Palace of Fine Arts and he'd feed bread to the ducks.

When did he last take the time to watch ducks or pigeons, let alone feed them?

His hands began to shake from the tight grip he had on the papers he held. The marriage certificate was on top. He moved it aside, exposing the sheet below, and began to read.

Certificate of Live Birth. Full Name of Child: Paavo Hampton Turunen. Maiden Name of Mother: Hampton. Place of Birth: San Francisco, California. Name of Hospital or Institution: Saint Francis Hospital.

His eye skipped down the document, past the address of the hospital, his birth weight, sex, and so on, to the next section, and then stopped.

Father of Child: Mika Turunen, age 26. Occupation: computer programmer.

Mother of Child: Cecily Jean Hampton, age 29. Occupation: housewife.

Pressure built behind his eyes and he quickly folded the papers in half, then in half again so they would fit into his breast pocket. This was what he had spent a lifetime wanting to know. The birth certificate Aulis had given him showed his mother as Mary Smith, his father as "Unknown."

Paavo Unknown, that was who he had been.

But suddenly, he had a name, parents, a history. He stood, his legs strangely rubbery as he started to walk away from the Civic Center, toward the Hall of Justice, toward the life he knew. Yet, even as he walked the familiar streets, his emotions roiled and he couldn't stop a dark, hollow sense from filling him, a sense that he, himself, had become a stranger.

Angie paced from the living room through the dining area to the kitchen and back, sure she was wearing a groove through the plank flooring. With each turn, she checked the time, but the clock scarcely moved.

She didn't like calling Homicide to ask Paavo where he was,

how he was doing, and when he'd be home. His job caused him to work long hours. If he was in pursuit of a murderer, he couldn't simply drop it because his girlfriend expected him to go home when it got late. She vowed not to hassle him about his hours, ever.

That didn't make it any easier to handle when he didn't call. He often phoned her sometime in the afternoon or early evening to check in, make sure everything was okay, give her some idea of his schedule, and to find out about hers.

Tonight, he hadn't done any of that.

After her visit with Donald Porter, she'd gone to the DeYoung and then to some smaller museums to look at Russian art and curios, trying to develop a sense of its esthetics—an interesting mixture of Europe and Asia. The museum shops had books that would help, and she bought several. She tried concentrating on them, but all she could think about was her music box and Paavo.

When Paavo told her about his visit with the professor yesterday, she realized she'd made an important mistake in her assessment of what was going on. She had thought of the two Russians, *her* music box, and then her, Paavo and Aulis. She should have thought of the two Russian, *Cecily's* music box, and the three of them. In the past, there had been a clear connection and political animosity between Cecily, the Finns, and the Soviets. Why, though, should that be an issue today? The music box was the key, but the key to what?

The ticking clock brought her back to the moment. She went to the window and looked out. How strange it was to be in the city and not see a busy street with an endless stream of cars. The quiet here was unnerving.

She turned again to a book about Faberge and other Russian artisans and their work.

Only when she heard the front door open, did she realize

she'd fallen asleep on the sofa. "Paavo," she murmured, and sat up.

He paused in the darkness of the doorway. "I lost track of time," he said, his voice subdued. He took off his sports coat and hooked it on the closet doorknob.

She stretched and got to her feet. "It's all right." She approached him, placing her hands on his shoulders, then down along his chest, feeling his warmth through the blue and white striped cotton shirt. "I'm making one of your favorite dishes tonight—pasta with prosciutto and sun-dried tomatoes." As she lifted her face to his, the bleakness of his expression struck her like a physical force and she reared back. "What is it?"

"Nothing." He kissed her lightly, then headed for the kitchen. "Is there any Scotch in the house?"

"Cousin Richie stocked this place quite well. Soda, too." She showed him where the liquor was stored, then twisted an ice tray to pop out a couple of cubes for him. "Did you go see Aulis?"

"Yes. He hasn't changed at all, and his doctor says there's still hope for a full recovery." He reached for the glasses. "Would you like a drink, too?" She shook her head, and he poured himself one before continuing. "A couple of his friends stopped by, guys he used to work with at the bank, and even a nun was there. She said you asked her to pray for him 'even though he's Lutheran.'"

Angie shrugged. "Why not?"

His smile didn't reach his eyes. He sipped his Scotch and looked even more desolate.

"Tell me what happened today," she said, watching him intently as they moved into the living room. She sat down on the sofa and expected him to join her.

Instead, he went to his coat and pulled some papers out of the pocket. "The lady professor phoned." He chuckled derisively. "It's a good thing she watches commercials. Some Finnish race car driver helped her remember the name of my father."

"Oh, my." She stood again. He'd been shaken enough by yesterday's conversation with her. Today, to have been given a name... "Oh, Paavo."

He handed her the papers. As she read the marriage and birth certificates, the full impact of what this meant to him washed over her and tears filled her eyes. She carefully folded them again. "I'm glad you finally know," she said huskily.

He finished his Scotch, then opened the French doors and stepped onto the deck. The sky was overcast and drizzly. He sat on a chair, leaning forward, arms on thighs, and stared into the blackness.

She stood in the doorway. There were times, like this, when the past he'd tried to bury came through, and she could see the child who grew up an orphan, whose troubled sister met an early death, and who still had an empty, dark place deep inside him because of it.

Usually so glib, her mind had emptied of words to say. She had never thought she could ache so much for him.

A world of information was at his fingertips at work, and she wondered if he'd made further discoveries today. She was almost afraid to ask, but she had to. Her voice was scarcely above a whisper. "Did you find out what happened to them?"

After a long silence, he spoke. "I couldn't, Angie. I thought about it, and typed their names to search the database more than once, but I couldn't hit the send command. I wanted to think of them alive, for one night, at least."

She squeezed her eyes shut a moment, then stepped behind his chair and wrapped her arms around his neck, bending forward to kiss the side of his face, to press her cheek to his. "I know," she whispered, her throat so thick she had to force the words out. "I know." He interlaced his fingers with hers, pressing them to his chest. She could have cried aloud, and ranted and raged with fury at the hurt this was causing him. Why did they do it to him—all of them, Aulis. Cecily. Jessica, and maybe even this Mika Turunen? She would blame each one for not telling a small boy who he was and blame his parents for walking out and leaving him all alone.

"I need to find out what happened to them, Angie. Why did Cecily write to Aulis the way she did? I've gone this far. I want the truth."

"We'll find out." She moved around the chair to face him and crouched at his knee. "Give it time. Give yourself time."

"I thought I'd put it behind me, and now..." He bowed his head and she reached her arms around his back, just as he clutched her tight. She needed to make this right for him.

Somehow, she would find a way.

The woman shut down her laptop, then stood and paced. Her "security" work served her well now. She was able to find out all about the players—Angelina Amalfi and Paavo Smith in their cute little not-so-well-hidden hideaway. She smirked. Plus, a music box worth hundreds of thousands of dollars.

That was a big part of this, certainly, but it wasn't everything. Not by a long shot.

There was more, and as soon as she found it, all hell would break loose.

20

When Serefina Amalfi opened the front door Sunday morning, Angie threw her arms around her and hugged her hard. She had waited until she was sure her mother would be home from church and seeing her lady friends.

"Angelina, *che fai?*" The startled woman asked. Angie's mother was short and heavy, her black hair pulled straight back into a bun.

"Nothing, Mamma," Angie said. "I'm just happy to see you."

"Come inside. It's that burglary, isn't it?" Angie followed the dancing red-polka dots of her mother's rayon dress through the house to the family room. "It has you nervous. That's why you're never at home when I want to visit."

Angie still hadn't told her mother she was staying in one of Cousin Richie's houses, and definitely not that Paavo was staying with her. Her parents would worry if they knew about the break-ins at Paavo and Aulis's homes, and if they heard Aulis had been shot besides, they'd insist Angie move in with them. "I'm not nervous," she said. She'd passed nervous days ago and was hurtling toward frantic. "Anyway, a locksmith put great new locks on the door. It's just that I've been busy with my video restaurant reviews."

Serefina sat down at a new laptop. "I'm online. Can you stay for lunch?"

Angie's eyebrows popped up high to see her old-fashioned, won't try a "streaming service" mother sitting in front of a high-powered Apple. "I've got a reservation for lunch at a new Basque restaurant for another video review. Bianca's joining me. Would you like to come, too?"

"You know I don't like restaurant food," Serefina said, staring at the screen.

Angie knew it. She also knew her mother would have been insulted to death if she hadn't invited her. Angie failed to once, and the fall-out, which the family dubbed Restaurant-gate, had more whispering, hurt-feelings, and innuendo than any political scandal. "What is this?" she asked, glad to change the subject. "I didn't know you bought a new laptop."

Serefina pushed a few keys. "Caterina brought it over. You know your sister thinks everyone needs the latest of everything. She says everybody shops this way now. You push the button and things you want show up at your door. No work at all."

Angie sat down and watched her mother study the screens and navigate her way through a Nieman-Marcus site.

"Hah! Look at that! *Dio!*" Serefina threw up her arms, then slammed the top down. "What nerve! I'm not going to use it again."

"What happened?"

"I've heard how people steal things off these computers, and that once you put some information in, it's there forever. No way am I going to tell them what size dress I wear! *Ma che schifo!*" She smoothed her hands over her round waist and hips. "And anyway, I'm on a diet so I won't be this size much longer."

Angie suppressed a smile. Serefina was always on a diet. "I don't think anyone cares—"

"I care!" As Serefina lumbered toward the kitchen, she called out. "Let's have some coffee. Your cousin Gina sent some of her biscotti. *Buonissimo!* Like butter, they are!"

A short while later, Angie sat in the sunroom across from Serefina, munching cookies and talking the way they had done, time and again, over the years. She couldn't imagine not having this warmth in her life, not having this security and place to come home to. Thoughts of all Paavo had missed swept over her —the mother's and father's hugs never given, tears of joy and pride never shed, hands never clasped doing something as simple as helping a child to cross a street.

"Why are you looking so gloomy all of a sudden, Angelina?" her mother asked.

"I was just thinking of someone who isn't as lucky as I am."

"Lucky?"

"To have you and Papà, and to know that you both love me, no matter what I've done."

An eyebrow arched. "How much money do you need?"

Angie was taken aback. "No, really. I was just thinking of my childhood, with all the family around, with Frannie to play with, and our older sisters to look up to. I was very happy."

"You used to torment Frannie. She was so sweet natured, and you were such a little devil!"

"Mamma! I'm trying to tell you how much I love you!"

Serefina studied her a long moment. "Angelina, are you pregnant?"

Sundays in Homicide were always quiet since only the on-call team needed to be there, and right now, the on-call team was off investigating a suspicious death.

When he first arrived that morning, he did what he should have done the day before. He looked for records on Mika

Turunen and Cecily Campbell Turunen. He found death certificates for both of them.

Mika had been murdered. He died of gunshot wounds. The killer was never identified.

Cecily died in a car accident one week later.

So, now he knew, and the knowing left him drained and empty.

When he requested the homicide book on Mika, he found an annotation on the system to the investigation of Sam Vanse. Sam… Professor White had mentioned someone named Sam. He called for that book as well. Several hours passed before Archives contacted him to say the files were ready for pickup.

The casebooks were old and dusty, and the clerk at Records had handed them to Paavo with all the reverence of giving him the Holy Grail. He pulled out Vanse's file first. He wasn't yet ready to look at a report on his own father's death.

The reports were, for the most part, in chronological order. Paavo read quickly through the Preliminary Report. Vanse had been found on the street near San Francisco General Hospital dead from a bullet wound to the back of the head. He had a second, non-lethal wound to his shoulder.

It was assumed whoever killed him, pushed his body out of a car near the hospital, leaving the investigators no crime scene, and little else to go by.

Mika Turunen was murdered the day after Vanse's death. The two men had been friends and co-workers at the Omega Corporation, a high-tech firm in the city.

A number of people were interrogated—Paavo saw an Okko Heikkila, Joonas Mäki and Aulis Kokkonen among them, but no leads developed, and although there were references made to Vanse's earlier activism in anti-Soviet groups, no conclusions as to why he was killed were made.

Reading between the lines, the type of questions asked, the cross-reference to Turunen's folder, gave the appearance the investigators were speculating that Turunen killed Vanse, and then, in retaliation, was himself killed. The case remained open pending further developments.

Paavo's skin was chilled. Could his own father have been a murderer? The investigation gave no answers.

He shut the folder, not wanting to look at any more photos or the autopsy report.

Slowly, tentatively, he reached for the next folder, the file on the investigation of Mika Turunen's death.

He had handled plenty of old homicide investigation case binders, but this was not any old case. This man had been his father. As he touched the black cover, his hands trembled and his chest felt as if a tight band was around it, constricting the air from his lungs.

He cracked open the faded and stiff cover, and then skipped over the yellow, dusty pages of the Chronological Report and Preliminary Report, preferring to form his own conclusions from the base material. He turned to the first report and began to read.

The report had been filed by the patrol officers called to the scene by a motel owner. It began:

Victim, Mika Turunen, age 30, found Room 8, Cypress Motel, 6321 Bayshore Boulevard at 0717. DOA multiple gunshot wounds.

Next came the Death Investigation Report. The motel owner provided most of the information. Mrs. Turunen was in the office settling the bill since the family was about to leave. The children were making him nervous playing with the ice machine just outside. He wanted to get the family on its way, but he was having trouble accessing a phone line to verify the credit card.

Suddenly, he heard a barrage of gunshots so loud he ducked behind the counter. Mrs. Turunen ran out of the office. He assumed she went to her children.

When the shooting stopped, the motel owner lifted his head

to see a black Cadillac tearing out of the lot. He didn't see the faces—only that two men were inside. The door to Room 8 stood open, and some of the other motel guests were peeking from their rooms. The man from Room 5 ran into the office to tell him the guy in 8 was dead.

The motel owner phoned the police and then searched for Mrs. Turunen and her children, but he never saw them again. She never even came back to pick up her credit card.

Under next-of-kin, the investigators had written:

Spouse—Cecily Turunen, age 33.

Stepdaughter—Jessica Campbell, age 9.

Son—Paavo Turunen, age 4.

Paavo turned to the supplemental reports. The motel guests were all interviewed. No one saw the shooters. One person thought he saw the victim's wife and children outside the motel room after the shooters left, but he wasn't sure.

Twenty rounds of 160-grain hollow points had been fired into the room, five hit the victim's chest—heart, lungs and stomach penetrated, death instantaneous. The remaining shots were fired into the closet and bathroom, as if in search of anyone hiding there and killing them as well. Several shots penetrated the walls into Room 7.

Paavo leafed through reports investigating the victim himself. There were essentially two sets of reports—one immediately after Mika's murder, and another set after Sam's body was found and a connection with Mika had been made.

Turunen was on a work visa and had nothing negative at all on his record. Co-workers gave him high marks for job knowledge and productivity. Reference was made to Mika being part of a group of Finns working to help anti-Communists in Finland and the USSR. Speculation centered around a falling out between members of this group, since Vanse was also implicated in it, but no proof could be found. Joonas Mäki and Okko Heikkila were interrogated, but both had good alibis.

Cecily and her children abandoned their apartment and disappeared after the murder. None of the neighbors, including Aulis Kokkonen, had any idea where they had gone. No one mentioned Cecily's job with the FBI.

Suspicion immediately turned to Turunen's wife, even speculation that the deaths were the result of a romantic triangle—that Cecily could have ordered a hit on Mika after he killed her lover. Everyone realized some sort of professional hit had to have been made on Mika due to the number of bullets used and the deadliness of the attack.

The next page in the file caused him to sit up abruptly. A week after the murder, Cecily Turunen's car was found, upside down, in the Pacific just below Devil's Slide in San Mateo County—not SFPD jurisdiction. No body was retrieved.

The investigation basically ended there, although more questions were asked and more leads followed, but nothing new turned up, and the case remained officially opened.

Twice in the following year the case had been picked up and reworked without consequence. Since the victim's children were still missing and the wife's body had never been recovered, the unsubstantiated conclusion within Homicide was that after having her husband killed, Cecily faked her death and ran, taking her children with her.

FBI help to find Cecily Turunen and her children was sought. Eldridge Sawyer, her boss, had worked as the prime contact for the SFPD on the case.

Mika's autopsy report came next. Paavo skimmed it, not wanting the details. Even flipping through the thick report, though, his head felt a little light.

Included in the binder was a brown envelope, ten-by-twelve. He knew what it contained—the crime scene and autopsy photos. He couldn't look, and set it aside.

Next in the file was an inventory of the evidence. Fingerprints lifted from the crime scene and their CSI IDs; lists of slugs and their CSI numbers; the clothes Mika wore, and clothes and belongings left behind in the motel room by the family.

No clear prints other than the family's and motel employees were found. If it had been a professional hit—no matter who ordered it—they wouldn't have touched anything. Probably kicked the door open, or knocked on the door with some innocuous request, stepped inside and started shooting.

Paavo closed the file and ran his hands over his mouth, nose and eyes. As much as he'd tried to read the file purely as a cop, at times the enormity of what he was learning after a lifetime of questions, shook him to the core.

He took the stairs back down to Archives, glad for the chance to move, and searched for the San Mateo County's investigation of Cecily's death. Often, complete files were copied and stored in cases clearly connected like this; if not, he would have to contact San Mateo.

He was in luck, a copy existed.

Back at his desk, he read through it. It was small and incomplete by big-city standards, but he could see that the police who took the case had been thorough with their contacts and their questions. They simply weren't given answers.

Passersby had spotted Cecily's car at low tide and reported it. Her seat belt had not been fastened and the driver and passenger side windows were both open. It was assumed the tides had washed the body out of the car and out to sea. Some strands of the victim's hair had snagged onto the window, and tests showed blood on the windshield consistent with a face or head injury to a driver.

Tide currents shows that the body should have washed up within a couple of weeks just north of the Golden Gate. It did not.

When the connection between the missing victim and San

Francisco's two murders was discovered, the case was basically turned over to the SFPD, who added little to it.

He shut Cecily's folder, his mind filled with more questions than the reports answered.

The envelope with photos of Mika's autopsy still sat, unopened, on his desk.

Homicide remained empty. He hadn't even noticed that three hours had passed.

As if he were moving in slow motion, he lifted the envelope, bent the metal clasps forward, opened the flap, and slid out the photos.

A black-and-white 8x10 showed a man lying on his back, on a carpeted floor, his plaid-shirt and jeans-clad body riddled with bullet holes.

He'd seen plenty of photos like this one before, but never had bile risen in his throat. He kept his eyes riveted to the photo. Despite the carnage, the thing that struck him the hardest was that the victim was so very young. He was a thin man. His long hair, almost black in the photo, had spilled thickly around his head onto the carpet. His eyes were shut. No bullet marred the narrow, high cheek-boned face with a broad brow and high, straight nose. His eyebrows were dark, not particularly thick, and arched. He wore a mustache and a short, trimmed beard.

In short, except for the mustache and beard, Paavo could have been looking at his own face.

The photo blurred. His hand shook as he lowered it. Mika, in death, was younger than Paavo was now. He didn't feel like he was looking at a father—more like he should be a brother.

The shock, the grief, gradually faded, leaving emptiness inside him. Although the office was well-heated, he was filled with an incredible cold. Then he remembered the feel of Angie's arms circling his neck last night as he sat out on the chilly deck, remembered her warmth and sunniness, her compassion. He drew in a deep breath and continued to go through the photos.

He quickly leafed through the crime scene shots, all taken from different angles. Lamps, the headboard, the walls, the bed, the closet, and the dead man.

He stopped when he reached the first autopsy photo. He didn't want to look at those. He didn't think he ever could. As he gathered everything together to put them back into the envelope, he saw a five-by-eight white envelope.

He knew what was in it—a photo of the victim in life. Homicide inspectors often use them to talk to people when they tried to find out more about a victim. It was too unsettling for people to be asked what they knew about a person and to be handed a photo from the morgue, or even worse, the scene of the crime. Only police should ever have to see victims in such poses.

So, here was the photo the homicide inspectors thirty years ago had used to ask people if they remembered Mika Turunen. Paavo opened the envelope and removed the photo.

If homicide inspectors had asked him their question, he would have answered, "Yes. I remember him."

They weren't precise memories, not sharp or definitive, but more of a blur. Yet, he *knew*.

An odd sense of vertigo swept over him, a sense of being lifted high in the air by sure but gentle hands, and looking down into the big, blue eyes of the man in the photo. Echoes of laughter, adult and child, wafted in his ears. Another fuzzy memory came of a zoo, the strong musky scent of animals in his nostrils, and climbing onto a railing to look down into a pit where Siberian tigers were kept, and the feel of someone's large hand on his shoulder, holding him, ready to grab him if he started to tumble over. He couldn't quite remember the face that went with those hands... maybe not even the hands, exactly. Yet it wasn't an unfamiliar touch. It was one he'd known. One he'd felt safe with.

Then it was gone, and he never felt safe that way again.

How could he have forgotten his father? And why hadn't Jessica and Aulis talked about him?

The vague sense of knowing his father had been a part of him for years, but they had assured him that he was wrong. As he grew older, the perception faded, and he came to believe them.

Why had they wanted him to forget the father who had played with him, and loved him? He grew up thinking the man didn't care that he existed; that his father walked away and never looked back. Why had they done that not only to him, but to the loving man who had been his father?

Nausea roiled in his stomach, and once more his vision blurred.

"Hey, Paav! Can't believe you're here on a Sunday when you've got a woman waiting for you." Homicide Inspector Bo Benson came in carrying a tall cup of coffee. Paavo glanced up at him.

"What's wrong?" Benson asked. "You look like you've just seen a ghost."

"Maybe so," Paavo said. He slid the photo back into the envelope, carefully locked everything away inside a desk drawer, then picked up his jacket and left.

21

———————

"Make sure you leave me out of your freaking videos, kid." Cousin Richie punctuated the air with his steak knife.

Angie dropped her phone into her handbag after having recorded several unsuspecting diners in the Bella Rosa restaurant. Since Paavo had gone into work that day, after leaving her parents' house, she came up with a plan. "Why don't you want to be on TV?"

"I got my reasons. Hell, I'm surprised none of these customers punched you out." He took a big bite of his New York steak. Richard Amalfi, the son of her father Sal's older brother, wasn't one for delicate veals and sauces as his main course. Nearly forty, he was speeding toward the age when men fight middle age with a vengeance. His hair was shiny blue-black and curly, but a thinning spot near the back of his head was beginning to give him a complex. He wore an expensive suit, a Rolex the size of a pancake, plus enough gold against his chest and his pinky to fill all the teeth in a small city.

They had already finished a *minestra* of swiss chard and cannelli beans, rigatoni with mussel and basil sauce, and were into the main course. "So, when you going to tell me why you asked me here?" Richie asked, taking a long sip of Krug's cabernet sauvignon.

"How suspicious! I wanted to thank you for the house, that's all," Angie said between bites of veal roll stuffed with tomato, anchovy and parmesan. "We're loving it."

"Yeah, and I didn't say a word to Sal or Serefina, just like you asked." He gave her a wink. "If they ever find out, I'll deny everything."

"Absolutely. Oh, I almost forgot, but since you brought it up, I do have one teensy little favor I wanted to ask of you."

"Uh, huh." He smirked.

"Don't give me that look! This is important. Paavo's been trying to find a guy, an ex-FBI agent named Eldridge Sawyer."

"Eldridge? What the hell kind of name is Eldridge?"

"I have no idea. Anyway, the guy seems to have gone into hiding." She handed him a piece of paper. "Here's his last address. He owned the place and sold it. Paavo tried state records, but there was nothing."

"What do you think I am, some freaking private eye?"

Now it was her turn to smirk. "I think a pack of bloodhounds would have nothing on you, cousin. You're someone who has sources in real estate, who has friends who can see where this guy was when the title documents and other papers were sent long after he left his house, and who can, somehow, track him from place to place after that."

Brown eyes innocently gawked at her. "What makes you think realtors keep records like that?"

He was innocent as a retriever in a duck pond. "A lot don't, I'm sure," she said, adding more wine to his glass. "Your friends are special. That's all I know. I don't know anything else. Nothing at all."

He chortled. "That's my girl."

"You'll give it a try, then?"

"It'll cost."

"No problem."

He leaned way back, raising his hip in order to stuff Sawyer's address into his pants pocket. "An ex-special agent trying to hide? It'll be like taking candy from a baby."

A squatty two-story building designed to look like a Spanish hacienda with chipped stucco walls and a row of red tile edging a tar and gravel roof bore the sign Cypress Motel in neon letters. Below it, the single word VACANCY. The rooms all faced the center parking lot, and the motel office guarded the entrance.

From his car, Paavo studied the motel where his father had been murdered, and then walked into the parking lot. It was half-filled. Up close, the motel looked even seedier than from the street. He focused on the door to Room 8, then abruptly turned back toward the office. A small alcove, built between the office and the first rental, caught his eye.

As if against his will, he moved in its direction and stepped inside.

The alcove had an ice machine, and several vending machines for soda, candy, cookies and crackers. The vending machines were new... but this alcove... right next to the office...

"Looking for someone?"

Paavo spun around to see a middle-aged man warily frowning at him. He took out his badge. "I'm checking up on an old case. About thirty years ago a man was shot in this motel. Do you know anything about it?"

"Thirty years ago?" The man scoffed. "You kidding me? I don't give a damn about that. I only bought this flea trap ten years ago. Worst thing I ever did. They was supposed to put a shopping mall 'cross the street. Upgrade the area. Then it fell through. This area's getting worse than ever.

"I had a guy O.D. last year. A suicide three years ago. But no murder. Not yet, anyhow. Wouldn't surprise me, though. After being in this business, seeing the customers, nothing surprises me no more."

Paavo glanced again at the alcove with the ice machines—*the children were playing with ice*—then at the door to Room 8.

"You being a cop," the motel owner said, hands on hips, "I guess you know what I mean about the public being for shit. That nothing they do surprises you any more, right?"

"You're right," Paavo replied after a while. "Nothing surprises me much at all anymore."

He left the motel in a fog, his usual dogged clarity blurred and distorted by the past. His life had been nothing but a house of cards, and he was now in a game of fifty-two pickup. He couldn't say he remembered having been at the motel as a child, but an eerie familiarity about it haunted him.

As much as he wanted to see Angie, he needed a little time to digest all he had learned and seen that day. He drove, not paying attention to the streets.

The motel had brought back the reality of his past—the gunfire, the loss of his father, and soon after, of his mother.

Her loss must have overshadowed everything else for him. That was the only way he could imagine believing Aulis and Jessica's lies about his father. He rubbed his temple. It was all so very fuzzy to him, memories mixed together with lies.

What must have been going through his child's mind back then? And through Jessica's for that matter? She was nine, five years older than him, old enough to feel the full impact of everything that happened, old enough to understand, but not to have the maturity to handle it. That was probably why she'd been so close to him for so many years, closer than most brothers and sisters. Despite her youth, she'd learned how quickly those you love could be taken away from you.

Was that why she'd been so eager to live life to the hilt? Why she had burned as a bright young flame that died too soon?

Damn, if only she'd told him. If only he'd known the truth. Maybe he could have helped.

Somehow, he ended up on his street, in front of his own small home. The car that continued past him and stopped at the corner barely registered on his conscience.

Angie told him she'd sent a cleaning service over to haul away destroyed furniture, and pick up mattress feathers and other debris. He'd like to see his home again.

As Paavo got out of the car, he didn't look around him and particularly not to the end of the block. The shooter hadn't expected him to. That was why this parking spot was chosen, along with a M40A1 rifle with an Unertl 9X scope. The car engine remained running, as the black-clad sniper dropped behind the fender.

Paavo bounded up the steps to his front door, reaching into his pocket for the key. The scope aligned the back of his head in its crosshairs. He then watched as Paavo slid the key into the hole, turned and pushed.

The world exploded.

22

———

As Angie drove away from the restaurant, she noticed the headlights of a car behind her. Normally, driving in the city, she wouldn't have paid any attention to it. But nothing was normal now. The car stayed back some distance, but made all the same turns as she did, and seemed to speed up whenever another car tried to slip between them.

She made four lefts in a row. The car followed.

Going to the house she and Paavo shared was no longer an option. Instead, she headed for the Hall of Justice, unable to lose her tail the entire way.

Parking at the Hall was restricted to employees and people with special passes. Because it was an administrative building, not a police station as such, and fairly quiet at night, she didn't want to park in a nearly empty public lot either.

As she neared, she phoned Paavo to come down and meet her at the entrance. His phone rang, but he wasn't there to answer it.

Now what?

She could call his cell phone, but he could be miles away at some crime scene.

Hell, she had a fast new car, and she knew these streets like the back of her hand. Why not put all that to good use, just as she did when those jokers were outside her apartment? A freeway on-ramp was up ahead. Turning the wheel sharply, she darted through lanes of traffic and swung onto the freeway and punched the accelerator. The car following her sped up as well, cutting off other drivers to reach the freeway entrance. For a while, it succeeded in keeping up with her since she had to keep changing lanes to get around drivers paying attention to the speed limit. Once she passed the airport, however, the congestion loosened and her pedal hit the metal.

At one point she hit 105 in a 65 mph zone, and nary a CHP in sight... thank God. When she was sure she'd lost the car following her, she headed back to the Filbert Street cottage.

She was still pumped from her version of Mr. Toad's Wild Ride as she ran inside hoping to find Paavo. But he wasn't there.

Where was he? A homicide must have happened. She wished Yosh would hurry back to work. Having Paavo go off on calls alone made her even more nervous than usual. She held Paavo's cat, Hercules, close, scratching him behind the ears as she stood at the window hoping to see Paavo arrive.

She assumed he had caught a bite for dinner while he was out, but a warm, comforting dessert waiting for him when he got home would be a nice treat. She enjoyed cooking. Relaxing, yet engrossing, it required a degree of expertise and creativity to do well, much as handcrafters found with needlepoint or crochet. Her Amaretto-pecan bread pudding was a particular favorite of his. She happily mixed enough to fill a 9x13 inch-baking dish.

Hours later, the bread pudding had grown cold, and he still wasn't home.

At midnight, she called homicide, with no luck, and his cell phone was switched to go straight to messages. She went to bed, but her nerves were too on edge to sleep.

At two-thirty she heard footsteps on the front walk. She sprang from the bed to the window. It was Paavo.

They both reached the front door at the same time.

He grabbed her, buried his face against her neck, and held her tight.

23

———————

"That's the house," Angie said. She and Paavo parked across from the Liberty Street building where Cecily, Aulis, and the Finnish students had lived. "Do you remember it at all?"

"I don't know," he said. "I had a murder case up here about three years ago. A dentist. I don't know if the area feels familiar because of him or some other reason."

"Let's walk around a bit," she suggested.

Walking the quiet street in the sunshine, even though the weather was chilly, gave Angie time to reflect on all that was happening. Last night, she'd been frightened and horrified to hear about Paavo's close call. He had paid no attention as the purr of a car engine grew louder behind him, and then a gun fired and the streetlight outside his house exploded in a hail of glass. Instinctively, he'd hit the ground just as a bullet smashed into his front door, right where he'd been standing a split second earlier. More shots were fired at the end of the street, followed by two cars screeching away.

By the time he'd run to his Mustang, a couple doors down since his house didn't have a garage, the two cars were long gone. Everyone on the block, apparently, had called the police because half the Richmond station's black-and-whites roared to the scene. The slug found in his house was from a high-powered rifle, a sniper's weapon. The danger level of whatever was going on had just been upped tenfold.

Angie's freeway adventure paled in comparison, at least to her, although he seemed as worried about her as she was about him. That neither of them had any idea of what was happening didn't seem to matter to the person, or people, behind it.

Now as they walked around the neighborhood, they discussed again, in depth, the homicide files Paavo had read, as well as Cecily's. The police had based their conclusion that Cecily had gone into hiding on her having brought her children with her, but she hadn't. Did that mean she was dead?

Angie's head spun. They'd stayed up until dawn trying to put the pieces together, but nothing fit.

"When you were a boy, what did Aulis say when you questioned him about your parents and your name?" Angie asked as they walked.

"He gave me answers that, as a child, I accepted. He told me what to say when I went to school, and I did. It was only when I was older, that I began to wonder."

"Such as?"

"I learned that the Child Protective Services would never have allowed a neighbor to keep a child whose mother had abandoned him. Aulis told me that when Mary Smith disappeared, he had filed a missing person's report, but they never found her. We moved our things to his apartment and simply stayed. I now know that would have been impossible."

"He had no family of his own, right?" Angie asked. "No one to question or complain about you and your sister?"

"He was alone. I always thought he saw us as the children he might have had, had his life worked out differently. He told us about his past many times when we were growing up."

"Oh?" she asked, her voice lifting. He smiled at her obvious curiosity about the tale.

"Aulis left Finland in the early 1970s," Paavo began. "He was engaged to a woman named Müna, a neighbor. The two of them grew up together, always knowing they would marry. But Finland had troubles after the second World War. Parts of Finland were ceded to the Soviets. People were displaced, their land taken away, their freedoms lost."

"How frightening," she said.

"Aulis decided to leave the country. He told Müna he would send for her. He had little money, so it took a year before he made it to the United States, and a year after that he'd crossed the country to San Francisco."

Angie nodded. Her own family had many stories of Italian relatives working their way to America.

"Aulis arrived, got settled, and wrote to Müna. He had complete faith she'd waited for him. Instead, she'd gotten married a year after he'd left. She'd assumed he'd been killed."

"How awful," Angie cried.

"He swore he'd tried to forget her, but after so many years of loving just one person, the disappointment seemed to take the heart out of him."

"He's such a nice man. How could other women not have noticed?"

"Maybe they did, and he ignored them," Paavo said. "He used to tell me and Jessie that we reminded him that there was more to the world than his own self-pity."

Hearing those words let Angie understand how much those children must have meant to Aulis—the fun-loving Jessica, and the quiet, somber little Paavo. Her hand tightened on his. "I'm glad—for all of you."

When they reached the intersection of Sanchez and Liberty, Paavo gave a long, last look down Liberty street, then shook his head.

"Let's go. I just don't remember this area," he stated.

"First, I'd like to try one more spot," she suggested.

They got in Angie's car and she drove westward, first to the Lutheran Church, which Paavo remembered Aulis taking him to as a boy, and then continued for another mile to a two-story brown-shingle home. "Pastor Eschenbach lives there," Angie said.

Paavo stared at it a long while. He shut his eyes, leaning back against the headrest. "I don't know, Angie. There's something familiar about it—something I don't like about it—but I've covered so many areas as a cop, who knows what it is."

"The way the wife acted troubles me. She seemed to know something, something that frightened her."

"It's weird. When I look at the house, I think of a lion, which makes no sense."

She gasped. "But it does! The door knocker is shaped like a lion's head. You were here! Aulis must have brought you here. But I wonder why?"

He stared at the house. "Whatever it was, I hated it. I wanted to go home... but I couldn't." He shook his head, and a look of such profound sadness came over him that it tore at her heart.

She was about to suggest that he could go home now, to *their* little home, when to her surprise, he got out of the car.

"Let's find out what this is all about," he said, marching straight for the house and its lion head door knocker.

Mrs. Eschenbach's scowled ferociously when she saw Angie, then turned toward Paavo. She gasped, her eyes wide. "Oh, my," she murmured, pressing her fingers to her mouth.

"I do remember you," Paavo said. "From church."

She rested her hand on her bosom as if to calm her heart. "My God, you look so much like your father now, you startled me."

Paavo drew in his breath, then murmured, "I'd like to talk to you about him."

She stiffened, casting another angry glance at Angie. "All right."

Angie expected to be led to the back of the house to see the Pastor, but Mrs. Eschenbach brought them into the kitchen and gestured for them to sit at the table. "It's such a shock seeing you again, Paavo," she said as she darted about, flustered and nervous, and then poured them each a glass of red wine from a jug. "What do you do for a living now?"

He glanced quickly at Angie. "I'm a homicide inspector."

The elderly woman paused, then slowly nodded. "I'm not surprised," she murmured, and Angie wondered what she meant. She joined them at the table and lifted her wine glass. "Skoal!"

They responded and sipped the heavy burgundy.

"What can you tell me, Mrs. Eschenbach?" Paavo asked. "I'm trying to find out what happened all those years ago."

Her lips tightened a moment. "All I know is that Aulis brought you and your sister here one day. He asked us to hide you and said no one, no one at all, was to know you were here. I had read about your father's murder in the papers, and the day after you came here, we received word that your mother's car had gone into the ocean. I asked Aulis about her, but he just shook his head. We needed to forget everything we ever knew about her or your father. They were gone, and the only way to keep you children safe was to change everything about who you were and who they were. You stayed here for ten days, then he came and got you. I didn't see you again for almost five years, when Aulis again began to attend our church. We never spoke of those times with him."

"What was he so afraid of?" Paavo asked.

She shook her head. "He never said, and we were afraid to ask. All we knew was that it was very, very bad, and the people involved were completely ruthless." She turned to Angie. "When I heard your questions, the fear we had lived with during those days came rushing back to me. Our lives were in danger—Aulis knew it, and so did we—because of the children. That was why I asked you to stay away."

Her wrinkled hand touched Paavo's, and her eyes grew teary. "I'll admit that, right now, I'm glad you didn't listen."

Paavo showed up in Homicide that afternoon to find a message from Tucker Bond's secretary. He answered her call, and was faxed a list of names and phone numbers of people who had worked with Cecily.

They all gave the same responses to his questions. None of them knew her. They remembered that she was a research clerk, but they didn't remember her being in the office, or even where her desk was situated, or what she did. The few times they saw her she was pleasant and likable. They knew she'd worked for Eldridge Sawyer, but nothing more.

Paavo phoned Tucker Bond. "Hello, Inspector," Bond answered. "Did you get the information from my secretary?"

"Yes, thanks. I was calling with a different question about Cecily Campbell," Paavo replied.

"Oh?"

"There's nothing in her file about her second marriage."

"Second marriage? I don't remember anything about that. She must have chosen to keep it from us."

"Why would she?"

"Well, some women believed they'd go further in their career if unmarried. I don't know if that was true in her case--"

"She married a Finn. He was here on a work visa."

"Not an American. Well, that might have bothered us if she were placed in any sensitive areas. But she was just a clerk, Inspector. I'm afraid I don't understand your interest in her at all."

Paavo didn't bother to explain. "Did you know her body was never recovered?"

"Now that you mention it, that does sound vaguely familiar. I'm afraid that detail slipped my memory. There was no question about her death that I was aware of."

"You didn't know the SFPD asked Sawyer's help, treating her as a missing person?"

"I knew he was asked about her, but he was her boss. That wasn't unusual in a situation that might have been suicide for all anyone knew."

"What can you tell me about Eldridge Sawyer?" Paavo asked.

"Actually, our prior conversation got me to thinking about the old days," Bond said. "Sawyer was mixed up with a lot of strange business back then. I suspect he had Cecily Campbell researching quite a bit of odd stuff. If you ask me, find him, and you'll find the answers you're looking for."

"What kind of strange business?" Paavo asked.

"If I knew the answer to that, I might be able to help you, myself."

"One last question," Paavo said. "How long after Cecily Campbell's death did Sawyer quit the Bureau?"

"How long?" Bond didn't say anything for a moment. "Well, as I recall, it was soon after. I can't imagine, however, that the two were in any way connected."

24

"Maybe there's a better way," Connie moaned, elbows on the bar, head in her hands.

"The better way is to drink tonic without gin in it," Angie scoffed. "You're getting sloshed."

"I'm just doing my part to help find Paavo's mama," Connie said, swirling the toothpick-skewered lime wedge in her drink. She wore a short, sleeveless black dress that fit like a wide band of Spandex. "Anyway, if neither of us drank, for us to come to a bar would look very suspicious."

"If you'd stop making googly-eyes at all the men, they wouldn't be sending over so many drinks." Angie's Versace icy peach outfit had an equally short, shiny skirt, and sleeveless, v-neck top. The heel of one high, ankle-strapped shoe was hooked on the rail of her stool, while the other foot waggled impatiently.

"I come to bars for one reason, and it's not to quench my thirst," Connie said. "Anyway, I'm not making eyes at anyone. This is just how I look."

"Hah! If you were any more kissy-faced, we'd have to run your lips through a mangle iron to straighten them out."

Connie stopped listening when a blond hunk entered the bar.

Angie took another sip of her virgin piña colada. The entire evening had been a waste of time. They were on Noe Street, in an area of neighborhood shops, bars and restaurants just a couple of blocks from Liberty.

After learning that Paavo was nearly killed the night before, she wasn't about to sit around tonight nervously pacing and cooking and praying he made it home in one piece. She was determined to do something. To find out exactly what was going on here. Whatever it was, had drawn in people who lived in this neighborhood thirty years ago. And as Bianca had said, people talk. They knew a lot more about what happened in their neighborhoods than the police ever imagined.

She would discover what the police hadn't. Aulis and his Finnish friends had lived here. Most were young men and, except for Mika, were bachelors. She didn't know any bachelors who didn't go to neighborhood restaurants at least once in a while, and often to bars as well. The Noe Valley area was filled with friendly neighborhood establishments, and enough singles to make them interesting. The area hadn't changed that much in the past thirty years, from all she'd heard.

She made a list of long-established nightspots and restaurants.

She and Connie began the evening at a listed bar, asking if the owner or anyone else there had lived in the neighborhood some thirty years earlier. No one had. They worked their way through other places, asking about customers, owners, and other establishments as they went. A few "old-timers" remembered some Finns in the neighborhood, but no one remembered their names or what happened to them. At The Golden Spike restaurant, the chatty owner suggested a nearby Swedish smörgåsbord. No Finnish restaurants existed in the city, now or thirty years ago, or Angie would have gone there first.

The Swedish restaurant's owner was active in the community and the Lutheran church. He knew Aulis, but that was as far as it went.

Back to barhopping, they came across some people who'd been students back in the 1990s and who remembered a Finnish guy named Sam. All they remembered was that he had been killed—they thought by another Finn.

Angie doggedly dragged Connie to the one last restaurant and three last bars on her list, tearing her away from a number of gallant men who offered drinks and anything else they wanted.

"We're so close," Angie cried with frustration, shoving her piña colada aside. "But this just isn't panning out. Let's go home."

"Good idea." Connie stood, but was a bit wobbly on her stiletto heels. "I don't even like the guys in this place. We could go back to that second bar, though. Did you notice the Polynesian-looking fellow who kept smiling at me? To die! Or, wait, was he at the third?"

"Forget it, Connie." Angie looped her arm around Connie's and the two of them tottered outside.

As they reached Angie's car, Connie rubbed her stomach. "I don't feel so good."

"You aren't going to be sick, are you?" Angie asked in alarm.

"I don't think so. It must be just a stomach ache. From all that herring at the smörgåsbord. I should never eat herring."

"And everyone knows herring doesn't mix with gin and tonic."

"Oh, please!" Connie turned several shades of green.

A small grocery store was at the corner. "Let's get you some Pepto-Bismal. It should help until you get home and lie down."

The grocer took one look at Connie's sickly pallor and tipsy state and pointed Angie in the direction of the medicines.

Connie leaned heavily against the counter, her shoulder

against a bread rack. "We're here trying to find anyone who knows Cecily," she said, her words a little slurred. The grocer was a middle-aged Chinese man. He stared silently at Connie, clearly torn between wanting her gone before she squashed the bread, and human curiosity as to how long she could stand upright. "You don't know Cecily, do you? It was a long time ago. No, you're too young to remember her."

"Did she live around here?" he asked.

Connie rubbed her forehead. "She sure did. Right up there on Liberty Street, according to my friend, Angie. She was young and pretty—I mean Cecily, not Angie. Angie's single. I was married once, though. A real shithead. My ex, not Cecily's. She was nice. She had a couple of kids, and a Finnish friend. But then she left, or died, or something."

"Oh, *that* Cecily," the grocer said.

Angie walked up with the biggest bottle of Pepto-Bismal she could find. She couldn't believe her ears. "You knew Cecily Turunen?" she asked and shoved the bottle into Connie's hands.

"I didn't know her personally, but I knew who she was. My father used to own this store, and I worked here after school. She used to come in with her kids. She was a nice lady. Then, it seems something or other happened, and they all disappeared— her, her husband, their friends. It was weird. Everyone talked about it for days."

"Oh, my God!" Angie cried, scarcely able to believe her good fortune. "You did know her!"

Connie was fighting with the bottle top. "See, I told you it was a bad idea to go to all those bars and restaurants."

"I didn't *know* her," the grocer said. "Not really. One of my customers was a good friend of hers. Why?"

"We could have simply gone grocery shopping," Connie murmured, whacking the side of the cap on the counter. "But no-o-o-o-o."

"I need to find out more about Cecily," Angie said. "Lots more. Can you tell me how to reach that customer?"

He thought a moment while eyeballing Connie who had finally gotten the bottle open and was now glugging pink stuff like it was water. He winced and said, "Well, I couldn't do that, but if you want to leave your name and phone number, I'll see if I can locate her and tell her about you. I'm afraid I haven't seen her in a while. But anyway, she'll need to decide if she wants to contact you or not."

Angie quickly wrote down the information and gave it to the grocer. "Thank you so much. Tell her it's very, very important that I speak to her. It'll just take a little while, and I'd be eternally grateful."

"Sure thing. By the way, I think you friend is going to need more than Pepto-Bismal."

Angie had forgotten all about Connie. She swiveled around to find her still standing, but her eyes were shut and her forehead rested on a flattened loaf of Wonder Bread.

25

―――――

On the northern, Mendocino coast, five miles past the fishing town of Gualala, Paavo turned Angie's Lexus onto a small paved road that snaked uphill into the coast range mountains. Ten minutes later, he reached a gravel-packed private road.

He and Angie were headed toward a home he'd visited a few times as a teenager with Aulis. The area had changed very little, and the route came back to mind with surprising ease.

A large wooden gate stood open in the barbed wire fence, leading to a wood-framed house. Beyond it, the forest was thick and dark with pines. Joonas Mäki opened the front door and walked toward them.

He greeted Angie, then clutched Paavo's arms and gave him a kiss on the cheek just as he used to when Paavo was a little boy. He was lanky, with a full head of bushy salt and pepper hair. His eyebrows were gray, the individual hairs thick, coarse and corkscrewed and, as Professor White had remembered, met in the center.

Paavo and Angie followed him into the house Aulis had helped him build. Paavo was about eight or nine years old at the time, and had enjoyed coming to the country to play while the men worked.

Before that, Joonas had also lived in San Francisco.

Memories flooded Paavo's head as he entered the main room with a pot-bellied stove in the corner and small double-hung windows. Originally, the house was one big room with an outhouse in the back, but when Joonas married, a bathroom was among the new additions.

Joonas's wife waited in the house for them. She'd prepared a hearty brunch, and they caught up on old times and Aulis's condition as they ate. Afterward, Angie gave Paavo a nod. She and Hannah took care of the clean-up while Paavo and Joonas put on heavy coats and went outdoors.

They walked to a bluff overlooking highway, beach and ocean. In a mesmerizing rhythm, waves crashed onto tall boulders standing in the water, sending magnificent white plumes high into the air. The land was lonely and isolated and cold, but it was also incredibly beautiful. Both men took in the vista before them in a moment of mutual awe.

"Did you know that Finland was created by the Water Mother, Paavo?" Joonas's voice smiled.

"No. I've not heard that."

"Water and wood and winter. That's what Finland is all about." He seemed lost in thought.

After a respite, Paavo said, "I've learned a little about my parents, factual things, but not about their character. Some of this present danger, I've come to suspect, goes back to them and their causes, and their deaths. Help me understand, Joonas."

Joonas's gaze fixed on Paavo, sorrowful and wistful. "You are so much like your father, sometimes it makes me think I am still a young man. How could I be this old when I look across the room, and there is Mika, just the way I remember him?"

A sudden anger gnawed at him. "All these years you knew, and you kept it from me. Why?"

"I had to. Aulis made me promise."

He tamped his ire. "Tell me about him."

"There were four of us," Joonas began, hands tucked into pockets, eyes fixed on the sea. "Myself, your father, Sami Vansha who Americanized his name and called himself Sam Vanse, and a fourth man, Okko Heikkila. The four of us worked to help our people back in Finland."

"You had family there?" Paavo asked.

"Okko and Sami did. Okko's grandfather had been imprisoned by the Soviets and died in the Gulag. Sami had family, too, but where Okko was quiet, Sami was a hothead. Any chance to cause trouble, Sami was right there. I imagine that's what got him and Mika killed."

He fell silent. Paavo waited.

"When I was in Finland, when the Soviets occupied the lands our government had ceded to them, I will never forget how my father kept a suitcase packed with warm clothes and canned and dried food near the door, ready to grab it and run if necessary. He had been a vocal opponent of the Soviets, and knew he could be arrested at any minute. Although it never happened, he lived only to age fifty-three. My mother said he died because all that happened to his country broke his heart."

Paavo remained quiet as Joonas's thoughts drifted to the past.

"She died not long after helping me get passage to the United States."

"And Mika?" Paavo asked finally.

Joonas hesitated, and then said slowly, "After the Soviets finished fighting against the Germans, Mika's parents lived in Soviet-occupied territory. Many people tried to escape the madness of those years, and were killed. Mika's parents were among them."

A chill stabbed through Paavo, and he hunched deeper into the thick fleece coat. He told himself it was the icy ocean wind.

"Mika was just a child," Joonas said. "Other refugees fleeing the country, friends of his father, took him with them. He lived in England until he graduated from school, then came to the US on a student visa. He was the only one in his family to make it to this country, although it had been the dream for all of them. That was one reason, I believe, that he was so passionately against the Soviet Union. He blamed it for his parents' deaths."

Paavo nodded silently. So his father had lost his own parents. At least he had known why. Paavo mentally gave a shake of the head. He was not here to judge or accuse, but to learn the truth. To find out as much as he could about the man who was his father.

"I saw what an all-too-powerful government could do to the rights of individuals," Joonas continued. "Even after the Soviets returned some of our land, Finland still lived under its shadow. That was why I joined with Mika and the others. That was why we worked together for our homeland, and its freedom."

"Did Mika have any living relatives in Finland? Any here?"

Joonas sighed. "None that he knew of. He left the old country as a child alone. I expect you might have some distant cousins, but I don't know who."

For the second time in this visit, he was shaken. He hadn't thought about having people related to him, not even when he had asked Joonas. He'd asked as a cop, seeking facts, but suddenly the thought of having cousins, however distant, was inexplicably welcome.

"I am sorry I don't know more, Paavo."

He stared out at the water before answering. "Don't be. I never expected to learn who my father was, let alone his background or what he looked like."

"He had your eyes. Very big, very blue. His hair was dark brown, almost black." Joonas paused, then grinned with warm affection. "You have your father's nature. He was always serious, very intense. He had a high idealism as well, one that remained unshaken. As time went on, things began to happen, dangerous things, and more and more dangerous people became drawn in, for reasons far different from Mika's and the group's original reasons."

"Who were these people?"

"What can I say? They were in it for the money. Money began to be a part of our work. I was not working with them at that point. I got out. I told Mika to do the same."

"But he didn't."

They walked along the windy bluff a while before Joonas answered. "He felt it was wrong to ignore the sorrows of people back home. Your mother tried to turn him around, but Sami... Sami was like a cancer, always eating at him, always reminding him of what had happened at home, that his parents had been killed by the Soviets, and that he needed to take revenge on them for what they did to Finland, as well as his family."

Paavo sucked in his breath, finally reaching the point to ask the question he came here for. "Who killed Mika and Sami, Joonas?"

"Aulis never wanted you to know. He was afraid for you."

"It's time I learned," Paavo said.

"We worked with Russian smugglers—they, like us, hated the Soviets. We knew they were criminals, but we also thought they alone had the strength to help us. As I said, we were young and idealistic. In time, it became clear they belonged to the *Organizatsiya*. There's nothing worse than them. Not the Italian mafia, none of it. The only thing worse, maybe, was the old KGB. But they're gone, and the *Organizatsiya* continues to this day."

"Who are they?"

"These days, you call them the Russian mafia."

Paavo was staggered. "They killed my father? You're sure?"

Joonas's eyes softened, his voice low. "I believe so. I understand your mother witnessed it."

Paavo's stomach clenched at the horror of it. "Tell me about my mother," he said after a while.

"All I know is that she died. She loved you and your sister very much. That was the part that hurt the most, telling you she was no good, that she had abandoned you and your sister. But it was the only way Aulis believed you would not try to find her, the only way to keep you safe. If he told you she was dead, as you got older, you'd say where is her grave? Where is her death certificate? Her will? How did she die? He knew you might ask a million questions he had no answer for. So he told you your name was Smith, you were illegitimate, and that your mother had walked out. It was the kind of story you wouldn't be inclined to pursue."

Paavo sucked in his breath. Aulis's assumption was accurate. "The police thought she faked her death."

"Did she?" Joonas asked. "Or did the *Organitziya?* Or, did she truly die? I don't know. I don't *want* to know. I was scared. Once they want you dead, they never stop hunting you. I moved up here, bought this land."

Paavo closed his eyes briefly. Joonas, more than any document or FBI file, had made these people come alive for him. "I need to find out what happened back then."

Joonas turned a world-weary gaze on him. "Okko might know more. He worked with Mika and Sami and was much closer to all they did than I was. He can tell you more about those days. Let us go inside and call him. You two need to meet. He lives high in the Sierras. He, too, has spent his life hiding."

Joonas found the number and phoned, but an answering machine came on with a long beep, as if filled with messages. Joonas dialed Okko's close friend and neighbor to ask if he had any idea when Okko would return. The neighbor said he didn't know, but that Okko had left suddenly, and had been gone for over a week.

26

"I don't believe this," Angie said the very next afternoon as she and her cousin Richie sat by the window in a coffee shop in the town of Gideon. Four hours ago, she hadn't even known there was a town called Gideon halfway between Sacramento and Mt. Shasta, and now that she'd seen it, all two blocks of it, she didn't *want* to know it existed.

"Eat your banana split, but not too fast, we might be here a while." Richie adjusted the red bandanna on his neck. "This thing is too damn tight. How do cowboys wear them? Don't they have Adam's apples?"

Angie tried not to laugh. Last night, a message from Richie said he'd see her in the morning, that they were going to the country. Since she'd just returned from a journey to Mendocino with Paavo, traveling the next day with her cousin was hardly appealing.

It became even less so when, shortly after Paavo left for work, she heard a knock and found Yosemite Sam in her doorway. Richie announced he wanted to fit in with the locals. Somehow, a nearly middle-aged, olive-complexioned Italian in a butternut leather vest, blue and white striped Ralph Lauren shirt, red bandanna, starched and creased Calvin Klein denims, beige hand-tooled cowboy boots, and a silver rodeo belt buckle big and bright enough to signal distant planets, was not her idea of how to fit in with anyone, anywhere, ever. She gave thanks he wasn't also wearing a white ten-gallon hat and a hip-hugging holster.

He swore he knew what he was doing. She felt positively conservative in her twill trousers, turtleneck sweater, boots, and new purple parka.

Things went from bad to worse when she walked out to the street.

A red Ford F350, one ton long-bed truck with purple and yellow phantom flames, a silver grill guard, and monstrous off-road Super Swamper tires awaited them. He practically had to lift her into the extended cab's passenger seat.

"What's going on?" she asked, peering out the window to the sidewalk far below. She'd been on lower Ferris wheels.

"You'll see," he said with a grin, crawling into the driver's seat. Then they were off. He spent the rest of the trip talking into his phone, making deals, buying a stock he'd gotten a lead on, betting on horses...

From Gideon's only restaurant, Linda's Eats and Sweets, they had a clear view of the post office. Richie's so-called real estate connections had tracked Eldridge Sawyer to "Edward Sanders" with a post office box in Gideon. It was up to Richie from that point. He began by mailing Sawyer a 9x12 fluorescent pink envelope filled with information on discounted rifle and ammo supplies. He then called the Gideon post office and learned that mail became available around noon each day.

"If he don't show up today," Richie said, "we're going to be stuck here over night."

"What do you mean by that?" The horror of being stuck here

while Paavo was going through so much, was more than she wanted to contemplate. "There's a chance he's not here?"

"Well, see, when I was sweet-talking the lil' gal at the post office to find out when the mail would be delivered, I casually mentioned it was for Ed Sanders—something he wanted right away. And she said that was odd because he was away. He'd told them hold his mail. But then she checked the hold, and it was over today."

Angie gaped. "You got a postal employee to give you that information?"

He beamed. "Women love me."

She bit her tongue. "I hope she was right." But then she remembered a story she'd heard right after Christmas. "Speaking of women, I heard you had an interesting Christmas Eve with one of Paavo's co-workers, Rebecca Mayfield."

Richie's mouth pursed. "Yeah, well, it was definitely interesting."

"Rumor has it, you two got along rather well," Angie said with a wry grin. Her cousin and Rebecca Mayfield doing anything but murdering each other at first sight was hard to imagine.

"Where did you hear that?"

"You know you can't keep anything from this family. They'd use Morse code if they had to, when there's a good story to tell."

Richie grimaced. "Well, I hate to disappoint everyone, but there's no story to tell. We spent one day together, and one evening. End of story."

"Did you call her?"

"Of course not!"

Angie knew when she'd pushed Richie far enough and looked outside at the still-empty post office. "I don't know how much ice cream I can eat before the owner here starts to suspect something. If she doesn't already."

"Don't worry about it."

She was nibbling on her banana split, while Richie had finished his and was now slurping the end of a chocolate malt when he stiffened, his eyes fixed on the post office. A tall, powerfully built man wearing a camouflage jacket, pants, hat and jackboots—a real friendly looking guy—stood on the sidewalk, glancing through mail that included a fluorescent pink envelope. He stuffed it inside his jacket and started walking.

"Okay, babe, it's Saturday night!" Richie tossed some money on the table and was out the door, Angie chasing after him. Once on the sidewalk, he grabbed her arm and practically dragged her across the street toward Sawyer's truck. She was too stunned to try to stop him.

Sawyer climbed into the truck and started the ignition just as Richie shoved Angie hard against his back fender. "You bitch!"

With a shriek, she fell to the ground.

"You talk to me like that and you won't say anything for a week!" His face was purple, landing his fist hard on Sawyer's fender as he leaned over her. "Get up!"

He lifted his foot as if he was going to kick her.

"Don't!" She screamed, her arms thrust out protectively. Had he gone crazy?

Suddenly, Richie flew about five feet into the air, to land sprawled on his backside. Sawyer stood over him. "That's no way to treat a lady."

Richie slowly sat up. "Hey, can I say 'that ain't no lady, that's my wife'?" He gave a quivery chuckle.

Sawyer wasn't having it, but turned away from him with contempt. "You all right, lady?" he asked, holding out his hand to help her stand.

Angie nodded. He grasped her wrist and her entire body left the ground as he pulled her to her feet. When she landed, she thanked him and brushed herself off.

"Hey, she don't like my new truck." Richie, also standing, pointed to his flashy long bed. "I don't have to put up with shit like that!"

Sawyer jabbed a finger into her cousin's chest, his nose nearly touching Richie's forehead. "Listen, rhinestone cowboy, you take your problems somewhere else. Gideon doesn't want your kind around here."

"I want to go home," Angie said, stomping toward the truck.

Richie lifted his hands, stepping back out of Sawyer's way. Sawyer looked from him to Angie in disgust, then got into his truck and drove off.

"What was that all about?" she asked when Richie joined her.

"Sleight of hand. Hope I didn't hurt you none. Follow me."

Just around the corner was a ten-year-old black Chevy sedan. He unlocked the doors. "Hurry."

Her head was reeling as she jumped into the passenger seat. Richie flipped a switch on something that looked like a radar detector and headed back to the main road, turning in the direction Sawyer had gone.

The detector beeped.

"Where did you get this car? And what's beeping?" Angie asked.

"It's easy to pay someone to drop off a car for you," he explained, cruising away from the town. "The rest of it, we had to do on our own. You got to be ready to improvise. You were pretty good back there."

She decided not to say she wasn't acting.

He continued. "The beep means we're connected with a little homing device under Sawyer's back fender. Soon, we'll know where he lives. After that, it's up to you and your boyfriend. On the way back, let's stop at that restaurant again."

"Not another banana split?"

"No. I saw some tutti frutti on the menu. I haven't had any of that since I was a kid."

Although it was late when Angie returned to the city, she contacted Paavo and agreed to meet him in Aulis's hospital room. She'd felt bad that a couple of days had gone by since she'd last been there. Cousin Richie dropped her off on the sidewalk, refusing to drive up to the entrance. "Hospitals are bad luck," he said. "I leave them alone, and they do the same for me."

She had just turned onto the corridor with Aulis's room when she saw a little man wearing work pants, a black watch cap, and denim jacket sneak inside. He quietly shut the door behind him.

No guard was present. The city couldn't afford to continue with one full time, so Paavo's friends on the force stopped by regularly. The stranger must be one of Aulis's friends, she told herself, and he wasn't being sneaky, but careful and quiet, perhaps not wanting to disturb a man in a coma...?

Angie teetered in the hallway, torn between going to find a nurse to enter the room with her, or bursting in immediately to find out who the man was. How long would she have to wait before convincing a nurse to join her? If the man meant harm, how much damage could he do while she dithered? She had no choice.

Hitting the door hard, she swung it open. The little man was bending low over Aulis. "Who are you?" she demanded.

At the sound of the door flying open, he turned his head, his eyes startled. Suddenly, he bolted toward her. She swung her tote bag, smacking him square in the stomach and knocking him back into the room. All she could think of was to escape and yell for help. She spun around and ran smack into a brick wall.

Familiar hands caught her. "Paavo! Quick! That man is trying to hurt Aulis!"

She jumped into the hall before looking back into the room

to see the little man clutching the foot of the bed with one hand, the other pressed against his stomach.

"Paavo?" he whispered.

Paavo stepped toward him. "You are?"

"Okko Heikkila."

27

Angie, Paavo and Heikkila spent time with Aulis, who still hadn't wakened, and then went to a Japanese restaurant with small, individual tatami rooms. There, they could talk uninterrupted and unobserved by others. Although Heikkila agreed to go with them, it was clear he was nervous about it. Once they arrived, both Heikkila's and Paavo's demeanors were even more serious, and the two said little as they ordered dinner.

No more than ten words passed between the two until the cocktail waitress brought a flask of warm sake, and small porcelain cups. She poured them each some, then left. Heikkila drank his cupful in one gulp, then poured more rice wine for himself.

Angie hated such silence. She tried to relieve the tension by talking about the beauty of the Sierras where Heikkila lived, asking him about the level of snowfall this year compared to others, and anything else innocuous she could think of. The anxiety level at the table remained high, thickening the air.

The waitress brought misu, and replenished the flask of sake. Angie noticed that Heikkila was already beginning to feel the effect of it.

The misu was followed by a platter of sashimi, and then the waitress heated the center hotplate for shabu-shabu, in which the diners dip paper-thin raw meat and vegetables into boiling water, cooking their food and creating a broth as they eat. It was a leisurely, congenial meal, and soon, as Angie had hoped, the food and wine began to loosen the taciturn Heikkila's tongue.

"What are you doing in San Francisco?" Paavo asked.

"Can't a man take a vacation? I heard Aulis was hurt and came to visit him." He glared at Angie. "Didn't know I'd be hit by a cannonball hurling harridan for my trouble."

"Well, you scared me, and then you tried to run," she protested.

"I don't like strangers," he said.

Paavo quickly poured them both more sake. "I'm interested in Omega. I heard you worked at the tech company with Mika and Sam."

Heikkila sipped his wine. "I'll tell you. Those days were different. Better. People did real programming. Computers were monsters kept in refrigerated rooms. We thought IBM was the greatest company known to man."

Angie suppressed a smile, considering she had a smart phone that, she'd been told, could outperform some monster systems of the past. She hoped her phone hadn't been damaged by his stomach.

"Did you and my father know each other before going to work at Omega?" Paavo asked.

"Mika and Sam met at San Francisco State. Later, I was hired. Sam was a flaky, impulsive guy, always emotional. It made sense he got us mixed up with sympathizers against the Soviet government. You got to remember, it was the late-eighties into the nineties. People had causes. Students and American-born Finns held protests, petitions, sit-ins. And meetings. Meetings to stage more meetings. Joonas, Mika, Sami, me, even Aulis, we hated the Soviets." He swished some beef in the hot broth,

"What were your ideas of support?" Paavo asked, doing the same.

Heikkila smiled wryly. He didn't have to say it, but Paavo heard the sentiment: *serious, like your father.* "For vacations, Sam always went back to Finland to visit family. He made connections with an underground movement, led and driven by the 'intelligentsia' as he put it. Having an American work visa drew attention. Sam thought of himself as an intellectual, a radical poet. He would have loved Paris in the twenties—except that he didn't know French and he wasn't a poet. But he lived for being a radical and making contacts. That was his thing, contacts. Before long, he recruited others, especially Mika. While Sam played with intrigue and heroics, Mika was all idealism and patriotism. You know, his parents were killed by the Communists—"

"Yes," Paavo said softly, "I've heard that."

Angie watched his face and could see how much Heikkila's simple words troubled him. Even for herself, listening to Heikkila made Mika and his parents so alive that she, too, felt the grief of their deaths. And Sam, she could have wrung his neck! Didn't he ever consider what might come of his toying with people's lives and emotions?

"So Sam led the rest of you to the movement against the Soviets?" Angie asked.

"That's right. The dissidents needed communications equipment for their *samizdat* movement. Sam had his contacts—a group of radicals called themselves the Kalevala. The name was from the epic poem that gives the legends, myths and folklore that make up the soul of the Finnish people. Perhaps Joonas was the old and wise Väinämöinen, a powerful seer with supernatural origins, and I was Ilmarinen, a smith and forged the "lids of heaven" when the world was created. Sam was Lemminkäinen, an adventurer-warrior and charmer of women. And Mika was the tragic hero Kullervo, who is forced by fate to be a slave from childhood and avenge his father's death."

Paavo broke into the old man's reverie. "So, when Sam came back with this idea of helping this *samizdat* movement, what did all of you do?"

"For a long time, our help was fairly minimal. If we could get our hands on equipment the dissidents needed, they'd give us money to buy it, and then connect us to some Russians who'd smuggle it into the USSR. That all changed after Sam met Harold Partridge."

"Partridge? The big name in computers?" Angie glanced at Paavo, not sure she heard right, but Paavo too was staring with surprise at the name Heikkila had just spoken.

"See, we didn't have personal computers then," Heikkila said. "But Partridge had already started with his business. Before anyone knew what hit it, he bought Omega and all the main-frame programmers switched to personal computer operating systems. But I'm getting ahead of my story."

Thinking of the pictures she'd seen of the diminutive, bespectacled titan of Silicon Valley and famed philanthropist and collector, Angie said, "It's hard to imagine Harold Partridge being caught up in anything like this."

"He was different then," Heikkila explained. "Young, ambitious and greedy. Now, he lives in Silicon Valley with so much money he doesn't know what to do, other than to worry that someone somewhere might steal it. He came from a wealthy family and spent years traveling around the world looking for something to interest him."

"Did he find it?" Angie asked.

"He found two things—computers and Russian art. Computers because he had enough financial savvy and vision to know they were going to be huge, and Russian art because it was the one thing he couldn't go to a store and buy. He could only get it through devious means. And being devious was what he did best."

At the words Russian art, Angie and Paavo caught each other's eyes.

As they continued with the meal, Heikkila explained. "When Sam learned that Partridge was willing to pay good money for Russian art, he realized that if he could get his hands on Russian artwork, statues, and jewelry, he could sell them to Partridge for big bucks and buy whatever the dissidents needed. He went to his contacts about 'exporting' some artwork to Partridge, keeping Partridge's name a secret from everyone. I only found out by accident, overhearing something. Before long, a man named Gregor Rosinsky showed up."

"Rosinsky?" Paavo couldn't hide his shock, while Angie let out a small gasp. "The jeweler?"

Heikkila snorted, then his eyes bored into Paavo. "He was a smuggler! One of those guys who moved goods into and out of Russia for money. He learned all about Russian artwork and jewelry doing that job, and could tell a genuine piece from a fake at fifty paces. And if a piece was damaged during transport, he had to learn to fix it. Why not go into business?" Heikkila chuckled wryly.

Angie couldn't believe the stooped, soft-spoken jeweler had once been a smuggler.

Suddenly Heikkila asked, "Do you know who killed him?"

"Not yet," Paavo said. "Nothing was stolen, except perhaps, a Russian music box that belonged to my mother. Angie took it to him for repairs, and it's missing."

The Finn's blue gaze went from Paavo to Angie and back. "That's disturbing news."

"Another Russian connected with jewelry was recently killed," Paavo added. "This one was a forger."

Heikkila nodded. "I know. Jakob Platnikov. He was also one

of the smugglers. We mostly dealt with five of them. Rosinsky, Platnikov, Nikolai Drach, Artur Masaryk, and Leonid Boldin."

"How did you know they were dead?" Angie asked.

Heikkila's gaze shifted from her to Paavo. "It was in the newspapers," he replied innocently.

"Joonas thought the smugglers were part of what became the Russian mafia. Do you agree?" Paavo asked after a pause. Angie's attention was glued on Heikkila.

"Absolutely. The *mafiya,* emphasis on the 'ya' as they say it, is the reason I live where I do. I don't want to be anywhere near them. I don't want them to even imagine I can be trouble for them. They're the scariest people I've ever seen. I know a story of some very dangerous men in the Middle East who captured a Russian businessman and held him for ransom, threatening to kill him if their demands weren't met. They didn't know that the businessman belonged to the *mafiya.* The *mafiya* found out who the kidnappers were and captured some of their relatives. They cut off a finger from one, an ear from another and mailed them to the kidnappers. They said that for each day the Russian businessman was not released, a package with another body part would be delivered. The guy was released immediately. That's how the Russian *mafiya* plays."

Angie felt a cold chill.

"Why did they kill Sam and Mika?" Paavo asked.

A weariness came onto Heikkila's lined face, and he said, "The Soviet government rounded up a group of dissidents and smugglers and imprisoned and tortured them. The *mafiya* thought we, the Finns, gave the Soviets the names. We swore we didn't, but they said they had proof. Next thing I knew, they killed Sam and Mika. And I ran to the Sierras."

Paavo stared at him in shock. "No one told the police any of this."

Heikkila gazed flatly at him. "Do you think we're crazy?"

"Rosinsky said the music box was museum quality," Angie added.

"It probably belong to the Romanovs—the Tsar or his wife. It sounds like the type of thing they smuggled." Heikkila shook his head with disgust. "But that was thirty years ago! No one could possibly still care about all that old history, no one but me, at any rate. It haunted my dreams for years, but in time, even I began to forget. Only once in a while, like when I saw Aulis in the hospital, does it all come back, and I replay the ideas of revenge I used to have."

"Revenge on the *mafiya*?" Paavo asked.

"Who else? Anyway, it's over now. I stay in the mountains because I've come to love them. There's no more to it than that."

28

Paavo re-read his notes on Jakob Platnikov's case and now turned again to Rosinsky's murder investigation. Rebecca had worked on telephone records and one annotation jumped out at him. Three days before Rosinsky was killed, he had phoned Harold Partridge's residence and Jakob Platnikov. Three days... the same day Rosinsky's office was broken into, and the same day Angie had brought him her music box.

Rosinsky would have known of Partridge's interest in Russian imperial porcelain pieces such as the music box. If Partridge were willing to pay enough to convince Angie to sell, Rosinsky easily could have received a generous finder's fee. That would have been a legitimate reason for the phone record.

Now, Rosinsky was dead, Jakob Platnikov was also dead, and the music box was missing. Could the music box be the key? Both men were suspected of being part of a group with ties to the Russian Mafia. And somehow, his father's and Sam's murder had included those same characters.

The answer to what was happening had to be right there in front of him, but he just couldn't see it.

One thing he did know, was that he needed to learn more about computer and software magnate Harold Partridge.

Paavo didn't wait for the elevator, but took the stairs up one floor to Room 558, where the Special Investigation Division Gang Task Force was located. Since the infamous Golden Dragon restaurant massacre in Chinatown years earlier, most of the task force's work concerned Chinese gangs. Two gangs, Joe's Boys and the Wah Ching, had opened fire on each other in a crowded Chinatown restaurant and innocent customers were caught in the murderous crossfire. The Golden Dragon carnage had announced that the city wasn't free of crime gangs. To have them in the heart of one of the city's landmark tourist areas stirred the city's government into action.

Paavo knew Joe's Boys had ceased to exist, but the Wah Ching were still in San Francisco and were now affiliated with more organized and more powerful crime groups in China and Hong Kong. And despite the Gang Task Force's efforts, new ethnic gangs had also emerged throughout the city, including the Russian mafia. He needed to find out to what role Partridge had, if any, in all of it.

Inspector Fogarty, one of the key members of the Gang Task Force, pulled out a file on Harold Partridge and handed it to Paavo. "We don't have Partridge down for doing anything illegal," Fogarty said, "but we have a file on him because his name turned up so many times while investigating the Russian mafia. Partridge isn't too particular about the company he keeps. He ain't no Partridge in a pear tree."

Paavo groaned. "Bad jokes aside, just how active is the Russian mafia in the city?" he asked.

"We got some problems. Nothing like the east coast, luckily. The Russian mafiosi were already hardened criminals when they arrived. Their leader calls himself Koba--'protector of the little people.'"

"And Partridge works with them?"

"There's no doubt in my mind—just no proof he's done anything illegal. We share what we turn up with the FBI. I haven't heard back from them, though. Either they think he's clean or just have other fish to fry."

Paavo sat down to read Partridge's file. While Partridge had a long history of association with reputed members of the Russian mafia, keeping bad company was no crime, even if the unlikely socializing between a Silicon Valley magnate and Russian crime lords reeked with suspicion.

"Thanks for the information," Paavo said as he handed the file back.

"I just hope you nail the bastard, Paavo. He's dirty. I know he is."

Harold Partridge lived in a massive white stucco house on a bluff above Silicon Valley.

Silicon Valley was not so much a geographical feature as a state of mind, an exciting state of wild competition, startling innovation, cutthroat deals, fabulous wealth, and nearly unlimited power in government. It ran from San Francisco south to San Jose along the bay to fairly deep inland.

For Harold Partridge's home to look out over the place that had given him everything he could ever want made sense. The house was quiet as a mausoleum. An elderly butler opened the door and said almost nothing as Paavo showed his badge and asked to speak to Partridge. Silently, he led Paavo to the living room, then walked away.

The interior was more of a display center than a home. The floors were a smooth, dark hardwood, the walls bright white, with picture windows facing the hills. In the center of the room were two black-leather chairs and a matching sofa. One wall had a display of Russian triptych ikons mounted on it, another had shelves filled with collectibles, also in a Russian style.

Paavo slowly worked his way around the room, first studying the ikons with their religious scenes. The shelves displayed candlesticks, cloisonné enamel boxes, miniatures, pen trays, cigarette cases, and a variety of fancy bottles. Two Fabergé eggs, incredibly detailed and beautiful, were displayed in glass boxes.

When Partridge still didn't appear, Paavo wandered out of the living room into the hallway.

Across the hall, a plain, Shaker-like dining room stood in contrast to the room he'd just been in. Past it, the next room was lined with display cases.

The center case held jewelry. Three necklaces with diamonds and emeralds had center stage. There were also a variety of diamond earrings, brooches made with gold and diamonds, with aquamarine, silver and agate, and rubies, and a number of heavily jeweled boxes, many with portraits of Nicholas or Alexandra or both.

The value of the pieces was beyond his ability to comprehend.

"My, my, a policeman with a nose for art."

Paavo turned at the voice. Partridge, with a wiry build, wispy gray hair and oversized glasses, was an even smaller man than news photos indicated. His left eye twitched nervously.

"I'm Inspector Smith, Homicide, San Francisco," Paavo said, holding out his hand.

Partridge's hand felt as soft and squishy as Brie cheese.

"Homicide? I take it you're investigating someone's death?" Partridge's voice quavered, and he tried to laugh it off. "I don't think I know anyone who's died under unusual circumstances, do I?"

"It has to do with the death of Gregor Rosinsky, owner of Rose Jewelry in San Francisco."

Partridge gasped. "Yes, I know that store. As you can see, I collect Russian pieces, and the owner of the shop was an excellent craftsman, an expert. He could tell me if the pieces I was interested in were genuine, and I always went to him to have them cleaned and repaired, if necessary. I'm afraid I haven't spoken to him recently. Not for a couple of years." He took a breath. "You said he died. A homicide? How horrible! What happened to him?"

"He was shot in his store. We're looking for any possible leads and are contacting recent customers. His telephone records show that he called this house three days before his death."

"They do? I never received any such call. I spend a fair amount of time at the Industries complex. If he called me, he didn't leave a message."

"Is there anyone else he might have spoken to?"

"My butler should have told me about any phone calls, although he's getting a little forgetful. Still, after so many years of faithful service, how can I complain? The same is true for my housekeeper. She would definitely have given me a message, unless he didn't leave his name or anything. That's probably it. I can ask her if she remembers such a thing. She's out grocery shopping at the moment, I'm afraid."

"Please do," Paavo said. "But tell me more about Rosinsky."

"I have nothing more to tell. I'm sorry."

"If he found a piece of porcelain that you would be interested in, do you think he'd call?"

"I would imagine so. But my pieces are extremely valuable. I doubt he would come across a piece I'd want. In the early part of the twentieth century, when the Bolsheviks took over Russia, a great many people escaped to the West and brought jewels, art, and beautiful collectibles with them. They had to sell them to live. What a treasure trove that was for collectors like myself! But, that source has dried up. And the few new pieces that emerge are outrageously marked. Everyone's gotten into the act, I'm afraid."

"What about the *samizdat* movement some years ago? I imagine you've heard of it."

"Ah, I see. You are now talking about those who were anti-USSR and stole artwork to sell to get money to keep their cause going. From what I know, they pretty much died out." Partridge gave a mousy smile. "Let's just say I don't ask the sellers where the art came from originally. They give me assurances I will become the legal owner, and I accept them."

"I see," Paavo replied. Something about Partridge annoyed him. He decided not to ask about the music box at the moment. "Thank you for your time. Let me know if your housekeeper spoke to Rosinsky. For now, I'll ask your butler."

Partridge's eyes narrowed. "Of course, Inspector. I'll ring for him."

Partridge hovered about as Paavo questioned the butler, but the servant had no memory of a telephone call from Rosinsky.

———

"They're all closing in." Partridge sniveled into the phone. "Paavo Smith was just here! He doesn't know yet, but it's just a matter of time."

"What do you expect?" the voice bellowed. "You try to kill a cop, and you think they're going to sit back and play Tiddly Winks? Keep away from everything and everybody! Too many questions are being asked, too much old shit being stirred up. I'm doing what I can to put a lid on it, *but you have to stay clear!*"

"None of this would have happened if it weren't for Rosinsky and Platnikov!" Partridge whined. "You're taking too long! You've got to stop him—and, from what I hear, he's got a girlfriend who sticks her nose into as much or more than he does."

"I'll handle them both. Leave everything to me." The connection went dead.

Partridge glared at the phone. *Like hell I will!*

29

———

"Inspector Smith, Homicide," Paavo said, showing his badge as he stood at the front door of the home of Craig Weston, the onetime owner Omega Computing. "I'd like to speak to Mr. Weston."

"Homicide?" The man cocked his head, peering hard at the i.d. He was darkly tanned, his head bald. Rounded shoulders caused a stooped posture, and the skin around his eyes and mouth hung in loose, rubbery folds. "I'm Craig Weston." His voice was gruff. "What's the problem?"

"There's no problem. I'm investigating a murder case in San Francisco," Paavo said, "the murder of a Russian jeweler. In the course of the investigation something came up that happened many years ago. It doesn't involve you, but I did have questions about some of your former employees."

The man visibly relaxed. The way people became uptight when first contacted by police never ceased to surprise Paavo. They could be perfectly innocent, but you wouldn't know it from the way they looked.

"Come on in," Weston said. The house was a simple ranch-style, the type that carried an affordable, middle-class price tag almost anywhere but in Palo Alto, the home of Stanford University and many Silicon Valley executives and managers. Weston walked straight through it to the backyard. Across a concrete patio was a clapboard workshop. "We can talk in here so the wife won't be listening and butting in every two seconds."

The workshop looked like a junkyard for old desk top computer parts. A couple of complete systems were up and running, but most of the room was filled with miscellaneous pieces, soldering irons, tools, and electrical equipment. "I'm working on a new invention. Soon, it'll be ready to market."

Paavo nodded. Weston removed a crumb-filled plate, utensils and an empty coffee cup from a chair near the work area, and motioned for Paavo to sit there.

"What do you want to know?" Weston asked, easing his bulk into the chair in front of one of the computers.

"About the Omega Corporation."

"Omega?" Weston leaned back in the chair. "That was years ago."

"You had some Finns working for you there."

Weston looked surprised a moment, but then he nodded. "Okay, now I get why Homicide is here. You're talking about three of my programmers. Yeah, they'd get to talking Finnish, I didn't have a clue. They were good, though. Smart boys. They even stayed with the company after I sold it. I heard a couple of them were killed about a year after that. I suppose that's why you're asking. I didn't know anything about it, though. I was long gone by then, thanks to Partridge."

"Partridge bought Omega, I understand."

"Right." He bent forward, suddenly steely eyed. "Partridge forced me out. To this day, I'm not sure how he did it, but he decided he wanted Omega, and went head to head with us, contacting my customers and undercutting my deals even if he was losing money on them. The customers didn't care as long as they got a better bottom line. After a while, I couldn't afford to make my payroll. Guess who showed up to offer to help?"

"Partridge."

"You're damned right." Weston reached for a pack of Marlboros and matches on the work table, shook out some smokes and offered one to Paavo. Paavo declined. Weston lifted the pack to his mouth and wrapped his lips around one cigarette, pulling it free from the others. "I had no choice, so I borrowed from him. He was a smooth bastard, offering help, saying he understood. What he understood was how to run me out of my own company. Before long, I owed him more than my share of the business."

Weston paused long enough to light the cigarette bobbing up and down between his lips. "He became the owner and booted me out the door. Made me an offer—not nearly what the place was worth. Back then, I was young, but didn't have the business sense to jump from here to there. Look at Altair or Osborne or Commodore computers—they owned the early days. Where are they now? It was the same with a lot of us. Me included."

Paavo nodded. Weston was simply stating the facts and there was no recrimination or resentment. Even his dislike of Partridge was coldly clinical...like a computer.

"I never understood how Partridge made a go of it. The bastard couldn't tell the different between computer parts and those of a toaster." Weston gazed at the far wall and shook his head. "I always suspected he had an insider with our government so he could get some of those lucrative contracts. But why? He was just a nerdy computer builder in California. I don't get it."

"Neither do I," Paavo admitted. "But it's a good question. One that bears looking into."

"Good luck, fella. I used to try to wise up folks in the industry—hell, anybody who'd listen—about Harold-The-Shit-Partridge. All it got me was a rep as a bitter loser. Everybody loved Harold—and if you didn't, you faced his lawyers or got blackballed in the Valley or both."

"Paavo, I'm at the Au Claire restaurant, Union and Grant. I've heard it's delicious." Angie spoke quietly into her phone. "Are you free to meet me here?"

"I am. I'll drop my things off at the house and walk down. I should be about twenty minutes."

"Great. Love you!"

"You, too."

She listened to the receiver disconnect, and couldn't help but smile. He still wasn't one to get mushy on the phone. Or ask questions. Cops—they always act as if their phone is being tapped.

She was soon seated at a table by a window where she could look out at the night life of the "upper Grant" part of the city. But instead of enjoying the view, she opened the photo app on her phone. Although she wouldn't use this spot as one of her review subjects since it was near the house she and Paavo were sharing, and she might want to come here fairly often. Still, she couldn't pass up the chance to take a few shots.

As she panned the room, she became aware of someone standing behind her. She stopped the video and glanced over her shoulder. The older man who had been seated at the next table now stood frowning at her. "I'm sorry," she said, guessing he didn't like her recording. "It's just that it's a lovely restaurant."

To her surprise, his frown changed to a smile. He was a big man, in his late sixties or so, with broad shoulders and a thick chest, waist and hips. His hair was the color of steel, receded quite far at the temples, and had a slicked-back center tuft. His eyebrows were gray, and his lashes so pale she could scarcely see them. His brown eyes were thin slits in a fleshy face.

"No need to be sorry. I'm the one who should say that! I hope my ugly mug didn't break your phone." His voice was deep, and his enunciation beautifully precise in a British mixed with some sort of European accent. "Does it take good videos?"

"It's the latest model phone, so yes."

"Can I take a look?"

"Sure." Angie handed it to him.

He slid out the chair across from her and sat. "They haven't brought my dinner out yet," he murmured, lost in studying the phone, which Angie found odd. It wasn't anything at all unusual, simply an upgraded model. "This is nice. Quite nice. I should tell my son about this. He fills his car with equipment."

"Is he a professional photographer?"

"Yes. He takes videos at weddings, bar mitzvahs, all that sort of thing. He enjoys it."

"I don't suspect he'd want to use a cell phone for that kind of work." Angie took her phone back, as the idea of becoming a photographer filled her. Maybe she should forget about food-related jobs. It wasn't as if food-related jobs were getting her anywhere. But making a living going to happy occasions and getting people to smile sounded easy and like fun… until she thought of her sister, Caterina, and how she tended to scream at photographers for always catching her with the most unflattering expressions.

Actually, Angie always found the photos to be quite accurate.

"My name is Nick," the old man said. "I must say, I don't understand your country."

That surprised her. "You don't? Why not?"

"Because a beautiful young woman like you should not be sitting alone in a restaurant. Back home, when I was young, you would have been circled by men like roosters around a hen."

A hen? How unflattering. "All pecking at me?"

"Not pecking in a bad sense... pecking as in a kiss."

Her eyebrows rose up, and then she burst out laughing. "You do have a way with words, Nick."

He chuckled. "That's what the ladies used to say. Those days were great fun. So, why is someone as beautiful as you alone?"

"I won't be for long. My fiancé is going to meet me here." She held up her hand with her engagement ring.

"Ah! My bad luck! I should have noticed—actually, I did, but a fellow could hope, right?" he said with an impish grin. "Well, I won't keep you. I see they've finally brought out my salad. I'd better leave. I wouldn't want your fiancé to get the wrong idea." He held out his hand. "It's been very nice talking to you, Miss...?"

"Call me Angie." She reached her hand out to shake his.

"Angie." He gently revolved her hand, clicked his heels, bowed forward and kissed the back of it. "My pleasure." Then he walked away.

Instead of returning to his table, he continued toward the back of the restaurant. Going to the men's room, she supposed. She had to smile. It had been a long time since she'd met anyone who knew the proper way to kiss a lady's hand, or, for that matter, knew any of the old-world mannerisms on how to treat a lady. Nick. She liked him. Ah, if he were about thirty years younger, watch out, Paavo.

Since Nick wasn't there to make her feel self-conscious, she took a few more video clips of the restaurant. It had a warm charm to it.

The waiter brought out the lobster bisque she'd ordered, and soon, Nick returned to his table. She returned his smile as he sat and began to eat.

He seemed to forget about her, and she took a few more shots of the restaurant. She had no sooner finished the salad than the waiter brought her crab-stuffed filet of sole. She tried to eat slowly, waiting for Paavo, but he was taking much longer than he'd expected. The man seemed to think he had wings and forgot that annoyances like traffic jams could slow down his progress. Although he had said he'd walk…

She nibbled at her sole. Had she been able to concentrate on it instead of Paavo's whereabouts, it would have been delicious. Nick sent a bottle of Chalone Vineyard Reserve Chenin Blanc 1996 to her table.

She had the waiter ask him if he'd like to join her and share the wine.

Quietly, and smoothly, the waiter moved him to her table, and poured them each a glass of the wine. Nick had ordered *frutti di mare* with white beans. "I don't know where my friend is," Angie said, as he settled in across from her, "but it seems a shame for both of us to be eating alone."

"You are very kind to an old man. Most young people don't give us a second thought these days," he said.

"You're very kind to send me this wine. It's excellent."

"You seemed to be someone who would know and appreciate a fine vintage."

They talked about wines, and food, and music, and Angie discovered that Nick liked classical as much as she did, and they launched into a discussion of the San Francisco Symphony and the many fine conductors who had led it over the years. Nick, who admitted his name was actually Nikolai, and that he was of Russian descent, had grown up with classical music. Angie had come to it because of violin lessons as a child. Later, when her family realized that she had no ear for music, they switched her to ballet lessons. Neither worked out at all—her musical talent was nonexistent and her dancing ability was even worse—but she did learn an appreciation of classical music.

As they talked, she caught a view of a tall man walking along the sidewalk toward the restaurant. "Oh! That's my fiancé now," she said. She picked up her phone, set the viewer to enlarge the picture. She began taking a video of him as he approached.

"You're videoing your friend?" Nikolai asked with amusement.

"Won't he be surprised?" she said.

"I'm sure he—"

"Oh, my God!" she cried.

"What?"

She stood up, still looking through the viewer. "Help! Somebody! He's being attacked!"

"Attacked?" Nikolai stood as well and looked out the window. The other customers put down their forks and knives and stared at Angie.

"He's fighting with some guy!" she yelled. "Waiter! Stop them!"

"I'll call nine-one-one," the waiter said, but instead of doing either, he rushed to the window with other customers.

Angie grabbed her tote bag, a heavy lethal weapon in itself, and ran outside, determined to swing it at the attacker and send him flying away from Paavo.

As soon as she reached the sidewalk, the attacker fled. Paavo was standing a bit wobbly, his hand pressing his mouth as if to make sure his teeth were all still there.

She grabbed his arm. "Are you all right?"

"I think so," he said.

"There's some blood on your lip," she said. "Let's get you inside the restaurant."

Inside, she led him into the women's room. He hesitated, but she dragged him in and locked the door. She drenched a paper towel with water and dabbed the blood from his lip and chin.

"What was that all about?" she asked.

"I have no idea," he mumbled.

"Did he try to rob you?" She angled his head and patted cold water on his cheekbone where a weal was already building.

"No."

"Did you recognize him at all?" Angie asked, pressing the wet paper towel to his lip once more.

"Uh, uh."

"Well, for what it's worth, I've got his picture on tape. I was making a video of you walking toward the restaurant when he attacked."

He pulled the towel out of her hand. "You didn't stop?"

"I was too stunned to do anything. I'd set the focus to blow up the picture a lot and I could see better looking through the lens than not. Still, it took a moment before I realized exactly what I was seeing. Then, I put the phone down, yelled for help, and ran outside."

He looked at her strangely.

"Do you feel up to eating dinner? Or do you just want to go home?"

"Home."

As she led the way to the table to pay the bill, she saw that Nick and his place setting were gone. The waiter was clearing his spot and setting it again for Paavo until Angie told him they weren't staying. "The elderly gentleman took care of your bill, ma'am," the waiter informed her. "He said to tell you he had a very nice time, and he was sure you'd want to be alone with your young man."

Angie was strangely touched by the message, and the man's generosity. "How very kind. I'd like to thank him. Does he come here often?"

The waiter shook his head. "I've never seen him before."

30

———————

Paavo drove them back to the bungalow in Angie's car, taking a circular route to be sure they weren't being followed. After arriving, Angie immediately set up the video on her phone to cast to the TV as she and Paavo sat on the sofa to watch. Immediately, Angie saw that the stranger had approached Paavo, said something to him and tried to leave. Paavo decided to stop him. That was when the fight broke out.

The lighting was poor, but as the two men struggled, they moved near a storefront that was lit up and the other man's face became clearer. He was enormous, with the physique of a body-builder. Finally, he pushed Paavo hard and half-stumbling, ran away.

Paavo didn't follow.

"What did he say to you," Angie asked.

"'Back off and you won't get killed.' I wanted him to explain himself, but he was feeling shy."

"Hmm. I might be imagining things, but I think I've seen him before." She rewound and played the fight again. "Muscles like that don't show up every day, especially not in this city. They're quite remarkable."

"You've established you like his looks," Paavo said, "now, where did you see him?"

"Actually, bubbly muscles like that don't do it for me. I prefer--"

"Angie!"

Clearly, he wasn't in the mood to be teased. "I've got an idea," she said. "Let's take a look at some of my other restaurant shots." Going to her restaurant video reviews, she fast-forwarded through them until she reached the Basque restaurant she'd gone to with her sister a few days ago. Seated alone at a table was Paavo's studly combatant. "Voilà!"

"Damn, I don't get it." Paavo leaned back, arms folded, and glared at the TV.

"How did he find us tonight? That's what I want to know," Angie said.

"He must be following you," Paavo surmised. "It's the only explanation. He could have been waiting to go into the restaurant, or watching you from the sidewalk. You'd been seated at the window the whole time, right?"

"That could be," she said thoughtfully.

Paavo fingered his swollen lip where his teeth had hit and caused the bleeding. It made him mad all over again. "Could you move that video to a USB drive? At work tomorrow, I'd like to have a search run on Jesse The Body. You'd better stay put in the house. Order out if you don't want to cook, but keep away from restaurants."

"Stay home? No way!" Angie was appalled. "I *should* go out. Now that I know I'm being followed, I'll be extra alert. If the guy shows up again, I'll hurry to a safe place and call you. Then you can arrest him and find out what's going on."

"It's too dangerous," Paavo said.

"But if I stay home, I won't be able to learn things the way I did yesterday with Eldridge Sawyer, or earlier with Connie."

"Uh, oh," he murmured. "What now?"

"It's what I'd hoped to discuss with you at the restaurant." She excitedly joined him again on the sofa. "I learned your mother had a girlfriend who lived near her on Liberty Street. Unfortunately, she moved and the grocer I spoke with could no longer locate her."

"Who?"

"He gave me her name, Irene Billot."

"Now that you mention it, I remember seeing Irene Billot's interview, but it had nothing at all noteworthy in it."

"I'm sorry to hear that," Angie murmured. "Unless she was lying. I mean, the FBI and the Russian mafia were both involved, it seems. Heck, I'd lie, too."

"Damn it!" Paavo slammed down the knife he had used to cut the sandwich in half and faced her. "That's exactly what this is all about. Lies. Thirty years' worth of lies! I'm fed up with the lies and the people making them. Damn them all!"

"Paavo!" She was shocked. He almost never raised his voice.

"Hell, Angie. Think about it. You're caught up in this, too. You're in danger and can't even go to your own apartment because, years ago, people didn't have the balls to level with each other, or with me! What does that make them? Or me?"

"It's not your fault," she began, not sure she followed what he was saying.

"I'm not talking fault. I'm talking deeper. Who *are* these people, Angie? A mother who lies to her husband? A father who goes off on some idealistic mission and gets himself killed?"

She didn't speak, giving him the chance to open up, to vent all he'd been holding in since this began.

"I was better off not knowing," he said grimly. "I don't want to know about them, not like this! I don't want you to be a part of it. And most of all, I wish they hadn't been so goddamn stupid!"

She reached for his hand, but he got up and walked into the

living room. She shut off the gas beneath the soup, put his sandwich on a plate, and followed.

"You don't mean any of that," she said.

"I sure as hell do!" He paced. "But I'm not giving up. I'll find out the truth now that I've come this far. It'll tell me who I am."

"What they were has nothing to do with you," she cried, following him back and forth across the living room, the plate still in her hands.

"It has everything to do with me!"

"No. You're wrong!"

"You just don't get it," he yelled, facing her. "You, with a city filled with Amalfis—more cousins than you can count—cannot begin to understand what it means to have no one. No one, Angie. I can't look around and see anyone else with the same features, the same blood. No one with the same background that made me who I am and what I believe. I don't *know* who I am. It's all buried. And now that I'm trying to dig beneath it, it keeps getting worse."

"You're who *you* created," she cried. "And you did a damned fine job, Inspector."

His voice turned as cold as she'd ever heard it. "Don't patronize me, Angie. That's one thing I will not tolerate."

"I'm not patronizing you!" She waved an arm in frustration. "I'm trying to tell you that whatever turns up about your parents, your past, doesn't matter as far as who you are!"

"It does to me. Can't you see that? How can you not understand something so simple, so basic?"

"Oh, I understand, all right. I understand this is an excuse of yours. You skitter away like a feral cat—"

"A *cat?*"

"Whenever I try to talk to you about our future—about setting a date for our wedding, I face a wall!"

He looked like he couldn't believe his ears. "What does a wedding have to do with anything?"

"It has everything to do with how you're feeling about your-self. About us! I love you. I don't give a damn about your ancestors. I want to marry you, not them."

His mood was too ugly to listen. "You're obsessed with the subject."

"Obsessed!" The word exploded. "I'm trying to tell you how I feel, to let you know I see that you're hurting, and I understand."

"The only thing you understand is a white dress and wedding veil."

She was literally hopping mad. "You're being an arrogant jackass!"

"My, my. From cat to jackass. Sounds like I'm moving up on the food chain." He folded his arms, looking so smug she picked up half his sandwich and threw it at him. He ducked, and it sailed past him to land with a splat on the television screen.

"Hah!" He shouted in triumph just as the second half hit him square on the chin. The sandwich opened up as it flew, and mayonnaise and mustard caused the bread slices to stick a moment before dropping to the floor.

Realizing what she'd just done, Angie covered her mouth as he slowly wiped his face. He looked at his greasy hand, then at her.

She backed up.

He stepped toward her.

She took another step backward. "Now, Paavo."

Suddenly, his eyes filled with mirth and to her surprise, he shook his head and began to laugh.

She put her hands to her mouth and joined in.

They laughed so hard, tears came to their eyes, relieving the tension. When they stopped, their eyes met and held.

And that was when he picked her up and carried her to the bedroom. Mustard and mayonnaise be damned.

Jane Platt awoke with a start. A strong, icy cold hand covered her mouth and nose, smothering her. The child's eyes flew open to see a woman's face looming in front of her eyes.

"Stop struggling!" the woman hissed, pressing Jane's head further down into the pillow. "Stop struggling and I'll remove my hand. Will you do that?"

Jane tried to nod as tears rolled down her cheeks. She wanted her grandpa. If he was still alive, this woman wouldn't be here scaring her. No one would ever scare her.

The woman eased back a little, and when Jane didn't call out or try to get away, she sat on the edge of the bed.

The bedroom window was wide open, and Jane realized that was how the woman got into her room. She tried hard to stop crying, but it wasn't easy. The foster family she'd been sent to wouldn't like it if they found out that someone broke into the house because of her. They wouldn't want her anymore, she feared, just as her aunt didn't want her.

"Now, Jane," the woman said in a harsh whisper, "we're going to talk about your grandfather, and a fancy music box. Do you know what a music box is, Jane?"

31

The next morning, Paavo walked into the crime lab with the USB drive with Angie's video tape from the fight he'd been in the night before. His friend, Ray Faldo, ran the video until they found a clear shot of the man Paavo had fought with. Faldo froze the frame and made a copy. While Paavo phoned contacts in the FBI and Interpol and transmitted copies of the photo to them, Faldo put the suspect's characteristics into the face-recognition program database. He found no hits in the state or city mug shots.

The homicide book on Mika's murder was still on Paavo's desk, and he reread the interview of Irene Billot. The woman had given the homicide inspectors no information beyond being a neighbor and recognizing the family if she passed them on the street. She wasn't mentioned at all in the investigation on Cecily's auto accident, conducted mostly by a different police force due to the jurisdiction of her death.

On a hunch, he decided to see what, if anything, the SFPD had on Irene Billot. The information that turned up surprised him.

Records of her calls to the Mission Station about Cecily

existed—dire warnings, conspiracy theories, fears for her own life—contact after contact, all dismissed as a troubled woman who couldn't cope with her friend's sudden death. The beat cops who talked to Irene weren't given access to the background of Cecily's disappearance. They were simply told her car had plunged off a cliff into the Pacific. Faced with Irene's weird ravings, they half expected her to announce aliens had abducted Cecily. Irene's own words didn't help her case any, and Paavo couldn't reconcile the difference between the alarming, shrill woman the neighborhood police reported, the woman who "knew nothing" when a homicide inspector interviewed her, and the sweet woman the grocery clerk had told Angie about.

He had just finished reading the reports on Mrs. Billot when Interpol contacted him. They had a photo match on Mr. Muscle and faxed him the information.

Leonid Stavrogin: Russian mafia enforcer. Right-hand man to the leader of the West Coast mafia, known only as Koba, the Russian Robin Hood "little people's protector" figure the Gang Task Force inspector told him about.

Stavrogin, despite his physical strength, wasn't a man who gave out verbal warnings. He shot people. Why should a man like that have given Paavo a warning?

More distressing than his remark, though, was the knowledge that he must have been watching Angie, and had following her.

Paavo had to find out why.

Angie felt as if she were walking on air. She was in the television studios of Bay TV. This was her milieu, she decided. Television. It's what she'd been born for, lived for. After all she was a child of the age of television. She simply had to find herself a job here and all would be well with the career part of her life—she just knew it.

Paavo didn't know about this. He had already gone to work when she received that morning from BayLife Today. Their scheduled guest had just cancelled, and they needed an immediate replacement. Was she available? Her heart was in her mouth, but she managed to croak out, *"Yes!"*

It wasn't a prime-time news show, and it wasn't a major syndicated program. Instead, it was an area "events" show on a local cable channel. As cousin Richie would say, "Hey, a start's a start."

Bended-knee begging and a hefty tip got her an immediate appointment at her hair dresser's, plus a manicure. Careful not to destroy her hair, she rushed from the beauty parlor to Sissy's of Maiden Lane for a new suit. A peppermint pink Anne Klein looked properly Leslie Stahlish.

She signed in at the guard station on the ground floor and a casually dressed fellow with dreadlocks greeted her and silently led her up to the studio.

"Which way is make-up?" she asked.

He looked confused. "The women's room is down that hall."

She glanced where he pointed. "Oh?"

"The studio's in there." He gestured toward double swinging doors at the end of a wide hallway filled with computer terminals. No one sat at any of them, though.

The dreadlocks fellow disappeared. Angie gaily bustled into the studio and promptly tripped over a maze of cables on the floor. To avoid stumbling again, she minced toward the brightly lit set.

A woman with hair shorter than Paavo's, wearing a beige smock tied around her much like a butcher's apron, ran up to her. "Miss Amalfi?"

"Oh!" She put her hand to her chest. "You recognize me!"

The woman looked at her strangely. "Well... you *are* the only guest on the show tonight. I'll take your restaurant review tapes to the producer. You can sit over there. You've got a half-hour before the live show. Any questions?"

Angie looked at the chair the woman pointed at. It was in a dark corner. "Aren't we going to rehearse?"

"Rehearse? No. We like spontaneity."

"Aren't we at least going to run through my video?" She held up the USB flash drive.

"A thumb drive. How precious." The woman smiled and took the drive from Angie. "No need to run through anything. You know what's on it. You tell us when to run it, and we will. Then, you explain to the audience what we're seeing. It's simple."

Angie had her doubts about how simple it would be. The first inklings of panic began to tickle her. "Where's make-up?"

"Make-up? You're fine." She dashed off and left Angie clutching her make-up case.

She always wore make-up and wore it with care so that it didn't look like she had it plastered to her face. TV make-up was different, or should have been. She thought it was supposed to look plastered so that when the lights washed out the color, she would look alive rather than ghostly pale.

In the women's room, she darkened her make-up, then returned to the studio to sit and wait. She practiced her opening lines—a clever, witty little speech about who she was and what her video restaurant reviews were all about. She wished she could talk someone into a teensy-tiny rehearsal.

The technicians were running about shouting incomprehensible jargon at one another, and the woman who took her flash drive was nowhere to be seen.

Carol Metcalf, the star of BayLife Today suddenly appeared and stepped onto the set, the lights bright on her face. One instant, people dashed in frenzy, and then next, all fell silent. The program had begun.

Angie could scarcely breathe. Hers was the third segment.

She sat, without moving a single muscle through the endless television ramblings and bad jokes until she heard the announcer say, "Next San Francisco's own restaurant reviewer, Angelina Amalfi, will be here to present a *video* restaurant review. We'll see for ourselves the restaurant Angie went to and hear what she has to say about it! Stay tuned!"

Her legs wobbled as she approached the set and sat beside the star. Carol turned to her. "Now remember, keep your answers short, and be as outrageous as you wish."

"What?" Angie looked at her blankly.

"No speeches," Carol ordered. "And be controversial."

Angie nodded, taking deep breaths. The opening she'd prepared was a bit lengthy, but surely, she could introduce herself. No one would object. Nevertheless, she grew so nervous, she was sure perspiration glistened on her face. She remembered a scene from an old movie in which a guy had spent his entire career thinking he could be a news anchor on TV. When he finally got his chance, he sweat so much, viewers began to call the station thinking he was having a heart attack. She prayed she wouldn't be like that.

When production assistant called out, "Five seconds!" Her mind went absolutely blank. Her only coherent thought was *Get me out of here!*

She was hyperventilating when Carol Metcalf began speaking into the camera. "Angelina Amalfi is, herself, a gourmet cook and frequent restaurant reviewer for *Haute Cuisine* magazine. Angie, which restaurant did you go to?"

"Thank you, Carol," she said. Her mouth felt like it was filled with uncooked Quaker Oats. "I--" Her voice came out in a high squeak and she just hoped it would drop an octave. Or two. She began her introduction. "I'm here to give a video restaurant review. I--"

"Yes!" Carol interrupted. "I've never seen one before. So, you went to an interesting restaurant, I take it?"

"I did." Her eyes caught the camera and all she could think of was all the people in the bay area watching her at that very moment. She tried to return to the introduction she'd practiced. "Video restaurant reviews are a new concept."

Carol frowned.

Angie hurried on. "They're something I just dreamed up for this very program. For you. And for your viewer... viewers." She was dying inside. She wished she could die on the outside, then, at least she'd get sympathy instead of being laughed at.

"How nice, Angie." The woman's jaw was tight. "*Where* did you go?"

Panic set in as she noticed that the veins on Carol Metcalf's neck were beginning to protrude. She threw away her set speech, but nothing filled what now felt like a huge, empty gap where clever bon mots and turns of phrase should have been. "I went to a restaurant that is called"--*Oh, God, what, what, what?*-- "Pisces. It is the zodiac sign that features two fish." She took a deep breath. Time for the videotape. "Here are some scenes from it." *I hope.*

Like magic, her video began to roll.

She tried to think of what Carol had said. Short answers. Controversial. "See how pretty it is. See the waiter. See the customers. See them eat."

Carol Metcalf kicked her.

She was ready to cry.

"Did you like the restaurant, Angie?" Carol asked.

"Yes. I liked it very much. This is my waiter now. He is bringing me steamed lobster with a saffron-tomato broth." Angie racked her brain for something interesting and contro- versial to say. She definitely wanted to make it big on TV, and she had to make up for her blown introduction. The camera stared at her. "The lobster was a little mushy and a little stronger than lobster should be. Sounds disgusting doesn't it? And..." Her voice rose. "There was too much thyme in the broth.

It overwhelmed the saffron. Usually there's not enough thyme for anything... ha, ha. Get it? Time..." *Oh, Lord!*

Carol looked stricken. "How was the dessert?"

"I had a hazelnut torte a la mode." *Controversial! Be controversial!* "It was um, um, uh, a little stale. A little like chalk. Here is my waiter bringing me my dessert." He slammed it onto the table—her video recording had irritated him, Angie recalled—and the ice cream slid from the torte and off the plate onto the tablecloth. He scooped it up, stormed away and soon was seen bringing her another plate. He made faces at her phone and then left.

Angie wracked her brain, then blurted out, "He must have thought this was a Candid Camera revival, ha, ha!"

Carol gave her a long withering stare, then signaled the camera to focus on her. "And now, for our weather report. Here for an *expanded* report is our meteorologist...."

Angie stopped listening. All she wanted to do was curl up and die. Thank God she hadn't told Paavo she was going to be on TV tonight. Unfortunately, she did tell her parents, her four sisters, several girlfriends, a number of cousins, the grocer, her hairdresser, the woman who did her nails, and some guy selling newspapers on the corner. When would she ever learn to keep her mouth shut?

32

———

After calling it a day in Homicide, Paavo went to visit
Aulis.

His condition hadn't changed any. The doctors
were growing increasingly alarmed about his continued
inability to wake up.

Fear and frustration flooded through Paavo as he stood in
that sterile hospital room and watched over the man who had
raised him, now looking so small and shriveled under the white
sheets. Usually, Paavo didn't notice the lines on Aulis's face or
the thinness of his white hair. He still saw Aulis very much as he
had appeared when Paavo was growing up: an older, but spry
man. Now, Paavo observed all the changes, and thought about
the fact that someday he was going to lose the one who'd been
there almost forever for him.

He wondered what Aulis had known all those years about
Cecily and Mika, and why in God's name he had kept it
hidden.

He sat alone by the bed for about twenty minutes. But then
he realized it didn't make any sense for him to just sit there and
do nothing. Once Aulis woke, he'd want to know who had done

this to him, and had the assailant been caught? Paavo didn't want to have to answer, "No."

After about five more minutes, he decided it was time to go home.

Home. He wished he didn't get a kick in the gut each time he thought about the cottage. He liked being there more than he ever dreamed he would, and more than he really wanted to admit. He had found a place away from the world's cruelty and losses where there was love and laughter, and he wondered how long he could accept it, or if he would soon want to retreat to his own quiet solitude once more.

In no time, he'd driven across town, and parked on Montgomery Street, right in front of a four-story apartment house that looked like a ship, and had been used in an old Bogart and Bacall film, *Dark Passage.* Maybe, someday, he'd rent the movie and see what all the fuss was about.

He fairly ran down the Filbert steps to the little house, and burst into the living room to find Angie sitting on the sofa, Hercules on her lap, staring at the wall. She didn't look at him, didn't say a word.

"What's wrong?" he asked. Angie was not one to sit silently. Usually, she greeted him with a hug and a kiss.

"Nothing," she replied.

Sure, and there's no ice in the Arctic.

She sighed heavily and mumbled something about coffee. He followed her into the kitchen. "You can tell me about it," he said as she filled the carafe with water.

She silently measured coffee into the filter. *We're together,* he wanted to say, *so we can talk to each other when we're unhappy or disappointed or just need a shoulder to lean on.* He didn't say that, though. He didn't quite know how. Instead, he waited.

"I blew it," she murmured, and flipped the On switch.

He captured her. "Why don't you start at the beginning?"

She leaned her head against his shoulder. "I was awful."

"Awful? You mean you did something awful?" he asked, confused. "What did you do?"

"I went on television. Oh, God! Why, why, why did I ever dream I could do TV? I'm just not Katie Couric. Not even Carol Metcalf."

"Who?"

"She's on BayLife Today."

"Ah."

She covered her face. "I was so hideous! My mind went blank. I couldn't get the words out. What came out was like listening to a tape that someone had slowed down. I can never show myself in public again! Heck, I don't even want to see me!"

His arms tightened around her. "I'm sure you weren't as bad as all that. You're always your own worst critic."

"If I wasn't so bad, why did Carol kick me?"

He had no answer.

She stepped back and made her hands into fists. "I should have seen it coming, but did I? No! Not until it was too late. Then, I saw it. Here I go again, I said to myself. Angie Amalfi, looking foolish. Why do I do it?"

"You aren't foolish, Angie."

He lightly stroked her hair, and she leaned into him again. "I so much want to do interesting things," she said, burrowing against his chest. "I want to be accomplished, an achiever. I want to be a person who is independent and successful, and good at her job—not daddy's privileged little rich girl. Not that that's so tragic. But I'm more than that, aren't I?"

"Of course."

"I'll take that as an enthusiastic yes." She sighed heavily. "I know I try too hard sometimes. Maybe a lot of times. I know I push it. Occasionally, I even leap before thinking. It's fun sometimes, but not when I disappoint myself."

He placed his hand under her chin and forced her to look at

him. "You never disappoint me, Angie. Promise me you'll never change."

Those were the words she needed to hear. They held each other in the lengthening silence. "Maybe I should just go to bed," she said finally. "This won't look so bleak in the morning."

"Want company?" Paavo offered.

She glanced up at him. He grinned. She couldn't help herself and smiled back. "I'll turn off the coffee."

A loud bang woke them both. Paavo was on his feet while Angie clutched her pillow, probably trying to figure out if she was dreaming or if the roof had just fallen in. She lifted her head and looked at him. "What was that?"

He pulled the bedroom drapes aside to see a strange glow in the sky.

"Call 911. Tell them it's a fire," he said as he put on trousers and shoes, then grabbed his badge and gun.

As he pulled a heavy sweater over his head, Angie put on her bathrobe and followed him to the door. "Don't go out there." He ordered. "Call."

He ran up the Filbert steps to Montgomery Street, not believing the sight before him.

Angie's new Lexus was a ball of fire, flames stabbing the night sky. Behind him, others emerged, sleepily confused and chattering, a few venturing too close to the burning car. He held up his badge. "Police officer! Stay back! Go back inside!"

The crowd wasn't about to disperse, but it didn't move any closer. He walked around the car to its far side.

A man's body lay on the ground. The body must have been close to the car when it exploded, and he had been flung aside like a rag doll. The clothes were still burning. Paavo turned away. One look and he knew there was nothing that could be done for the man. His hair was gone, his facial skin black and charred, his eyes dark pits. The smell of burnt flesh hit Paavo's nostrils.

"Oh, my God!"

Paavo spun around at the sound of Angie's voice. She had put on slippers and a robe and stood at the top of the stairs. He ran to her and grabbed her arm, not wanting her to see the horror on the far side of the car.

"What happened?" she cried.

"I'll tell you when I find out. Right now, go back inside."

"No. It's my car! My beautiful car!" Then she seemed to notice people's reactions to something on the opposite side of it. Paavo stopped her from approaching.

"Don't," he ordered. "A man's dead. Burned. You don't want to see him."

Shock and horror filled her face. Fire sirens and the shrill sound of police cars could be heard over the crackle of flames, and murmurs of the still gathering crowd. She backed away from the street and waited.

The police and fire trucks arrived at the same time. The firemen immediately began hosing the car with heavy water pressure.

Paavo met the uniformed officer and showed his badge. "The car is, was, my fiancée's. I can give you the particulars. We were asleep when it happened. I don't recognize the victim."

"Does she?"

"The way he looks right now, I don't think his own sister would recognize him. I haven't asked her to look."

The policeman glanced at the victim, then nodded.

Once the car fire was out, Paavo moved closer to the burned man. A couple of patrol officers joined him. "Looks like a car bomb went off," one of them said. "I wonder if the vic was just passing by and unlucky, or if he'd been trying to rig a bomb up and had slippery fingers."

"Or if something caused an accidental detonation." Paavo pointed to a small hole in one side of the dead man's skull, and a larger hole opposite it. It looked like entry and exit wounds from a large caliber handgun or rifle.

Instinctively, the officer looked over his shoulder. Up Filbert were more steps and a little beyond that, the circular road to Coit Tower on the very top of Telegraph Hill.

"That's right," Paavo said. "A shooter could have easily stood anywhere up there and found a clear shot. The question is, who was he?"

"There's another question, too," the officer said, looking at the shell of the car. "Who wants your girlfriend dead?"

33

———————

"We have a make on the marshmallow," Yosh said to Paavo, hanging up the phone. They were seated at their desks in Homicide. Yosh had returned from vacation and had quickly been brought up to speed on Paavo's cases, and also on Aulis's condition.

Toshiro Yoshiwara, a second-generation Japanese-American, was Paavo's partner. They'd had an uneasy start when Yosh first joined Homicide and was given the spot that had been held by Paavo's best friend and partner of many years, Matt Kowalski. Matt had been killed while investigating a murder, and Paavo had been reluctant to establish deep ties to a new partner. Since then, Yosh had proven himself to be an outstanding detective, a good partner, and an even better friend. He was a big man, "from the Sumo wrestler part of Japan," he often said, with close-cropped hair, a thick neck and powerful chest and arms.

"He was a Russian with ties to organized crime," Yosh said. "His name was Yuri Krakovar."

"Christ! Aulis being targeted was bad enough," Paavo said, "but now it's Angie. If I knew who was behind this, I'd say here I am, come and get me and leave the others alone. But I don't know how to stop it." The crime scene technicians had determined a plastic explosive device that would have been set to the ignition had blown up Angie's car.

"These Russians are scary," Yosh said. "You've got to get Angie out of there before they come back. Better yet, get her out of town."

"I brought her over to her friend Connie's house this morning. But I'll get her out of there as soon as we figure out what to do. I don't want her family or friends mixed up in this."

"Any idea how the Russians found her?"

"She was on live TV yesterday evening. Apparently, they were running promos about the show all afternoon. Someone who knew they were interested in Angie might have heard about her appearance. I'm guessing it was just a lucky break for them. Not for Angie, though."

"She was on TV?"

"She did a restaurant review. Someone could have had her followed when she left the studio and went home. Or"—he thought of the photos she'd taken of the mafioso Stavrogin sitting in restaurants where she'd been—"they've been watching her all along and for some reason decided to take action last night."

"This is weird, pal. First, someone shoots at you, then a Russian enforcer warns you off, and the next thing, another Russian's trying to blow up Angie's car. I thought the Cold War was over. What the hell is this all about? But still, why would anyone go after Angie?"

"She's been asking questions about this case, about the past. Maybe she's getting closer than we realized."

"Don't worry, pal," Yosh said. "We'll find out who's targeted her."

"That's half of the million-dollar question," Paavo said.

"Half? What's the other half?"

"A bullet killed the bomber before he rigged it up to the car. Who pulled the trigger?"

Yosh nodded. "That's right. Whoever did, had to have been a good shot."

"They found the slug—identified it as a Federal Premium hollow point. It's high-powered rifle stuff—a sniper's weapon. Just like the slug that ended up in my front door."

"You don't see many people walking around San Francisco with one of those."

"That's what I would have thought, but all of a sudden, we seem to be holding a convention for them, starting with Leonid Stavrogin."

"Why would Stavrogin take out his own man?"

"He wouldn't, unless there's been a falling out within the mob. I think whoever killed the bomber wasn't part of the Russian mafia. But, if not, who was it?"

"Shoot," Yosh said, rubbing his temple. "With friends like that, who needs enemies? I don't want to have a war going on in the middle of this city between those guys."

"A cat-and-mouse game with the Russian mafia is too dangerous to play. And I won't have Angie being the goddamn mouse. I've got to get her out of the way, then go after them directly. I want a piece of those bastards!"

"Whoa, Paavo. You're making this personal." Yosh eyed his partner steadily. "We know personal gets cops killed. Watch yourself."

"Yosh, it *is* personal."

"I don't want to do this, Paavo," Angie insisted. "Filbert Street is home, now."

He didn't like it either. He had come to love the cottage and the garden-filled Filbert steps that led to it. But it was known that Angie lived there, and he couldn't take any chances.

"And I don't want you dead." He hustled her and her luggage into the enormous red, gold and marble lobby of the Fairmont Hotel. He chose the big hotel since they could enter from a number of entrances and not be noticed. A place in which Angie could simply get lost among the crowds of tourists.

Angie had called ahead for a reservation, then registered as Mrs. Nancy Yoshiwara, using one of Yosh's wife's credit cards. The desk clerk looked questioningly from her to Paavo, but didn't say a word.

"I don't want to stay here," Angie repeated quietly while the clerk stepped away to process the registration. "I want to be with you!"

Paavo didn't answer as the clerk returned with the keycard for the room.

They headed toward the tower elevators. "You can leave as soon as I know it's safe," Paavo said. "In the meantime, keep out of sight. I don't want you in any more danger."

They stepped onto the elevator. Angie pushed floor eight.

"It'll be hard for me to travel very far anyway, with no car," she said moodily.

"Good!"

They stopped talking as others got on. On the eighth floor, Angie had a question the minute they got off. "Will you come back tonight?" she asked.

"I'll try, but if I don't make it, be ready to leave early tomorrow to pay a visit to Eldridge Sawyer."

She frowned. "What about Aulis? Can I go see him?"

Paavo found the room and unlocked the door. He went in first. "They know you'll be wanting to go there," he said as he checked closets and the bathroom. "They'll be watching his room. I don't want them following you the way they did when you were on TV."

"You don't know that's what they did."

"I don't for sure, but it's a good guess. Keep away from Aulis. He's in a coma and won't know if you're there or not. If he wakes up and you still can't see him, I'll explain why not. He'll understand."

Angie sat on the bed. The hotel room was lovely, but it wasn't her apartment, or Paavo's house, and not even the cottage they'd shared. "I don't like this, Paavo. I feel lost here."

He put his hands on her shoulders. "It's better you feel lost than I lose you."

She gazed up at him. "Be careful."

"I will."

"I love you."

"I love you, too," he said. "That's why I want you here and safe."

He kissed her, then left the hotel room. She put the dead bolt on the door and turned around to face the tiny room alone.

34

The next morning, Angie and Paavo reached the town of Gideon. Just looking at the restaurant made Angie's stomach rebel.

Past Gideon, the road wound higher into the hills, through a heavy pine forest. Angie had to watch carefully for the turnoff and even at that, she nearly missed it. She felt as if they were looking for the Phantom of the Forest. Someone singing "The Music Of The Night" wouldn't astound her any more than she already was by all this.

After another mile, a log house became visible through the foliage. They got out of the car and were approaching the house when the cocking of a shotgun behind them shattered the bucolic silence, followed by the order, "Don't move!"

"No need to shoot," Paavo shouted while he grabbed Angie's shoulder, stopping her from taking another step. He didn't need to. She was shaking too furiously to move. "I just want to ask some questions about a woman you worked with years ago in the FBI."

"You've got the wrong man," the voice hollered.

"Don't play games, Sawyer. I don't like it, and you don't either," Paavo said, still with his back to the shooter. "I just want to talk, then we'll be on our way and forget we ever spoke to you."

"How did you find me?"

"Let her turn around and you'll know." Paavo gestured toward Angie.

"All right."

Angie put her hands up—she'd watched a lot of cowboy movies—then turned and, despite the weirdness and the danger, called out. "Hello! You were such a hero the other day, I can't believe you'd shoot me now."

Paavo turned too, but Sawyer remained hidden.

"Where's the other guy? The flashy one?" Sawyer asked.

"He's my cousin," Angie said. "He's back in San Francisco."

"Good place for him." Sawyer moved forward, and for the first time, Angie fully understood why his garb was called camouflage. "Okay, you two, you got more balls than brains coming here like this. What's it about?"

"I talk better if I'm not looking down the barrel of a double-gauge shotgun," Paavo said.

"And I don't want to talk to you at all," Sawyer responded.

"It's about Cecily Campbell. I know a little about her. I want to know more. I understand she worked for you."

"What of it?"

Paavo hesitated, then replied, "She was my mother."

Sawyer stared at them both a long while, then turned the shotgun so it rested across his chest even as his finger stayed near the trigger. "Let me see some I.D."

Using two fingers, Paavo eased his badge from his jacket pocket. Sawyer motioned for him to toss it, and he did. Sawyer looked at the name and his eyes darted quickly to Paavo's face. "I still don't see why I should tell you a thing," he said, throwing the badge back to Paavo.

"You ordered her to take actions that eventually cost her her life. I want to know why," Paavo said. "The whole story."

"Me? Hah! You're wrong. I rarely saw her. I wasn't important enough for the likes of her."

"You were her boss."

"Only on paper."

"What do you mean, you weren't important enough?"

"I mean she was a conniving, scheming bitch. She slept her way to everything she got, and then it blew up in her face."

Angie gasped and watched Paavo's reaction.

"Who was she sleeping with?" he asked coldly.

Sawyer's mouth twisted. "Tucker Bond is one. He was as ambitious as she was."

"Bond acts as if he scarcely remembers her," Paavo said.

"Scum rises, Smith. So do con men and liars."

"No one else ever said anything like that about Cecily," Angie added, unable to keep out of this any longer.

Sawyer's heavy legs were in a wide stance, his chin high. "Maybe they didn't know her well enough. Or, maybe it's not something most people would tell a son. But, hell, you two asked. It was all a long time ago. A lot of things happened back then that I didn't like."

"That's why you left, why you live up here like this?" Paavo asked.

"It might be a common story, Smith," Sawyer's tone was sneering, "but there was nothing common in what went on in the FBI."

"The old boy network in full force?"

"More than that."

Angie watched the strange male dance continue, both men establishing what they were about.

Paavo turned their discussion to Cecily, Mika and his murder. "I understand the Russian mafia was a part of it, and now they're back, after us."

"If that's so, it's not my problem," Sawyer said.

"If we found you, so could they."

"What happened back then is nobody's business but mine. I'll tell you one thing and one thing only because you should know it. Cecily was working with Bond, giving him info about the Russians the Finns were working with. He told her she was doing it for her country, helping the FBI find the enemy. He also assured her that her husband and his friends would be safe. They weren't. After Cecily saw the Russians kill her husband, she was going to go into the Witness Protection Program. But something scared her. She came to me for a different set of fake documents—different from the ones the Bureau was making for her. She was all broken up, said she was betrayed. Her lover didn't come through, I guess. She wouldn't give particulars. I helped her. I'm not even sure why, except that she'd been used and was paying big time for it. No one had ever trained her, taught her the way an agent would have been taught. She was thrown to the wolves and ended up being shredded by them. So, I gave her a driver's license and birth certificates for her and her kids showing the name Smith—Mary, Jessica, and Paavo Smith. *Yours.*"

Angie felt a chill all the way to her toes.

"She nailed a couple of the bastards that killed her husband," Sawyer continued. "Did you know that?"

Paavo stared without speaking a long while. "I had no idea."

"Yeah. Two of them. Then she disappeared—or died. Either way, after offing those Russians, she was dead. They would get revenge, no matter how long it took."

I'm a dead woman. Angie remembered the chilling opening words of Cecily's letter to Aulis.

"So you don't know, either, what happened to her?" Paavo asked.

Sawyer paused, then said, "My guess is, she's dead."

"Killed by the Russians?"

Sawyer looked evasive. "Probably."

"What scared her about the Witness Protection Program?"

"Look, Smith, you're like a bad penny showing up here after all these years. I've said all I'm going to. I don't want to hear from you—or anyone else—again."

"You know where to find me, Sawyer," Paavo said as he motioned to Angie and the two got into his car. "Think about it."

As Paavo and Angie rode back to the city, they tried to put together the pieces they'd learned.

"I don't believe Cecily was having an affair with anyone," Angie said. "I don't know how much I believe any of Sawyer's story. Maybe it was a mistake to come here."

"It wasn't. It's another piece of the puzzle. An important piece. Mika was killed, Cecily retaliated against the Russians, and somehow, she ended up with the music box."

"Then I brought it to someone who worked with the Russian mob years ago, and he recognized it," Angie said. "Damn!"

"And he called Harold Partridge," Paavo added. "Then a Russian jeweler/repairer and a Russian forger were killed, Aulis shot, and our homes ransacked. Partridge is a collector. He surely wanted the music box, but he wouldn't have to kill for it. He could easily afford to buy it. What am I missing?"

"Sounds like you need to visit Mr. Partridge again soon," Angie said.

Paavo agreed.

35

If Paavo thought Angie was going to cower in some hotel room while he went off to work, he still didn't know her very well. She spent a while thinking through her plan, stopped in the Fairmont gift shop for an "I Left My Heart In San Francisco" hooded sweatshirt, put it on, hood up, and then headed for the hotel entrance where taxis flocked like hungry vultures.

As she rode across the city in an Uber, she kept glancing through the back window. She quit looking when the driver started staring at her in his rear-view mirror. Judging from his smirk he must have thought she was completely paranoid.

When the car stopped outside Aulis's apartment, she paid the fare and ran indoors.

Aulis had hidden Cecily's letter in a Ford mailer. Other important clues could be lying all around, waiting for someone to find them.

She began with the drawer filled with important papers. An hour later, she'd gone through every envelope, then continued on to the rest of the bureau, checking under clothes and even pulling out drawers to look under and behind them. She found nothing.

In the living room, Aulis had a small desk where he kept bills and such. Going through each item there met with the same result.

Several cabinets lined the kitchen walls, but the house contained only one large closet. She headed for the bedroom.

Two boxes leaned against the back wall of the closet. Christmas decorations filled the first one. The next held year-books, report cards, and class projects from Paavo and Jessica's school years. Angie was awestruck as she went through them, glimpsing this part of Paavo's childhood. He was so skinny during early adolescence, she wondered that he didn't stab himself with his elbows. His haircut was probably cool at the time, but it made her laugh now. She had to force herself to stop reading school papers, or she'd never get through this.

At the bottom of the box was a large paper bag. When she opened it, her heart lurched. She lifted out a little boy's blue and white striped tee shirt and jeans. They had a slightly gummy feel to them as she unfolded them and smoothed them over her lap.

Next she took out a pale yellow tee shirt, larger than the blue and white one, but not big enough for an adult. Girl's light blue jeans were under the tee shirt.

She checked the sizes, a child's 10 for the girl's clothes and a 6 for the boy's. Didn't lots of boys wear that size when they were about four years old? The significance of the clothes—of the age—hit her.

"Oh, my!" A little brown stuffed bear, only about six-inches tall, lay in the bag, right next to a half-dressed, scraggly haired Barbie doll. She picked up the bear. One black-button eye was loose, and the red ribbon he wore around his neck was limp and bedraggled. He looked like an often-played with little bear. Angie's chest tight-ened. He must have been a well-loved bear besides.

She smoothed his bow and felt tears form in her eyes. Could these have been the toys, the clothes, the children brought when they came to Aulis? Or an extra set Cecily sent with them? Was that how they ended up, forgotten, in this box?

Angie gazed at the spotless clothes. The memory came to her of how Paavo once described his childhood. That he was the boy in school whose clothes were too big or too small, who wore sneakers with holes, and socks that didn't match. He said he was the boy who other kids stayed away from. How different his life would have been had his mother lived, or stayed with him.

She put her hands in the pockets of the little boy's jeans. A Bazooka bubble gum was in it, plus a shiny black rock. Her hand tightened on them.

In the girl's jean's pocket was a pink plastic wallet with 101 Dalmatians on it. She found herself smiling as she looked inside. A picture of Paavo and Jessica was covered in clear plastic, in the spot where "big people" would put a driver's license. It was an adorable photo—Paavo, about age 3, sat on a carousel pony, Jessica behind him, her arms around him, holding him in place. She leaned forward, cheek to cheek with him. They were both smiling broadly.

She searched the other compartments in the wallet, but all she found were three movie stub halves, one adult and two child tickets, with the letters SLEEPLES before the tear, and BHT plus a string of numbers along the other edge of each.

What movie could the children have gone to back then with that title? Sleeples? Was that even a word? But no sooner has she thought that, than the word "Sleepless" came to her. *Sleepless in Seattle.* An odd choice for kids, but maybe Cecily wanted to see it, and brought them along. Jessica probably appointed herself the keeper of the tickets. Angie liked to be similarly 'in charge' when she was a child.

She tried to remove the photo from the wallet, but it stuck to the plastic cover. In the kitchen, she found a sandwich-sized Zip-lock bag, put Paavo's pocket treasures in it, then placed it, the ticket stubs, and the wallet in her tote bag. She picked up the bear and put it in as well. Paavo should see these things again. It wasn't all misery and sadness in his childhood. Happiness existed, too, and he shouldn't dismiss it so readily.

And it just might be good for Paavo to know his mother had a romantic streak and saw movies like *Sleepless in Seattle*. This wasn't the time to talk to him about love and romance, or to think much about them, but day-by-day in the little cottage, she could all but see the word "wedding day" appearing on his forehead with more and more clarity, no matter how much he outwardly nattered about it.

From Aulis's house, she took a taxi to the hospital.

She firmly believed that even though Aulis was in a coma, he had awareness, at some level, of what was happening around him. The idea that this man could be lying there feeling frightened and abandoned was more than she could handle.

The moment she realized she was going to go against Paavo's wishes and leave the hotel room, she decided to visit Aulis as well. For the sake of his recovery, calming his fears and letting him know how much he was loved and cared for was important.

When she reached the hospital, the knowledge that she'd been followed in the past caused her to pulled up the sweatshirt hood and draw the strings tight around her face. On the main floor, she slipped into the women's room near the cafeteria and removed the sweatshirt, black chinos and running shoes she'd been wearing, and changed to cream-colored tailored slacks and high heels. She put the running shoes into her tote bag, and the other clothes, rolled up, under her arm. She hoped to have a chance to speak with Aulis's doctors. Although in the great scheme of things, it didn't matter how she dressed to meet with them, for whatever reason, it did to her.

She left the bathroom and rode the elevator to Aulis's floor.

In his room, she put her tote bag and clothes on a chair in the back, then walked to the side of his bed and took his hand. He looked thin and terribly frail, yet the way his eyes were closed and the peaceful look on his face made it seem he was simply asleep.

"Hello, Mr. Kokkonen," she said. "It's Angie. I know it must seem like it's been a while since I was here last. Believe me, I came back as soon as I could. Your doctors are wonderful. They keep Paavo and me informed of how well you're doing. You're going to be fine very soon. They've assured us of that. You know how Paavo is. He wouldn't let the doctors get away with anything less than your full recovery. It will take a few more days, though. You have to be patient. We all do. We're so much looking forward to you coming home once more. I'm sure you are looking forward to it as well."

She bent over and kissed his cheek. The doctors weren't nearly as upbeat as she had just said, but it would do Aulis no good to hear the truth. What he needed now was hope, and it was her job to give it to him.

"I love you, Mr. Kokkonen, and so does Paavo." She had to wait a moment to control her voice. "He loves you very much, so please be strong for him. Fight this. Come back to us. We want to talk to you and laugh with you. We're here waiting. Please come back to us."

She waited, but as always, saw no reaction whatsoever. She let go of his hand and turned around. To her surprise, the nun she'd met earlier in the hospital was standing in the back of the room beside the chair where Angie had placed her belongings.

"Hello," Sister Ignatius said, stepping toward the bed. "I didn't want to disturb you, but I also didn't want to leave without Aulis knowing I'd been here."

"Please stay. I'll move my belongings from the chair."

Angie hurried to her tote, but mistakenly only grabbed one

strap. As the nun was saying, "Don't bother, I have some other patients to visit," the bag tipped over and dumped the contents onto the floor.

Lipstick rolled, the cell phone took a wicked bounce, Paavo's bear tumbled, Jessica's wallet opened and rotated end over end, and little pieces of paper fluttered and skittered around the room like snow in an updraft.

"Oh, my God!" Angie cried, running about, gathering up pieces of her belongings.

"Let me help you," Sister Ignatius said, as she picked up the bear and gently smoothed the bow, and then Jessica's wallet. She studied the photo silently.

"My boyfriend and his older sister," Angie explained.

"What lovely children they were," the elderly nun said softly.

Together, they quickly dumped everything back into the tote bag. "Thank you, Sister," Angie said. Then she glanced at Aulis and again her face fell.

"Somehow, this will all work out," Sister Ignatius said. "Have faith, Angie."

They both smiled at that, and the nun said good evening.

Angie stayed a short while longer, then went in search of his doctor.

Afterward, she returned to the women's room near cafeteria. Once again, she changed into her black chinos, sweatshirt and sneakers, and walked out of the cafeteria with the hood covering her head.

36

It was all Paavo could do to stand in Bond's waiting room while his secretary announced his visit. Visit—hah! He wanted to punch the guy's lights out—but Bond was a SAC. Paavo wouldn't be doing any investigating at all if he was locked up in a Federal prison.

The secretary told him he could enter. Bond glared at him as he marched into the room. "What's this about? My secretary said you insisted on seeing me. That isn't how I operate, Inspector Smith."

"Your memory isn't what it should be, Special Agent Bond," Paavo said coldly.

Bond stiffened.

"You seemed to have forgotten not only that Cecily Campbell-Turunen was married, but that she spied on her husband and his associates and he ended up killed by the Russian mafia."

Bond took a nail clipper out of his top drawer and began to trim his nails and cuticles. "I have no idea what you're talking about, Inspector Smith. *Turunen?* Are you getting this information from Eldridge Sawyer?"

"Where I get information isn't the issue," Paavo said.

Only the click-click of Bond's manicure could be heard. Then he put the clippers away. "I think someone's been telling you outrageous tales, Inspector. We don't use research clerks to spy on anyone. My understanding is that she was a research clerk, and nothing more."

"That's a lie. What I've said is the only explanation for what's going on now. For people like the Russian enforcer, Leonid Stavrogin, to accost me and follow my girlfriend. Or didn't you know about that either?"

Bond's face went white with restrained fury. "We keep an eye on men like him. If he confronted you, it was a warning, or you'd be dead. You've gotten too close to something. He could have simply put a bullet in you and ended any threats you might pose that way." Bond rubbed his fingers across his mouth. "Stavrogin had to know you'd recognize him as soon as you looked at some mug shots."

"I did."

"Damn! What are they thinking!" He ground his fist against his palm. "You understand this changes everything. The SFPD isn't equipped to handle the Russian mafia. Few local law enforcements are. Since they're a part of this, we'll have to take over from here."

"I don't think so," Paavo replied coldly. "This—now—is about me, my stepfather, and my future wife. I'm not backing off."

"You have no choice." Bond's eyes narrowed. "The Russian mafia is FBI jurisdiction."

"Just like Cecily Campbell-Turunen's death? The FBI was called in to help find her, and apparently scarcely bothered to look."

"I don't know what you're talking about."

"You should. You were the agent running her, but Eldridge

Sawyer was the SFPD's contact. I guess even back then, you knew how to keep above the fray, since you've been promoted to SAC, and Sawyer lives in a shack."

"Sawyer." Bond paled. He stood up then, his hands in his pockets, and walked to the window peering out onto Polk Street before he turned and spoke. "None of that matters, Inspector. It's ancient history. Stavrogin is our problem now. He's a killer. A sniper. He got his training in Afghanistan, fighting on the Taliban's side. The guy's too dangerous for the SFPD."

"No way I'm pulling out of this," Paavo said, bristling at the man's high-handedness. "I intend to find out what's really coming down and stopping it. With the FBI's help, or without it."

Bond folded his arms. "It could be Washington's choice. A few well-placed phone calls. Do you really think the chief of police will argue? Do you think the mayor will? They're political creatures. They'll tell you to keep your mouth shut and your nose clean, and you know it."

"Call whoever you want!" Paavo stood up and headed for the front door.

Bond stepped toward him as Paavo opened it. "The authority of the FBI—"

Paavo didn't bother to glance back as he walked out the door. "I don't give a damn about your authority."

Paavo was still struggling to control his anger when he walked into Angie's hotel room that same evening. "Paavo, what's wrong?" she asked, alarmed and also afraid to know.

"Bond—that FBI agent. Damn him! I'm sure he knows more than he's telling. If he'd just come clean, this would be so much..." His eyes caught hers. "You've got an odd expression. What is it?"

"Sit down."

His face went from anger to stark fear. Suddenly, she realized what he must have been thinking. "It's not Aulis. He's the same." She saw his immediate relief. "I know you asked me to stay here, but I just made a quick run to Aulis's house." She reached into her tote bag. "I found this."

She took out the little bear and held it toward him. She had sewn the eye back in place.

Paavo stared at it without expression.

Had she been wrong? She had nearly cried over the stuffed animal and he had no reaction. "He isn't yours?"

His hand reached out his hand. The toy seemed dwarfed in it. "He's mine." He smoothed the rumpled fur. "I used to sleep with him."

She knelt down on the floor near his feet, her hand on his knee as she watched a panoply of emotions flicker across his face.

"I'm amazed I remember him. I'd forgotten what my own father looked like, but I remember a crummy toy." He stared hard at it, as if waiting for it to talk to him, to tell him about the past.

"He's a very cute little bear," Angie said. "I know it sounds silly, but a part of me kept hoping you'd be glad to have him back."

Long moments passed. "I am glad," he murmured. "It's a silly connection, this child's toy, yet it brings me back." He struggled with the words. "As if I've gone in a full circle."

"And then?" she asked.

He rubbed the bear's ear. "I found *me*, all over again." He lifted agonized eyes to her. "I'm not making sense." He put the bear down on the table, but Angie noticed that he kept glancing at it, and every so often would fiddle with the ribbon or brush a miniscule speck of lint from it, even if only he could see it.

"I understand what you mean. And I'm glad," she said softly.

He drew in a deep breath. "Aulis didn't keep any other surprises like this, did he?"

"Wait until you see what I found in your pocket!" She gave a small laugh to lighten the mood.

He grinned back, curious. "My pocket?"

"A set of your clothes was there, along with your sister's." She quickly turned away and reached into her tote bag for the Zip-lock bag. "One rock and a petrified piece of bubble gum. I wonder which is harder?"

He took out the rock and rubbed it. She could imagine him doing that as a boy.

"And, look here. Your sister's wallet. It's got a great picture of you both, and wait until you see the movie you went to!"

He took the wallet from her and studied the picture. Sadness tinged his eyes, even as he smiled.

"I have movie ticket stubs," she said, wanting to give him something to laugh about as she dug through her tote. "I'm sure they were here. I can't have lost them! I hope they didn't fall out when my tote bag tipped over at the hospital." She began pulling things out of the tote.

"What do you mean, at the hospital?"

Her hands stilled. "Well..."

He waited.

"Oh, all right. After Aulis's apartment, I went to the hospital. Don't worry. I was very careful."

His shoulders slumped.

"I can't believe..." He cut himself off. "You're sure no one followed you?"

"I'm sure. I can't tell you what I put the Uber driver through."

"I can imagine, Angie." Unexpectedly, he asked. "What movie did I go to?"

"Of all things, the ticket stubs were for *Sleepless in Seattle*."

"*Sleepless in Seattle?*"

"It's about a couple who meet on the radio," Angie said. "A super popular romance when you were a kid."

"I've heard of it. It's nothing I'd want to see."

She grinned. "I think you already have."

37

———

The former museum curator Angie had spoken to earlier, called her cell phone the next afternoon. She thought he'd forgotten all about her, but then he told her he'd found a peculiar story in a Russian newspaper about her music box. A radical group of dissidents had removed it from the Hermitage, and while it was being smuggled out of the country, the smugglers were caught and arrested by the "new" Russian government. The article did not say, however, what had become of the beautiful music box that had once belonged to the Tsarina Alexandra, wife of Tsar Nicholas II. The assumption was that it had been returned to the museum, but since Angie had it, obviously that wasn't true.

"That's an amazing story," She thanked Porter and hung up.

After relaying this information to Paavo's voice mail—he was never around when she called, it seemed—she did something she'd wanted to for some time. She called an Uber for the trip across town to the Cypress Motel.

An up-close-and-personal view of the seedy area, however, made her question the wisdom of leaving the car.

"Drive around a bit," she requested. "I'd like to take a look at this part of town."

"You get a kick out of slumming, lady?"

She didn't bother to answer.

Cecily and Mika's apartment was not anywhere near this area. While Angie could understand the family going into hiding after Sam was killed, what had made them come to this part of town?

The driver circled around several busy streets, knowing how to increase a fare. In the middle of a block stood a barren theater, its lobby boarded, and the outdoor ticket booth a poster board for graffiti and cheap, homemade flyers. "Stop!" she yelled.

The words Bernal Heights Theater stretched along the top of the now empty marquee. BHT.

Why would Cecily have brought her children this far from home to a movie? There were plenty of theaters in her area, much nicer ones, too. This area hadn't deteriorated in the last thirty years. It was always bad.

"Let's go back to that motel," she said, deep in thought. "And I'd like you to wait for me."

The cab pulled into the parking lot. Her chest tightened at the sight of the places Paavo had mentioned—Room 8 and the vending area.

"You looking for a room?" A rumpled, middle-aged man stood in the office doorway. As he observed the quality of her Jil Sander pants suit and Gucci boots, he openly ogled her.

"Hi." Her cheerful greeting sounded forced as she introduced herself and handed him a business card. "I'm writing a book on places of some notoriety in San Francisco—exciting spots that people will want to come and visit for a few days."

"I've never heard of notoriety being a drawing card." He frowned, as if she could make his business even worse.

"Oh, but it is. The public loves that sort of thing," she said.

"But would they want to sleep here?"

"Trust me." She followed him into an office furnished in rattan with threadbare cushions in need of fumigation. He stepped behind the counter and swiveled his reservation book toward her. Hope springs eternal, she supposed. "I heard a famous murder happened right here thirty years ago—guns blazing, a mafia hit, Godfather-types barking orders."

"You're the second person who's asked about that this week." He stroked his chin.

"There you go!" she cried. "Instant fame." She bent close lowering her voice conspiratorially. "What can you tell me?"

"Nothing. I don't know nothing about it. I'll try to find out for you, though. Hundred bucks for tonight, special rate. I'll give you my best room. Tomorrow, I might know something."

She straightened. "No way."

"Yeah, well..." He shrugged as if to say it didn't hurt to ask.

"Tell me," she said. "Do you know people you can ask about what happened years back?"

"Not really. It was strange, though, this place." He shut the reservation book and shoved it in the corner. "When I first bought the motel, there were a lot of weird people hanging around it."

"Oh? What kind?"

"You know." He bent forward, elbows on the counter top.

"No, I don't." She casually leaned a hip against it.

"Guys with guns."

Her knees went weak. "Criminals? Gangs?"

"No, no. Not that kind. Suits."

She could scarcely believe her ears. "Suits? You mean government types? G-men?"

"Yeah. You know, they all looked like they walked off the set of *Criminal Minds*. They soon stopped coming after I took over, but for a long time I'd always wondered if this might have been used as one of those, uh, what do you call it...?"

She braced her palms on the counter. "A safe house?"

"Yeah! That's it!"

———

Harold Partridge sat in the glow of the lamp light in his big, empty house, a black lacquered Russian jewelry box nestled in his hands. It was just a little thing, with a design on its lid of a colorful, fairy-tale like village. For some reason, he loved this symbol of the natural, peasant-like life he never had, of a warm, happy home, of love and laughter.

Not like his own home, with two ex-wives and three kids who hated him. At times, guilt and sorrow over the way he'd treated them nearly caused him to apologize, but then, they didn't behave so well toward him either. They didn't understand the pressures he was under. The pressures of business, and all he'd had to do to make it a success.

It wasn't really his fault. None of it was.

He heard a sound and nearly jumped out of his skin. Leaping from the chair, his hand on his heart, he peered into the darkness, trying hard to see. A secret drawer in the lamp table held a gun, if he could only reach it.

"Who are you?" he whispered. The gun caught the light, but the face was in shadow. "Do you want money? How much? Name your price and go."

All was silent.

"What do you want of me?" he pleaded.

The last sound he ever heard was a gunshot.

———

That night, Paavo went to visit Aulis. A night lamp beside the bed cast a dim yellow glow into the room. In a dark corner, a nun sat quietly saying the rosary. He'd met her briefly once before.

"Oh my," she said, startled to see him. She jumped to her feet. "I'll be leaving. I don't mean to disturb you."

"You aren't, Sister. Please stay. I'll only be here a minute." He reached for Aulis's hand and held it as he greeted the old man. As ever, Aulis didn't stir in the slightest.

With a heavy sigh, Paavo sat down in a chair beside the bed and bowed his head, still holding Aulis's hand. He had spoken to the doctor on the phone and knew there was nothing that could be done but to wait, and hope.

"It gets to be almost too much, doesn't it?" Sister Ignatius asked, sitting down again.

"It does," he admitted. "It's maddening that I can't get through to him. Can't make him better."

"Sometimes it helps to talk, even if it's only to a sorry old nun who spends her days sitting in hospital rooms."

Her gentle voice warmed him. How could he trust her, though? Nun or not, he found it hard to open up to anyone, to tell others his inner thoughts and feelings. Yet, when he gazed at her, something told him he had could trust this woman. A sense filled him that he could confide in her as a person, not because she was a nun. It was disconcerting. He was a cop, not a psychic. Yet, was there really so much difference? Sometimes he thought his most valuable cop's tool was his discernment. To his surprise, he wanted to talk.

"There's not much to tell," he said finally, sitting straighter. He kept his eyes on Aulis.

"You love Angie very much, it seems." The nun's voice came to him from the shadows in which she sat.

Her words surprised him, but then he realized the two women probably had talked at some length. Girl talk, as it were. Angie was that way—very open and easy to converse with. "I do," he admitted.

"I heard you're engaged. Will you marry soon?"

He kept his eyes on Aulis, and Angie's description of Catholic confessionals came to mind. "She thinks she'd like that."

"You sound doubtful."

"At times."

"Why?"

The soft yellow nightlight caught his attention. "I worry about it. For one thing, I know that to Angie, being married means children. With my job, my background, I worry about doing right by her, let alone any child we might have."

"Your background?"

"I have almost no experience with families and how they work. I consider Aulis my father, but I lost my real parents when I was very young."

"Do you remember them?"

He paused, and silence of the night hospital descended over the room. "I didn't think I remembered my father. But recently, I saw a picture of him, and I discovered that I do."

"That... that's good." She sounded somewhat puzzled by his words.

"Only a few things, general things, a sense of him, if not the man himself."

"How old were you when he died?"

"Four."

"It's not surprising then, that you don't have a clear memory." Her voice softened. "And your mother?"

He thought a moment. "I remember missing her." His reply was spoken as quietly as her question. "I remember telling Aulis at times I was going to run away and look for her."

"You're saying she... isn't dead?"

"I don't know."

"You never tried to find her?"

"No. I'll admit I thought about it. But as a child, Aulis taught me to forget about her. He said she was a heavy drinker and hinted at a lot worse."

"I see," the nun murmured. "What about your sister? Does she remember your mother? Does she ever talk about her, or say she missed her?"

"We didn't talk much about her. When we did, Jessie would grow sad. She remembered her well. The way Jessie used to talk, she made me think mothers were some magical creatures who knew how to make everything better in your life. She said our mom—Jessie used to call her 'Mom'—would know when something was wrong even without us telling her, and she could make us feel better if we were sad. Jessie never gave up hope that Mom would come back. And then Jessie had no more time left to wait for her."

"I'm so sorry," the nun whispered.

She fell silent, and Paavo stared a long while at the nightlight. "I spent a lot of time questioning, and wondering, about my mother. Wondering about the responsibilities of a parent, and if she had any idea how her kids felt being dumped on some neighbor's doorstep."

The nun's voice was gentle and soothing. "She must have known. Her going left a terrible void in your life—and in hers, too, I would imagine."

"I tried hard to blame her, even to hate her. It never quite worked."

He bowed his head.

"Let me say that, if your mother is alive," she said softly, "I imagine she never gave up hoping to come back to you. Whether or not she succeeded was in God's hands. I think that if you were to believe, in your heart, that she wanted to return, you wouldn't be wrong, and it would be a comfort to you. I would imagine leaving you and your sister was the most difficult thing she ever did in her life, and it must have been for a very good reason."

He nodded. "Perhaps."

The room fell absolutely still.

After a while, Sister Ignatius stood and gathered her things. "Gracious, I didn't realize how late it is. Sister Agnes must be having fits. I'm always Sister Slowpoke. I'm glad we had a chance to talk, Inspector Smith."

"Yes, so am I," he said, feeling the empathy in her eyes. "Goodnight, Sister."

She nodded, and he heard the soft swish of her skirt as she left the room.

38

ngie awoke late in the day. Paavo had called her last night, but he hadn't come to see her. She suspected he'd spent the night at their temporary home on Filbert Street, puzzling over the gunplay and danger around them, and possibly waiting for someone to approach the bungalow. The five a.m. news came on the radio before exhaustion overtook her worry and racing thoughts and she slept.

Before that, she'd spent a lot of time thinking. One question kept returning to her—why had Cecily brought her children to the Bernal Heights Theater?

Why would the movie stubs from that particular theater have ended up in Jessica's wallet? The feeling came over her that, somehow, it all had to be connected.

As dawn lit the sky, Angie came up with a plan which seemed like a good one. Now, in the harsh light of day, she wondered if she dared try it.

Paavo turned onto Harold Partridge's driveway and immediately stopped. The large circular path was filled with blue and white cars from the Santa Clara county sheriff's office.

Paavo got out of his car and showed his badge. "What's going on?"

"Harold Partridge was killed. His housekeeper found the body this morning."

"Killed? How?"

"From what I've been told, a single shot, to the head."

Paavo left Partridge's home as soon as possible after talking to the investigator assigned to the case. The fellow looked stricken. Not only were there few murders in Santa Clara County's jurisdiction, no victims had been as famous as Harold Partridge.

Fortune 500 moguls getting assassinated in their homes by someone clever enough or knowledgeable enough to bypass top-of-the-line security, tended to create lots of questions, even in the minds of green investigators, and Paavo answered as many as he could. He explained his presence by saying that he was investigating Gregor Rosinsky's murder, and that the jeweler had phoned Partridge three days before he'd been killed. He kept any mention of the Russian music box out of the story.

He also emphasized that he was unaware of any connection between Partridge and Rosinsky's murder, but he was merely getting background information on the jeweler. He convinced the county investigator to let him leave before the press got wind that a San Francisco cop was there. They would have a field day speculating on any statement he might give them— including a 'No comment.' The last thing Paavo wanted was any publicity.

The investigator agreed, and Paavo left, uneasy about his evasiveness and lack of candor. It nagged at him as he drove back to San Francisco and the Hall of Justice.

Back at his desk, he phoned the home number of his long-time FBI associate, Agent Bradley. It was already evening on the east coast. When Bradley came on the line, Paavo asked him for all the background files, paperwork, or reports having to do with the FBI's attempt to place Cecily and her family into the Witness Protection Program.

"First, little if anything is put in writing in cases like that, and second, I can't do it, Paavo." Bradley's voice was subdued. "There are too many questions being asked about these files already. Someone noticed that they've been moving. It sent up a red flag. Any more requests, and they'll want to know why. What you're doing isn't department business, and you're getting classified information. There's got to be a reason for it."

"There is a reason. Harold Partridge was murdered this morning."

"I heard. Hell, the whole country heard. You saying he had a hand in this?"

"That's right."

"Holy shit."

"Exactly. He was tied in, somehow, with what went down thirty years ago, and I need to find out what that was."

"Damn, Paavo, I can't do it. You know the penalty for unauthorized use of these files. It could mean my job, and if Partridge was a player as well..."

"A lot more than a job is at stake, Bradley. I've got to stop it. I think I've just skimmed the surface. The answer might be in those files."

"Look, I don't have those records, anyway. They're in San Francisco, if any exist at all. Background reports like you're talking about, thirty years old, would be in local files, not anything we'd put in our database. I can't help you."

"You can get me access to the files," Paavo demanded.

"I can't. They're there; I'm here."

"Fax me an authorization."

"I'm not high enough to authorize shit! I'm sorry, buddy, but you're on your own in this one."

Paavo hung up. Maybe he should try Bond again, see if he could get the guy to level with him. Bond clearly knew a lot more than he was saying, but until finding Sawyer, Paavo had no way to prove it. If he hurried, he'd get to the FBI before the office closed.

He went down to the parking lot, to the city-issue car he was using. As he walked toward it, he heard footsteps behind him.

He turned to see Eldridge Sawyer approach. "Let's go for a ride."

"What's this about?" Paavo asked. Sawyer was wearing a suit, carrying a thin brown briefcase, and looked like a quintessential FBI agent from a few years back.

"I've got some answers for you, but not here." Only the tough, wide-legged stance, the darting steel-gray eyes resembled the survivalist Paavo had met earlier.

Paavo nodded and unlocked the unmarked Ford. Sawyer got into the passenger seat. "Head toward the Embarcadero," Sawyer said, looking from side to side and back to make sure they weren't being followed.

Once they passed the congestion of the downtown area, Sawyer seemed to relax.

"Anytime you're ready to talk," Paavo said, "I'm listening."

"I thought a lot about what you were saying, and the fact that you found me. First, I'm moving on. Gideon's history. But I came across some files I thought you ought to see. They're about your mother."

"Files? Where did you get them?"

"There was a lot of shit going down when I was at the Bureau. I found out too much, and I didn't want to end up dead like Cecily and your old man. I would have been next."

"You worked a lot more closely with her than you wanted me to believe," Paavo said.

"What makes you think that?"

"If you hadn't, you wouldn't have known enough to be worried about. What was your role? Was she ever a research clerk, or did you know from the beginning that she'd be doing a lot more?"

"Take a right up there, then left at the next corner." Sawyer stared straight ahead as Paavo turned as directed. "You knew those times. We were suspicious of everything and everybody, especially those connected to student movements. Most of the groups behind them were no more students than I was."

"And if you could turn up some information no one else knew about, it would have made your career, wouldn't it?" Paavo asked. "You called Cecily ambitious and deceitful. But you were the same, right?"

"In the middle of the next block, pull over and park."

Again, Paavo did as Sawyer said. They were in an industrial area near the water, the Bay Bridge directly overhead. Sawyer removed a folder from the briefcase and handed it to Paavo. "I never meant for it to end up this way. Look at the file." With that, he got out of the car, and ran across four lanes of traffic to a white Chevrolet. The car started up and turned immediately onto the bridge approach.

Paavo could have made a U-turn and followed, but he saw no reason to. Whatever wrong or misplaced ideas Sawyer might have had in the past, he wasn't the one behind all that was going on now. All Sawyer wanted was to hide from those same people —a desire Angie and her cousin Richie had disrupted. That, and an obvious sense of guilt, had brought him here today.

Paavo opened the file. It was filled with photocopies of Cecily's reports, Bond's reports and notes about recruiting her for undercover work, and having Cecily befriend a female history professor as a way into the anti-Soviet movement.

Sawyer had most likely sanitized the file, but Bond's involvement came through loud and clear.

The investigative report at the end of the file stopped Paavo cold. It wasn't an FBI report at all, but an incident report, prepared by the Federal Building's own security staff. It detailed Cecily Campbell's attack on Tucker Bond.

As he read the eyewitness reports by Filomena Almazol and Roberta King from the typing pool, a clerk named Randy Fineman, and finally, Eldridge Sawyer, a startling picture emerged.

Cecily had approached Bond in the building's parking garage as he arrived at work early on the morning of October 8th, four days after Mika's death. As soon as he stepped out of his car, she ran up to him and began screaming at him.

All heard her accuse Bond of betrayal—that they'd met Thursday night at their secret spot, she'd told him 'everything' and he had betrayed her. The supposed safe place was the exact opposite—it was a set-up. Bond tried to get her to calm down, but she didn't. She was crying, and said it suddenly had all come together for her. Looking at the words used—a secret meeting, a rendezvous, and then a betrayal—Paavo could see Sawyer's conclusion that the two might have been lovers. But Paavo was more convinced than ever that Sawyer's conclusion was dead wrong.

Bond protested that he'd done nothing, and Cecily ran off, saying she'd get even with him and she'd make him pay.

When the security staffer interviewed Bond about the incident, he said he didn't know what Cecily was talking about, that he'd never met with her anywhere. In fact, on the night she'd alleged they'd met, he'd been out with a friend, and had proof.

Paavo went to the next page on screen to see Bond's alibi. As he looked at it, he suddenly understood exactly what had happened.

39

ngie would have liked to give Paavo a call, but she didn't dare dig into her tote bag and try to steer the used Cadillac SUV she was test driving at the same time.

She needed to buy another car soon. She needed one to visit her parents, or her friend Connie for some clear-eyed, not-caught-in-the-middle perspective on all this, and even to go car shopping at different dealerships. Trying to do all that in Uber was achingly slow. Besides, her hotel room felt like a prison cell.

And she wanted to see if she wanted to buy a full-sized SUV as her next "family" car.

And while she was test driving this one, she decided to make a quick stop. Last night, she'd thought of someone who might have a good idea of what Cecily had been up to the night Sam was killed.

Up ahead, the building loomed.

Street parking was all filled, as were nearby parking lots. An empty, yellow-painted loading zone took up most of the sidewalk. As far as she was concerned, the SUV was big enough to be a truck, and it was probably too late for deliveries, anyway.

She stopped the Cadillac at one end of the zone, locked the doors and hurried across the street into the building.

As she rode up on the elevator, she checked her phone and set it to silent so it wouldn't ring and disturb her meeting. Immediately on reaching the floor she wanted, she turned away from the reception area and walked down the hallway, reading nameplates on doors for the person she hoped to speak with. She found the right one and knocked.

"Excuse me, Miss," the receptionist stepped out of the public office and called to her. "You need to check in first."

"But this is the person I want to talk to," Angie said.

Just then, a tall, hawk-like man opened the door. He looked down at Angie, then at the receptionist. "It's all right," he said. "I'll see her." He meticulously rubbed a speck of dirt off the doorframe and then held the door wide for Angie to enter.

"Thank you so much," she said. "It'll only take a minute of your time. I wanted to talk to you about a movie ticket stub I recently found."

Paavo thought about Bond's alibi—a movie ticket stub with SLEEPLES right before the tear.

One edge of the ticket had a number on it, BHT00243. He knew many theaters used to number the tickets sequentially to account for box office receipts on a daily basis. If he could get hold of the ticket stubs for *Sleepless in Seattle* Angie had found in Jessica's wallet, the numbers would indicate if Bond and Cecily had attended on the same day or, possibly, together. The ticket could substantiate Cecily's story, that she *had* met Bond that night... and that Bond might well have betrayed Mika and caused his death.

Paavo rubbed his temples, needing to think this through.

Cecily had been an undercover operative. It made sense that

her contacts with her handler—Bond—would be covert. What better place than in a darkened theater? What better place to tell Bond that she, Mika, and the children were going into hiding?

Mika had been killed at the motel. In the attack it was apparent that killers were also seeking Cecily and possibly her children. Why else would the killers have unleashed firepower into every possible hiding place in the motel after already slaying Mika? Only pure, dumb luck had saved Cecily, Jessica and him.

After Mika's death, Cecily must have contacted Bond. He offered to put her and the children into the Witness Protection Program. Having them under wraps would allow him time to plan his next move. Was it an unconscious suspicion of Bond that had kept her from revealing where she and the children were hiding after Mika's murder?

Cecily must have been distraught, frightened for herself and her children. But in the days she waited as the WPP machinery moved to create new identities and a new safe place to live, she had time to think. Clearly. Coldly.

And what she came up with was chilling: Bond the agent; Bond the handler; Bond the betrayer.

Paavo could imagine just how desperate and alone Cecily must have felt as she pieced together Bond's pattern of betrayal. Paavo finally understood why she had decided to act as she did, as she realized that neither she nor her children dared to be placed under Bond's control. Worse, she had recognized that if Bond gained possession of her children, he would have a weapon against her to force her to his will—and probably to her death because of all she knew. Cecily also must have feared for her children themselves, particularly Jessica, who was old enough to remember too much.

Also, with Bond now the head of the San Francisco office, if word ever got out of what he'd done in that operation, he'd lose everything, and maybe would be imprisoned.

Paavo saw how his mother had analyzed her situation. From what he knew, he could all but envision just how she must have planned, and how she had set her plan in motion. First, to kill the Russians who'd fired the weapons that murdered Mika, and then with both the Russians and the FBI after her, she hopefully staged her own death, leaving Jessica with an all-important envelope for Aulis with their forged birth certificates and Cecily's letters. Her task completed, she disappeared.

Or… Bond tracked her down and killed her.

Paavo had to talk to Angie and have her read out the numbers on the movie tickets she had—hopefully she found them. They were the proof he needed to confront Bond.

He called Angie's phone but received no answer. He then called her room at the Fairmont. The phone rang until a message service came on.

He contacted Connie, and then Angie's sisters, but none of them had heard from her. His nerve endings crackled. Where could she be? She'd sworn she wasn't going anywhere.

Just then, Yosh called. "Has Angie reached you yet?" he asked.

"No. Did you talk to her?" Paavo asked.

"About an hour ago. She said she was going out—had a few errands and also had a serious question about something of Jessica's from Aulis's apartment. I hope you understand what she was talking about, because I sure didn't."

Paavo was beginning to feel a little panicky. "Unfortunately, I do understand."

He hung up and began to drive. If Angie was concerned about something of Jessica's, she had to be talking about the movie ticket stubs. He, too, had questions about those stubs.

It was time to get some answers.

Street parking near the Federal Building was all filled, as were nearby parking lots. An empty yellow-painted loading zone took up most of the sidewalk. It was too late for deliveries now. He stopped the car at one end of the zone, locked the doors and hurried across the street into the building.

He rode up on the elevator, and immediately on reaching his floor, turned from the reception area to head directly toward Bond's office. He knocked.

"Excuse me, sir," a security guard stepped out of the public office and called to him. "Why are you here? The offices are closed for the day."

He pulled out his badge. "Inspector Smith. I'd like to speak with Mr. Bond."

"I'm sorry, sir, but he already left."

The woman watched the cop park his car in the loading zone. She slowly drove past then pulled into a bus stop. A man waiting for the bus marched up to protest, but after one look at her cold, deadly eyes, then at the Glock on the passenger seat, he blanched and backed away, his lips sealed.

Within minutes, the cop raced from the building to his car. She waited until he drove by, and then pulled into traffic and followed, a couple of cars behind him.

40

———

"Will you stop fiddling with those dials and drive!" Bond demanded.

"There's something wrong with the car," Angie said, making her voice as high, whining and ditzy as she could manage. "I told you I can feel it straining." So far, she'd turned on the windshield wipers, hazard lights, headlights to high beam, seat warmers, and global positioning system. The car had a hands-free cell phone, and if she could keep punching enough buttons to slip in Paavo's phone number and then hit Send, she would. So far, even holding a gun on her, Bond had managed to undo most of what she'd done.

"Maybe we should stop at a gas station and have a mechanic take a look," she said.

"Drive!"

She did. Where was he taking her? They were going around in circles, and the sky was rapidly growing quite dark. She didn't like this one bit.

"Keeping me here is a stupid, ignorant and foolish thing to do!" she cried. She hit the windshield lever again, and the wipers screeched across the dry glass.

"Enough!" the man ordered, smacking the lever back to Off.

"You can't treat me like this!" She was shrill and nearly hysterical. "I'm an innocent person."

"Guess what?" His voice turned low, lethal. "I don't care. You know too much."

She tried pleading. "Let me go and I'll forget all about this. I promise I won't press charges."

"You've got to be joking."

"Who do you think you are?" she yelled.

"I think I'm someone who managed to pull together more wealth than you could imagine. Someone who won't let a twit like you stand in my way. Your friend, Aulis Kokkonen, is only alive because the sudden noise from a neighbor apparently made my man's shot go wide. Who would have imagined the old fool could hold on this long?" He moved his gun close to her side. "Believe me, no such distractions are here now!"

He had just pronounced her death sentence. Her hands tightened on the steering wheel, her voice meek as she said, "Oh."

Paavo swung into the parking lot at SF General and practically ran through the hospital to Aulis's room. Angie wasn't in it, but on the table near the chair where the nun often sat were three movie ticket stubs. They must have fallen from Angie's tote and were placed there.

He put them in his pocket and then went in search of a nurse. "I'm trying to find out if my girlfriend, Angie, came by this afternoon to visit Aulis Kokkonen," he said. "I'm worried about her. She's about five-two, a hundred fifteen or so—she swears she's one-ten, but I don't think so. Also, she wears these high, chunky shoes that add three or four inches, easy. She's pretty—beautiful actually—with short brown hair and big brown eyes, a classy dresser—"

"Stop," the nurse smiled. "I know Angie. I haven't seen her, but I've only been on duty since four."

"What about Sister Ignatius? Is she here? Maybe she's seen her?"

"It's strange you should ask. Sister Agnes was asking me about her as well. I'd assumed they were from the same convent, but they aren't. In any case, she hasn't been here all day."

41

"The air is outside will be chilly. I do hope you'll be warm enough in that jacket." Bond spoke as calmly as if they were headed for a sidewalk cafe. His voice was more chilling than the weather.

"I won't be," Angie said, now certain he'd simply been stalling for night to fall and the streets to empty. They were far from downtown, driving in a residential area near the ocean. Cheerful lights shone through windows of homes, and she could feel the warmth emanating from them, making her colder and lonelier than ever. "And I'm not a part of this, either. I really, really want to go home."

The older man laughed. "Don't be naïve."

For some time, she had noticed a car that seemed to be following her. Although it stayed far behind, whenever she turned, so did the black car with tinted glass. She would have liked it to be the police, but they didn't drive Mercedes.

"Is this about the music box?" she asked after a while.

"It's far beyond the music box," he said. "Partridge cared about it, not me. He was a nervous, simpering fool."

Angie was confused. "Then why are you doing this?"

"Why? Because I have to do everything myself, that's why! Those Russians are inept."

"But I thought Partridge was the one behind it all."

"Partridge was behind squat."

She was even more confused. "Are you doing this to help Partridge? If so, you're too late. It's been all over the news today that Partridge is dead. Someone killed him!"

Bond laughed.

———

Angie didn't like it here. To be in a dark, isolated and spooky place with a madman holding a gun on her was not her idea of a good time.

She knew where they were—on what was once the Presidio of San Francisco, and now a national park.

Bond had her walk towards the Pacific Ocean towards a gun battlement. They stopped on the concrete entry of one built along the edge of a bluff, a massive concrete structure upon which, at one time, heavy guns had been mounted to defend the coast against battleship and cruiser attack. Stairs rose up from the ground floor landing and at the top of each staircase was a gun mount. Protecting the guns facing the ocean were tall, wide concrete platforms. Metal ladders led to the tops of the platforms where artillerymen stood with a clear view of the ocean to direct and service the guns. At the lower levels were small rooms where men worked and for gunpowder and artillery storage. Long ago, the guns had been dismounted, and now the battlement stood like haunted monuments to a bygone era.

Moonlight on the salt-air weathered concrete gave the structure an eerie, whitish glow.

"Now, Miss Amalfi," Bond said. "Let's begin with you giving me the ticket stubs, then we'll talk about who else knows about them."

From his reaction when she first mentioned the movie tickets she should have realized her mistake. He wanted to photocopy them, he'd said, and when she told him they were in her tote bag in the car, he went with her to pick them up. Once she unlocked the SUV, he pulled a gun and told her to start driving.

She didn't dare tell him she'd lost the tickets. He'd kill her and that would be that. And she also didn't want him to set a trap for Paavo.

"They're inside." She pointed at her tote.

"Find them."

Slowly she lifted one item at a time from the bag and placed it on the concrete ground. The area was completely hidden from the roadway, and even that was little traveled. Still, they were in a city filled with people. Surely, someone would come by in time, perhaps for a moonlit tryst. Or so she prayed.

"Hurry up!" he ordered.

The surf pounded in the distance. He could kill her and drop her body into the water, just like Paavo's mother. She, too, would be missing, and never found again. Is that what Bond did to Cecily? Could that be what really happened?

Angie slowed down more than ever. "Everything got dumped onto the floor not long ago. I don't usually carry so much, but I've been living in a hotel and haven't had time to sort things out."

"Just find them!"

"They're here someplace, but I can't see without some light. We need to go someplace with better lighting than the moon. Let's leave this place. Once I find them, you can take the tickets and go. You go your way, I'll go mine, and—"

"Shut up!" Bond yanked the bag from her, and pulled out a make-up bag, phone, phone charger, lip balm, compact mirror, a container of feminine products, notebooks, pens, mechanical pencils, keys, business card case, credit card case, wallet, checkbook, keys, Kleenex packet, sunglasses, wet wipes, a mini first aid kit, and scraps of paper. He was fuming as he took out one thing at a time, being careful not to discard the tickets by mistake in his haste to go through her belongings. "The tickets have got to be here." Bond swore. "How can you collect so much junk? You and your idiot boyfriend are causing me nothing but trouble. He was gullible—just like his mother."

"His mother wasn't gullible."

"No? Could have fooled me! Damn, what are all these scraps of paper?"

"It's always necessary to have receipts for the IRS—for when I start to make a lot of money with my video restaurant review business. I need write-offs, you know. You work for the government. You know how it is."

"The IRS?" He looked at her as if she'd gone mad. "Who cares about them?"

"I do!"

"Lady, you know what they say about death and taxes? Well, guess what? You won't have to worry about taxes ever again."

Paavo's cell phone began to ring. Relief flooded him as he reached into his breast pocket to retrieve it. It had to be Angie. He'd left messages all over for her to call. The number calling wasn't one he recognized, but he hoped she was using someone else's phone.

"Smith," he answered.

"My name is Ralph Ernhart from MBC Motors." The sound of a man's voice was disappointing. "I'm calling about Miss Angie Amalfi."

Paavo tensed. "What is it?"

"She took one of our SUVs out for a test drive about three

hours ago, and still hasn't returned it. She did leave her credit card information, and excellent references, but still—"

"What's going on?" Paavo asked, his impatience showing.

"You were shown as a reference, Inspector. We're hoping you can convince her to bring it back soon."

"I don't know where she is. I've been trying to reach her."

"Oh, that's no problem. The has a GPS and tracking device, a satellite positioning system. She turned it on and hit the emergency button, so we know where she is. Don't worry. We know it's not an emergency because she kept driving. Just a new driver trying all the bells and whistles. Happens all the time. Drives our emergency operators crazy, but that's part of the cost of business—"

"Where is she?" Paavo asked.

"I'm really sorry to bother you with something like this, Inspector. I hope you understand. She was driving around most of the evening, but now that she's stopped we'd like our car back. Do you know how expensive these big Cadillac SUVS are? Worth every penny, too—"

"Stop!" Paavo said, then spoke slowly and emphatically. "Tell me where she is."

42

———

"They aren't here!" Bond was furious.

"They are! You just missed them. Ticket stubs are small and easy to overlook." She grabbed the papers he'd already gone through, shoved them back into her tote bag, and pulled it toward her.

"What the hell are you doing?" Bond yanked one handle from her grasp and tugged it back. "You've just made it worse. Let go!"

"Worse?" She pulled the tote toward herself again. "I don't think so! Everyone knows about these ticket stubs, and everyone knows I have them, so if anything happens to me, they'll come looking for you."

"And I'll deny it." Bond tugged back, being careful not to let the bag spill. He wouldn't want the wind to catch the ticket stubs—he wanted them safely in hand so he could burn them.

"They're proof of your involvement, and you know it or you wouldn't care." Angie spat the words at him. "That why Sawyer's been hiding, isn't it? We found him, you know. We spoke with him."

"I don't believe you!" Bond gave a hard yank and pulled the tote from her hands.

"Steel-gray eyes, six-three, stocky, his hair was probably sandy brown when you two worked together."

"Damn you and your mouth! I should shoot you right now!"

Paavo found the Cadillac SUV off-road in a remote area of the Presidio. Angie wasn't in it, and as he scanned the too-quiet landscape, his skin turned icy. Here were fifteen hundred acres of cypress, eucalyptus, and pine forests along the Pacific to the Golden Gate, filled with empty officer housing, barracks and other structures brought about by the end of over two-hundred years of military occupation. Countless possibilities existed to hide a person—or to bury a body.

The Federal Building security guard had told him a young woman who fit Angie's description had been seen around closing time, but there were hundreds of young women who met her description. There was no reason to think Angie had gone to see him. She didn't know Bond. But if she had questions about the movie tickets... and had used logic...

His heart dropped. She wouldn't have come here on her own. He feared her captor, Bond or someone else, had one purpose in mind, to kill her. Paavo couldn't imagine him waiting. He would shoot, then dump her body.

Whoever brought her here should want to use the Cadillac for his own getaway. So, there was some chance that whoever came with her was still nearby. That she was still alive. That he could find her in time.

He had never been to this part of the Presidio before, and wasn't sure which way to go. Instinctively, he walked away from the road and toward the ocean.

The lights of the roadway quickly dimmed, but up ahead the full moon lit an old gun battlement like a ghostly theater.

He walked up a hill to get a better view of the battlement before him, and when he did, he could have shouted his despair.

Snaking along the edge of the coast, hidden from view of the road were more and more of the concrete structures, with steps going up two stories to the gun mounts, and little rooms and tunnels tucked throughout.

How was he going to find Angie in there? And if he found her, would she still be alive?

43

―――――

Angie had no choice but to do what Bond said as he forced her to walk up narrow staircases and tunnels and ladders to the top of a strange, outdoor structure, and they now sat face to face near the precipice, pieces of her tote bag and belongings spread all around Tucker Bond. As his anger and frustration grew, in a fit, he threw all of Angie's other belongings over the edge of the structure.

She heard her things crack and bounce on the rocks as they plunged toward the water. The thought that she might be next was the only thing that kept her focused on keeping Bond talking, keeping him distracted and interested in her and her questions. At this point, she truly had no idea where the ticket stubs were, and gave thanks that Bond kept searching for them. The gun was at Bond's side, and she knew there was no way she could stand up and run before he'd pull the trigger and roll her off the ledge, just another "thing" for him to discard.

"I still don't understand your role in this," she said, trying to ease herself away from him. She knew she was somewhere on the grounds of what had once been the U.S. Army's Presidio. It was a now a park, but usually quite empty at night. Still, if she could hold out, someone might show up, someone who might offer help, or at least distract Tucker Bond enough for her to get away. She had to believe that, and not give up. "Did you work for Partridge?"

"*Me* work for him? No way!" His hands shook as he shredded her leather-bound pocket notebook, fastidiously ripping out gold-edged page after gold-edged page. "Think, Miss Amalfi! Where are the tickets?" He continued to rip the pages, his hands fisting around each sheet, his hysteria building.

"What was Cecily's role in all this?" Angie asked. "She was young and innocent enough to give you whatever you asked for from her, wasn't she?"

"She was smart and ambitious," Bond said. "She could have become a special agent, or grown rich working with me and Partridge."

"Was that where the music box came in?" Angie asked.

"Exactly," Bond said. "I was going along, just doing my boring, low-pay job and then, one day, Partridge told me about the Tsarina's music box. He was a collector, and somehow, the Finns who worked for him learned of his passion.

"Once they did, they realized it would be a way to get money to support the Finns and Russians who were against this new-Russian government—the 'new Soviets' now forming Yeltsin's government. They had contacts with Russian smugglers and learned about a pristine collectible. A Romanov music box. It still worked, just as when Nicholas and Alexandra listened to it in their St. Petersburg palace before the Bolsheviks killed them. It was, according to Partridge, a remarkable find. He was happy to give them $200,000 for it, which was worth way more thirty years ago than today. I suspect, they and the smugglers would split the money between them."

"How did you fit in?" Angie asked, sincerely curious at this point.

"Watching all this take place, an idea came to me, full-blown.

What they did makes no sense unless you know that this was the time when the USSR had fallen. It broke into a bunch of separate countries all warring with each other. Boris Yeltsin was named President of the new Russia, but his people were former Soviets. These former Soviets knew there were many dissenters against their government, plus lots of internal chaos and fighting. And many of the dissenters were in this country.

"Among those dissenters were many Finns. Finland was trying to walk a fine line between getting closer to the West but also appeasing the new Russian state, their neighbors. Young Finns, such as your fiancé's father, didn't want any appeasement. They had lost relatives and hated not only the old USSR but also the new Russia."

"I see," Angie said. "I didn't realize all that was going on back then."

"Oh, yes. It was quite the mess. Also, the new Russia wanted the names of any dissidents working against them. I was willing to get them those names, for a price."

"A price?" Angie repeated as a cold chill raced through her. "Now I get it. Cecily would give you the names of the Russian dissenters working with the Finns, then you'd give the names to the new Russian government."

Bond nodded. "I also let the Ruskie government know the music box was in danger of being stolen. They gladly gave it to me in exchange for the names. I then sold it to Partridge for a mere $195,000." Then, he smiled.

Angie shuddered at the thought of all the deaths the man before her had caused, and all the heartache. "I'm guessing the Russian dissidents must have thought the Finns leaked the information to the Soviets. Or"—she was aghast—"you planted the story that the Finns betrayed them. Is that what led to their deaths?"

The woman silently crawled over the battlements, hidden in the dark by her black clothes. She knew this area well. It was a place she'd come years ago, a good spot to meet in secret. She didn't know where the cop was now. He'd taken a look at it and turned away.

She wasn't about to turn away. She could smell her prey. She'd face him now. The weapon in her hand directed the way. For the first time in years she felt a frisson of excitement. Of triumph.

"I had nothing to do with the Russian smugglers," Bond insisted. "The Finns' deaths were an accident. They would have been fine if they hadn't interfered."

Angie stared at Bond as, horrified, she didn't have to guess any longer, but was learning the steps, one after the other, that led to the tragedy. "What do you mean?

"Sam Vanse somehow learned Partridge had the music box. He was a hothead and wanted to get the music box back, or wanted the money Partridge had promised him. He contacted Partridge. Partridge invited him to his home, but then called me. Partridge was terrified of what Sam might do.

"Sure enough, Sam saw the music box and became irate. Partridge shot him. At that, Sam grabbed the box and ran from the house. I tried to stop him. He made it to the car where Mika Turunen waited for him. He tossed the box in the car, but then he fell to the ground. I ran toward him to see if he was still alive. At that point, Turunen drove off."

It took all Angie's strength not to call Bond a liar. Paavo had told her about Sam's autopsy—that he had a flesh wound to the arm and then was shot in the head, which killed him instantly. If Partridge had fired the head shot, Sam wouldn't have made it to the car.

So Bond had to have been the one who fired it. Bond killed Sam.

Angie's eyes never left Bond's. "So Mika drove off with the music box. You must have gone half-crazy trying to find it back then. You needed to find Mika and used Cecily to learn where he was hiding. How did you do it?"

"I don't know what you're talking about," he said.

"I know exactly what she's talking about." A cold voice came out of the darkness, a woman's voice. "All these years I never knew exactly what happened that night. Now, I do."

Bond's face went white, his eyes dilated as they searched the darkness. With a half-sob, half-laugh, he lunged at Angie and, as she screamed, whirled her around, pulling her to her feet in a stranglehold, her arm twisted and her spine tight against his chest.

44

Paavo eased himself through the rugged land to the east of the battlements. Quietly, he called Yosh on his cell phone. He needed back-up, but not anyone charging in, setting Angie's kidnapper off, possibly hurting Angie if, in fact, she was here somewhere... and she was still alive...

He looked for light or movement, listened hard for any sound while staying within the shadows of the trees and brush, hoping against hope that he hadn't misread the situation...

"Drop your gun, Bond," the voice said.

"No!" He searched the darkness in vain, then pressed the gun to Angie's head. "Leave here or I'll kill her."

A woman stepped out of the shadows. She was tall and slim, dressed in a black flak jacket, black slacks and boots. She ripped the black cap from her short, gray-streaked hair. As she moved closer, in the moonlight, Angie could see her cold, green eyes; stern, narrow face; and the large automatic pistol she pointed at Bond.

"You!" Bond gulped air, tightening his grip on Angie, causing her to press closer to him. "I suspected it was you who ran over the Russian and shot the other one when he was trying to put the bomb in the bitch's car. Even you who stopped Partridge's hired sniper from killing the cop."

The woman's smile was wolflike. "Nice fireworks, weren't they?"

Bond backed up, clutching Angie in front of him like a shield.

The woman followed, her footsteps soundless. "All these years of waiting. Of needing to know the truth. Needing to know exactly who killed Mika and why."

Bond chuckled viciously. "So you finally put it all together, Cecily."

Cecily. Angie's heart thudded. Paavo's mother. The resemblance came as a jolt, but once she saw it, she wondered how she had missed it before. She could blame the disguise, she thought with a twinge of the same hysteria she knew Bond was feeling.

The nun. She was the nun who watched over Aulis and kept him safe from this killer. But the resemblance that Angie should have caught went beyond a disguise. They were there in the height and breath of her brow, in the firm set of the mouth, even the quiet, panther-like way she and her son moved.

Bitterness and hatred filled Cecily's eyes. "It was all a set-up." She glanced at Angie. "Let me tell you about that night, that horrible night. Mika phoned me after Sam was killed, he was terrified. He didn't know who Bond was—he thought the man who shot Sam was an agent of Russia's new government. He'd gone to Aulis's house to hide. Mika warned me to take the kids and leave our home, to hide. I told him I'd find a safe place for us. I contacted Bond, met him in the theater. He suggested the Cyprus Motel. I told Mika to go there, and you know what happened next."

Cecily then turned to Bond. "I trusted you, and you sent us

to the safe house to be killed. Who actually fired the shots, Bond? You? Your FBI agents? Or was it the new Russia agents working for you?"

Bond smirked. "It's too bad they missed you and your brats. We found the kids, by the way. About two years after you disappeared. Using the name Smith! How prosaic. But I admit, you had me fooled. When you didn't deign to show up at your own daughter's funeral, even I figured you were dead. Such a good mother!"

There were no tears, only an icy, brittle hardness, and implacability in her. "I knew there were others involved besides you," Cecily admitted. "But nothing I did in the past ever told me exactly who or exactly why. Not until *now*. Not until I followed Paavo and his woman, followed the clues to Partridge. He was your weak link. And you killed him." She trained her gun on Bond. "And now I'm going to kill you."

Both Angie and Bond spoke at the same time.

"Drop the gun, Cecily, or I'll kill the little bitch!" Bond yelled.

"No! Wait!" Angie cried. "Cecily, we can prove he's guilty."

45

Paavo heard Bond's voice. And another voice. A woman's. Eerily familiar. And then, a feeling that shook him to his core came over him as he realized who she was… and who she had pretended to be.

Finally, he heard Angie's voice. She was alive. As relief flooded him, as so many profound emotions roiled through him, he forced himself to remain steady and to move silently forward.

"I don't play games, Cecily," Bond shouted. "Drop it now, or I'll put a bullet in your son's girlfriend."

"No!" Angie was frantic, trying to wriggle free, but Bond's lock hold on her arm and neck only tightened.

Cecily didn't flinch, and the bitter realization that the woman didn't care hit Angie with a paralyzing force. Suddenly, she was as afraid of Cecily as she was of Bond.

"Listen," she cried. "We've got Jessica's ticket stubs! They have to mean something, or why would he be so desperate to get them from me? And we've found Eldridge Sawyer, too. He knows a lot about all this—it's why he went into hiding. Together we'll be able to convict Bond. He'll go to jail. He'll pay!"

Cecily didn't even look at her, but kept malignant eyes boring into Bond. Her voice was inexorable as death. "I didn't come back to put him in jail. That's too good for him."

A rush filled Angie's ears. Cecily was going to shoot. She was going to kill Bond and he, in turn, would fire.

"Stop!" Paavo stepped out of the shadows to one side, his gun drawn and aimed at Bond. "Put the gun down, Cecily. I've got this now."

"Paavo!" Angie struggled harder, but Bond's hold cut off her air and nearly tore her arm from its socket. No, she wanted to cry, straining to breathe.

"Yes, do as your son says," echoed Bond. "Do it or I swear I'll kill her."

Cecily didn't avert her eyes. "Stay back, Paavo. Don't get in my way."

Paavo stared at the woman in front of him, at the gun she pointed at Bond.

She was quite different from the photos he'd seen, not only in age, but much harder, much more world-weary. He had always wondered what color her eyes were. Now, she was close enough that he could see they were a light grayish-green color, and that her once-auburn hair was almost completely gray. But the shape of her face was the same as in the photos, as was her nose, her mouth. He should have noticed them earlier, even with the wimple. He should have realized why the sound of her voice in the hospital had such a strange effect on him. He should have known immediately who the nun really was.

This woman was alien and familiar at once to him. He saw traces of himself in her, and memories washed over him, overwhelmed him with a child's joy, a grown man's sorrow, and a cop's futility.

All these weeks of confusion, anger and longing, epitomized in this one moment. And this was all there ever was.

"Don't do it," he said again. He couldn't use a word like 'mother' or 'mom' to this woman. She was so filled with anger he could see how desperately she wanted to shoot Bond, who might reflexively pull the trigger of the gun pressed to Angie's temple. So, she was Cecily now—actress, fugitive, killer. The grief that pierced him was sharper than any knife.

Cecily's face, her voice, were terrible. "I betrayed Mika! I loved him more than life, but I gave him to this bastard. How can I live with that? How can I let him live?"

Angie couldn't stop her tears. "No, you didn't! You couldn't have known. You didn't know he was working with Partridge. It wasn't your fault." She wept for the family broken apart by one man's heinous mistake and another's callous indifference, for the lies and deceit, and for the innocent lives lost.

Bond sneered. "How touching! So you didn't come back for your precious son, Cecily. How does that make you feel, Inspector? I hate to break up this reunion, but Miss Amalfi and I are going to walk out of here now. If anyone makes a move, I'll kill her."

"You aren't leaving, Bond!" Cecily said. "Do you really think I can miss at this range? I've learned a lot these past years. I've worked in 'security.' I've learned how to kill. And you taught me all about being ruthless."

Angie saw the unyielding determination in Cecily's eyes and knew she would do as she said. Kill Bond. And she, too, would die. She didn't want the last sight of her life to the barrel of a gun, and cast her gaze on Paavo, giving him all the love she felt. She held her breath.

"No!" Paavo said with a passion that shook his voice as he moved closer to Cecily, knowing he'd step in front of her bullet if he had to. "Don't you do it! You, Aulis, Jessica, this gutless bastard—all of you deprived me of my *both* my parents a long time ago. Don't take Angie from me, too! Don't make me live alone for the rest of my life—just as you have—regretting what happened here every minute of every day. Regretting the trust I gave you. Please... mother."

Something flickered across Cecily's face, but Angie's eyes were too filled with tears to see clearly.

A loud report shattered the night.

Angie felt the gun barrel knock hard against her temple, felt shock waves blast through her body. Felt something wet and warm splatter all over her. She fell to her knees, her eyes squeezed tight. Not until she heard a thud and metallic clatter did she open then again.

Her gaze flew to Paavo. He stood staring at her, pale as death, without moving, without breathing. Then, when their eyes met, he was suddenly holding her, lifting, pulling her away from the body pinning her down, his arms wonderfully tight about her, his heart pounding so hard his body shook from it as he wiped the blood and gore from her face, thanking God none of it was hers. In a darkly shadowed area, he had her curl up as he hunched low over her, shielding her with his body. Gun raised, he peered into the darkness.

Cecily's gun was also raised, but toward the foliage beyond the battlement, her eyes searching it as she crouched and stepped slowly backwards toward them.

Angie didn't understand what had happened. She lifted her head and saw Bond. Shock pulsated through her at the open, unseeing eyes, at the blood-soaked mass where the entire side of his head had been blown away.

"Hold your fire. We aren't after you," a heavy, accented voice called out. A man came up the stairwell, and walked toward them, four others behind him, all fully armed.

As he neared, Angie saw it was the old man she had once met in a restaurant, the flirtatious Nick.

"Nikolai," Cecily said. She stepped forward. Gun in hand, Paavo moved to her side, telling Angie to run from them all.

"We meet again, Cecily," Nikolai said. He glanced at Angie who, instead of running, was now peeking around Paavo's shoulder. "And my *devuchka*, hello to you. My men saw Tucker Bond get into your car. They followed and called me, but unfortunately, we lost you for a while in this infernal complex. I'm sorry."

Angie was stunned. Her fingers gripped Paavo's jacket.

"Who are you?" Paavo asked.

"You probably know me as Koba," the Russian replied.

Cecily dropped her gun, then placed her hand atop Paavo's gun and pressed downward. Paavo lowered his arm. Angie realized why. Their weapons were of no use to confront this man. Koba—Nikolai—had a small army to protect him, all standing in the shadows behind him.

"I thought you were a better man than to work with a piece of shit like Tucker Bond," Cecily said to Nikolai, her chin jutting arrogantly.

He gave a loud laugh. "Perhaps now, older and hopefully wiser, I am." Then his eyes turned sorrowful. "We were all so young, then, my Sitsilija. Some terrible things happened. I'm sorry for that, and I do regret it."

She continued to glare at him with disgust.

"It was because of the Soviets," he continued. "They might call themselves 'new' Russians now, but they're the same Bolshevik scum they've always been. How I hated them! After they imprisoned our people, we couldn't think straight. Yes, we believed the Finns deceived us, but we didn't kill them. I didn't learn until later, after other things happened, that Bond was behind it. He worked with anyone he could use—the new Russian government, Partridge, even us." He glanced at Paavo.

"Your people call us the *mafiya*. And for us," he faced Cecily again, "we thought it was helpful to have an FBI insider on our payroll."

"Yet, you killed him?" Cecily couldn't hide her confusion.

"Bond was out of control and needed to be stopped, so we stopped him." Nikolai shrugged. "Such is life."

Cecily drew herself up tall. "So it is." She faced him squarely. "I suspect you want to shoot me, too, now. It doesn't matter, Nikolai. I've lived too long, anyway. But, you said you regret what happened in the past. I have a way to ease that regret. Let my son and his fiancée go. They aren't a part of this."

He turned the thin slits of his eyes toward Paavo and Angie.

"Just me, that's enough," Cecily said.

"Don't," Paavo said to her softly. She refused to look at him. All her attention on Nikolai, her expression uncompromising.

"Let them go," she said.

"Your son is very stubborn, Cecily. We tried to scare him off. I even had Stavrogin warn him to back off, but instead of listening, he tried to fight my enforcer! And he's a cop." Nikolai gazed at Paavo, then a long moment at Angie. "All right. He can go, and the young lady, too."

Cecily shut her eyes, but only for an instant. "Thank you for that. He's a good man. He reminds me so much of his father. Mika would be very proud of him."

Nikolai looked from mother to son. Then his gaze met Cecily's, and he nodded. But just as quickly, his expression hardened. "We will not meet again, Mrs. Turunen. The scorecard is not even between us. But I've grown far too old and fat and sentimental for all this. I will let you go as well, even though you know too much about my operation, and you've killed too many of my men. Some of my associates do not take kindly to having our men... intercepted, shall we say? And, as they say, the *mafiya* never forgets, and never forgives." He smiled at Cecily's silence, one professional to another. "Exactly. I will hold them off for twenty-four hours. Enough time, I'm sure, for you to disappear again. And it will be my present to Miss Amalfi for the fright we caused her today."

With that, he turned and left.

In the distance came the sound of police sirens.

Cecily faced Paavo then, without a word. Her large green eyes seemed to soften, and he knew he'd never forget the way she looked at him at that moment, with all the love a mother's eyes can hold. But also, he understood that too much had happened, too much death and murder, and she had no choice but to leave once more, just as she had so many years ago.

Emotions strong, unexpected and turbulent filled him. She had walked out on him when he was a boy, and hadn't been there all the times he had felt sad and lonely and needed her so much it seemed the center of his being was nothing but a huge, empty hole. She had grown old without him, just as he had lost his youth without her, but now he understood why she'd done it, and that made all the difference.

A moment passed, and then she straightened her spine and raised her chin. He saw that she kept herself under even tighter rein than he, that she had learned the hard way to be self-contained, and that if she were to survive, she had to continue to be stronger and tougher and more alone than he could imagine. Her look said everything and his heart filled with feelings long denied, filled until he thought it would burst. She nodded —once—then turned, and walked away.

Paavo's arms closed around Angie, gathering her to him, needing her warmth, her essence, her love. He glanced down at her, and when he saw her tears, they cut through all his defenses. As he shattered inside, tears filled his eyes.

When he looked toward Cecily again, she was gone.

46

A week later, Paavo sat on the edge of Aulis's hospital bed, Angie on a chair at his side. Three days earlier, the old man had come out of his twilight sleep, and with each passing hour had grown stronger and more lucid. His vital signs were excellent, and the prognosis was for a full recovery.

Propped up with pillows, Aulis was eager to hear what had happened since he'd lost consciousness. The doctors had finally given Paavo and Angie the okay to relate the whole story. What they told him, though, was a simple, sanitized version.

"So, when the music box stopped playing, I brought it to Rosinsky," Angie explained, "who was said to be the best of the best. We believe he phoned Harry Partridge, telling him he would sell him the music box that had eluded him thirty years earlier. Rosinsky then took the box to Jakob Platnikov, a forger, to make a copy. He would give me the copy, saying the box was now fixed, and then sell the original to Partridge."

"We suspect Partridge was in a panic at this news, and tried to find the music box, going from the jeweler's, to Angie's, then me, then you," Paavo explained. "When the Russians wouldn't tell him where it was, he killed them, and then contacted Bond to clean up his mess.

"Both men feared the story might come out that they were the ones who gave up the Russian dissidents to the new Russian government some thirty years earlier and then killed Mika and Sam."

Angie then chimed in. "Bond confessed that he had tracked down Paavo and Jessica and knew they were using the name 'Smith.' And he remembered that you, Aulis, were friends with Mika and Sam. Luckily, Cecily learned what was going on, and she kept an eye on you and Paavo, making sure you were both safe."

Aulis squeezed Paavo's hand at this. "I'm glad you finally know the truth," he whispered. "So many times I wanted to tell you, but I was afraid for you, and of what you might want to do if you learned. I think Cecily's way of handling this was right. If the people who were involved are still so dangerous thirty years later, her instincts to save her children were good ones. I'm glad she got to see what a fine man you turned out to be. You do Mika proud. It's like having him back again."

"Thank you," Paavo said, touched by the words about his father.

"The irony of it all," Angie added, "is that we had to make Tucker Bond a hero by saying he'd died trying to rescue me from kidnappers. His shooting has now been added to the long list of Koba's crimes. To blame the Russian *mafiya* was, unfortunately, the simplest explanation for his murder, and Partridge's, and all the earlier gunplay."

"I suppose it doesn't do much good for anyone to point out what really happened," Aulis said.

"None at all," Paavo replied.

"It's grim." Aulis shook his head, and they all silently thought about the strangeness that had transpired.

"What isn't grim is that Angie has a new business," Paavo said, trying to make the mood upbeat again. "She's on television!"

"Really?" Aulis smiled. "Well, she's pretty enough, that's for sure."

Paavo gave her loving smile. "She's doing video restaurant reviews."

Angie felt a little sick inside. It was a subject she'd carefully avoided, and had hoped Paavo had forgotten about. No such luck.

"Ah! I've never heard of anything like that." Aulis's voice was so filled with enthusiasm, she would have gladly crawled under the bed.

"That's the idea," Paavo said. "Angie came up with it all by herself. It's a winner."

"Paavo..." She looked from one man to the other. "I'm afraid I've given up that idea."

"You are? Why?"

"Well..." How could she tell him? She drew in her breath. "After I did my first review on TV, I was hit with four lawsuits. One was brought by the restaurant owner, who claimed I had no right to show the interior of his business on television." Her throat became dry. "Another was from the cook, saying I had slandered him." Beads of perspiration broke out on her forehead. "Another came from the waiter. He said he should have been paid standard actor's rates because he's a member of some actors' guild waiting for a big break. And the last"—the room began to spin—"the last plaintiff is a customer, who's suing for alienation of affection because my video caught him at the restaurant with a woman who wasn't his wife. Now his wife wants a divorce, and he says it's all my fault!"

Paavo sucked in his breath.

As Angie drank some water to compose herself, the old man

chuckled. "Well, at least, child," he said to Angie, "you did get back your Christmas present, didn't you?"

"Well, yes and no," she said, feeling a little better. "Paavo realized that the jeweler, Rosinsky, must have given the music box to the forger, Jakob Platnikov. Platnikov had a granddaughter who liked it and had wrapped it in a towel and put it in her backpack to show a girlfriend in school, knowing her grandfather usually didn't work on jewelry until evening. But when she came home, he was dead. Paavo explained to the girl that the music box was very valuable and had to go back to its owner. Even though she'd kept it hidden from others who asked about it, she gave it to him."

"So, you do have it?" Aulis asked.

"No. Its rightful owner, we learned, is the Hermitage in St. Petersburg. A friend, a retired museum curator, helped us send it back to them with a letter saying it was being returned compliments of Mika Turunen and Sami Vansha."

"Ah, that's good. Very good." Aulis shut his eyes as she spoke, and now, even though he commented and wore a smile on his face, Angie could see how tired he had grown. Soon, his breathing deepened, and he was asleep.

Paavo caught Angie's eye and motioned toward the door. She nodded, stood and moved quietly toward it. Paavo stopped in the doorway and took her hand. At the same time, he gazed back at Aulis. He loved these two and felt their love for him. And, for the first time in his adult life, he was able to accept the love they gave. It was such a cliché, he wanted to laugh at himself, and yet, knowing who his parents were and why they had left him meant more to him than he could ever have imagined.

It was as if he had needed to get over that hurdle before he could know where his heart was. And now he knew—with the people who mattered more than anything else in his life—with Angie, with Aulis, and with the mother who had stayed away to protect him. He would have liked to have spent time with her, a little at least, but he also knew the most important thing between them didn't need words. He now knew she loved him and always had, wherever she had gone, and wherever she might be now.

THE END

ITALIAN STYLE CHOCOLATE-AMARETTO BREAD PUDDING

Even people who aren't particular fond of bread pudding sit up and take notice when Angie makes this dessert. It's bread pudding with an Italian twist.

Preheat oven to 350 º

Ingredients for Bread Pudding:
1-1/2 pound loaf panettone bread (if none available, use a sweet French bread or challah) trim crust & cut into 1-inch cubes
1 cup chocolate chips
8 large eggs
1-1/2 cups whipping cream
2-1/2 cups whole milk
1 cup sugar
2 tablespoons amaretto liqueur

Ingredients for Amaretto Sauce:
1/2 cup whipping cream

1/2 cup whole milk

3 tablespoons sugar

1/4 cup amaretto liqueur

2 teaspoons cornstarch

Directions for Bread Pudding:

Lightly butter a 13" x9" x2" baking dish. Put bread cubes evenly in pan, then sprinkle chocolate chips over them, spreading evenly.

In a large bowl, add eggs, cream, milk, sugar, and amaretto, then whisk until blended. Pour the custard over the bread cubes and chocolate. Press the bread cubes gently to be sure they're all submerged. Let stand for at least 30 minutes, occasionally pressing the bread again into the custard mixture. (Can let stand up to 2 hours; but if much over 30 minutes, cover and refrigerate.)

Bake until the pudding is set in the center, about 1 hour. While the pudding is in the oven, it's time to make the amaretto sauce:

Directions for Sauce:

Add cream, milk, and sugar to a heavy small saucepan. Over medium heat, bring to boil, stirring frequently. Mix amaretto and cornstarch in small bowl, stir to mix and break up any cornstarch lumps. Stir amaretto-cornstarch into the cream mixture. Simmer over medium-low heat until the sauce thickens, stirring constantly, about 2 minutes. Set aside and keep warm. (If made ahead, store in refrigerator, and warm in microwave before serving.)

Putting it all together...

When the pudding is cooked, allow it to cool slightly, and then spoon the bread pudding into bowls, drizzle it with the warm amaretto sauce, and serve. While the pudding is best served warm, if prepared early, it can be reheated in the microwave before serving.

ABOUT THE AUTHOR

Joanne Pence was born and raised in northern California and now lives in Idaho. She has been an award-winning, *USA Today* best-selling author of mysteries for many years, but she has also written historical fiction, contemporary romance, romantic suspense, a fantasy, and supernatural suspense. All of her books are now available as ebooks and in print, and most are also offered in special large print editions. Joanne hopes you'll enjoy her books, which present a variety of times, places, and reading experiences, from mysterious to thrilling, emotional to lightly humorous, as well as powerful tales of times long past.

Visit her at www.joannepence.com and be sure to sign up for Joanne's mailing list to hear about new books.